## PRAISE FOR
# SVETISLAV BASARA

"A complicated take on the obsession that sees Rosicrucianism or freemasonry or the Illuminati everywhere, capturing both the talismanic appeal of the secret list and its satisfactory arbitrariness."

—Daniel Soar, *London Review of Books*

"*Chinese Letter* is often hilarious and always readable, even as Basara insists on asking big questions about life and death, art, and representation, the conflict between world and spirit."

—Ethan Nosowsky, *Bookforum*

"Serbian author Svetislav Basara's *Chinese Letter* is, first and foremost, a comic novel. . . . The novel's charm and inventiveness is due, in part, to the way it manages to combine elements of the Oulipian and postmodern comic novel."

—Brian Whitener, *Chicago Review*

"Basara is brazen in his borrowings, not trying to hide that this is a text built on the familiar. But he has a fine ear for creating just the right echoes."

—Michael Orthofer, *Complete Review*

**OTHER BOOKS BY**
# SVETISLAV BASARA
**IN ENGLISH TRANSLATION**

*Chinese Letter*

# THE CYCLIST CONSPIRACY

**SVETISLAV BASARA**

TRANSLATED FROM THE SERBIAN BY RANDALL A. MAJOR

Originally published in Serbian as *Fama o biciklistima* by Prosveta, Belgrade, in 1988


Published by arrangement with Geopoetika, Belgrade, Serbia

First edition, 2011


Library of Congress Cataloging-in-Publication Data: Available upon request.
ISBN-13: 978-1-934824-58-0 / ISBN-10: 1-934824-58-5

*This book was published with support of the Ministry of Culture, Media and Informatic Society of the Republic of Serbia.*

**Република Србија**
Министарство културе, информисања
и информационог друштва

Printed on acid-free paper in the United States of America.

Text set in Caslon, a family of serif typefaces based on the designs of William Caslon (1692–1766).

*Design by N. J. Furl*

Open Letter is the University of Rochester's nonprofit, literary translation press:
Lattimore Hall 411, Box 270082, Rochester, NY 14627

www.openletterbooks.org

*The Messiah will come at the point when he is no longer necessary.*
*He will not come on the last day.*
*He will come on the very last of all possible days.*
*—Kafka*

# CONTENTS

Editor's Preface . . . . . . . . . . . . . . . . . . . . . 1

## AT THE COURT OF KING CHARLES

Charles the Hideous: A Tale of My Kingdom . . . . . . . . . . 5

Majordomo Grossman:
A History of the Diabolical Two-Wheeler . . . . . . . . . . . 31

## ON THE THRESHOLD OF THE NEW ERA

The Manuscript of Captain Queensdale. Publisher's *Preface* . . . 43

*Preface* by the Unknown Copyist . . . . . . . . . . . . . . 44

The Manuscript of Captain Queensdale . . . . . . . . . . . 48

Arthur Conan Doyle: The Final Case of Sherlock Holmes. . . . 56

Sigmund Freud: The Case of Ernest M. . . . . . . . . . . . 62

*Correspondence*

From Mrs. Meier to Freud . . . . . . . . . . . . . . . 71

From Ernest to His Mother. . . . . . . . . . . . . . . . 73

From Freud to Mrs. Meier . . . . . . . . . . . . . . . 75

From Freud to Ferenczi . . . . . . . . . . . . . . . . 76

From Ferenczi to Freud . . . . . . . . . . . . . . . . 77

Jurgis Baltrušaitis: Fama Birotariorum . . . . . . . . . . . . . 78

An Analysis of the Ideological Orientation
of the Journal, *Vidici*, and the Newspaper *Student*. . . . . . . . . 90

Herbert Meier: The History of a Lie . . . . . . . . . . . . . 109

Çulaba Çulabi:
How I Became a Member of the Order of *Little Brothers*. . . . . 113

Çulaba Çulabi: The History of Timepieces . . . . . . . . . . 128

Sava Djakonov: The Pilgrimage to Dharamsala . . . . . . . . . 132

Afanasij Timofeyevich Darmolatov: Jubilee . . . . . . . . . . 142

## THE COLLECTED WORKS OF JOSEPH KOWALSKY

Kowalsky: A Biography . . . . . . . . . . . . . . . . . . . 157

POEMS . . . . . . . . . . . . . . . . . . . . . . . . . 177

PROSE . . . . . . . . . . . . . . . . . . . . . . . . . 195

Bicyclism and the Theology of Witold Kowalsky . . . . . . 197

Proclamations . . . . . . . . . . . . . . . . . . . . 217

A Letter to Branko Kukić . . . . . . . . . . . . . . . 228

## THE GRAND INSANE ASYLUM

Proclamation of the Evangelical Bicyclists of the Rose Cross . . . 243

The Metaphysics of the City . . . . . . . . . . . . . . . 245

L. Loentze: The Madness of Architecture –
the Architecture of Madness . . . . . . . . . . . . . . . 252

L. Loentze: The Plan of the Grand Insane Asylum. . . . . . . 260

A Tale of My Kingdom (subsequently found fragment) . . . . . 270

## APPENDIX

Mihailo Jovanović: Building:
"City Babylon the Great" Hospital – Technical Description . . . 275

Secret List . . . . . . . . . . . . . . . . . . . . . . 284

# EDITOR'S PREFACE

Endless are the secrets of provincial libraries. Filled with untouched volumes of classics and frayed copies of pulp fiction, in their unexplored cellars they also conceal books that it would be impossible to find in the bookstores of a metropolis or even in the catalogues of the university and national libraries. Just as one does not search for gold at the jeweler's but rather buys it there, while one finds it in distant canyons and alchemists' laboratories, so it is that one searches in vain for wisdom in the libraries of Babylon, where it is worn and discolored from use, where, as Berdyayev says, "The spirit is objectivized, fossilized, tied to the sinfulness of the world and the disintegration of its parts."

Books have a life and death of their own. Those whose authors did not believe in death have a life after the grave as well. Others, again, whose authors believed in reincarnation, get written again. It is impossible to separate the destiny of a book from the destiny of its author, and the destiny of the reader is also mixed into all of this. In other words, it is not the reader who is looking for a book, he is the one who is sought after, and there are manuscripts that hide in distant places for ages until they fall into the hands of the person for whom they were intended. Not being aware of this, one autumn in the cellar of the Municipal Library in Bajina Bašta (where I had taken refuge from a sadness the cause of which I still cannot mention), rifling through dusty copies of periodicals, I came across two little books. One was (in a crude paperback edition of "Slavija," Novi Sad, 1937) entitled *A Tale of My Kingdom*, without the usual publication data. The second, a first edition in German, *The Manuscript of Captain Queensdale*, printed in 1903 in Zurich, in a limited run of six copies. The copy I was holding carried the number 3. Interested in how a book of such a limited run, printed so far away in time and space, might come to Bajina Bašta, I asked a friend, a scholar of German, to translate the rather short text. I was surprised to learn that Captain Queensdale mentioned Charles the Hideous, whom I considered to be a completely fictional character. Then, I was even more surprised when two years later, in the magazine *Oblique*, I read the authentic text of Majordomo Grossman "A History of the Diabolical Two-Wheeler." To cut the matter short. I started doing research, the goal of which was to ease the boredom of rainy days, and which in the end – guiding me like Ariadne's thread through the labyrinth of history – ended up in the form of a voluminous almanac dedicated to the secret of the Evangelical Bicyclists of the Rose Cross.

In handing this collection over to the reader, I realize that several years ago, searching for colored pebbles, I came across a pearl, but also that the pearl had been awaiting a proper owner and found an improper one instead, who would turn it into a glass bauble by reduplicating it in an insufferably large number of copies. The only justification is that, in our time, which falls within the autumn of the *year of years* (about which Captain Queensdale speaks), even the sparkle of a glass bauble shines through the darkness gathering on the horizon.

S. B.

# AT THE COURT OF KING CHARLES

## CHARLES THE HIDEOUS
# A TALE OF MY KINGDOM
## (APOCRYPHAL)

Although the square kilometer as a unit of measure has not been invented yet, my kingdom stretches over 450 square kilometers. But no one knows that. Not even Grossman. I never desired to have a large kingdom. The size of a kingdom contributes nothing to the greatness of its king. On the contrary. Large empires gather all sorts of riffraff, and the emperor has all the shortcomings of his subjects. After all, I did not inherit my kingdom. I created it myself, with my bare hands and a lot of hard work. I spent all my savings. With the help of Grossman my majordomo, I even made my own throne from well-seasoned beech. Into the back of the throne, from behind, we nailed spikes in the shape of a cross, and then we hung the throne with thick rope from the ceiling like a swing. Nothing was left to chance, everything roils with symbolism. When I sit on the throne, the points of the nails drive into my back and I thus crucify myself; the pain does not allow me to relax. I think of the sufferings of our Savior and that forces me to be just and to be forgiving. And the fact that the throne swings indicates the inconstancy of Fortuna, of human life in general. You see, I began as a normal village boy. No one knows who my father was. Perhaps not even who my mother was. This will be interpreted in three hundred and fifty years by

Sigmund Freud, when he arrives in the world of the living: the conditions were right so that I never overcome my Oedipus complex, of which Grossman does not even dream. He thinks that Freud is a figment of my imagination. He does not realize that he himself, the majordomo, is a product of an imagination so powerful that he is tangible. It does not matter, if he knew, the flatterer he is, he would immediately come running, tuck his tail and cry out: "Sire, what an important prophesy! What a great prophesy!" Imagine what he would do if I were to tell him something about quarks and quantum theory! Never mind. I overcame my Oedipus complex with ease, possibly because I did not know at the time that it existed. I am a simple man and I figured like this: I have no father, I will be no one's father. End of story. Then I met Grossman. He had been studying theology at the University of Uppsala, and they had just thrown him out. Rumor has it, because of a deal with the devil. The deal was this: the devil gives Grossman a doctoral degree, Grossman gives his soul to the devil. A fair deal, but it was against the rules of the time. Since we did not have any income back then, we only had intentions, we found jobs at "The Four Antlers" tavern. We washed dishes, kept the fire burning, carried water and cooked oxen in pepper and dill. Grossman had the habit of killing time by asking me theological riddles. For example, how many angels can stand on the head of a pin? Or, *habet mulier animam*? He would ask in the middle of the rush, wrapped, as if in hell, by an opaque cloud of sulfur steam from the ox horns. Then the owner would interrupt our dispute with a flourish of curses, and theology would have to wait for the nobles to stuff themselves. And stuff themselves they did. I can still hear them slurping their soup, smacking their lips, the chomping of bones, it all resounds through the ages like an echo. I almost forgot, at the time my name was Ladislav, but I did not pay much attention to that. If someone were to accidentally call me, let's say, Ivan, then I would be Ivan. Ivan, Ladislav, Grossman, what is the difference? At that time, almost none. That is the very reason I became a king. So that I could rise above the average. But I remained average anyway. That is the *conditio humana.* Anyway, once the nobles had gorged themselves, I would answer Grossman in a whisper: "She doesn't have one, a woman has no soul. I am sure of it. Women have only a cunt. The cunt is the center, the sun of their planetary system around which, and because of which, all the other organs move and function. And since the vagina is nothing, an ordinary hole, the lack of anything, emptiness, not only does a woman not have a soul – she doesn't even exist." "You're wrong," Grossman shouted to me from the cloud of his reeking soul. Poor Grossman. He knew Greek and Latin well, but he knew nothing about women. Just like his languages, he was dead. I want to say: hardly anyone knew him, it was hard to communicate with him, but he was still quite useful. Grossman taught me to write. The first use I had of Grossman. I was not interested in the skill of making slanted-thin and straight-thick lines, but in making this book, I was indeed interested. Because of this book I clumsily wrote out my first letters with my gnarled hands. Not to mention the lack of writing materials. This will be well known by even the lowest village tutor in the 19th century. As a sign of gratitude, when I became King I raised a nice mausoleum for Grossman and had the stone engraved GROSSMAN, which soothes his vanity no end. Sometimes he closes himself up in it and practices being dead. He's careful, he leaves nothing to chance. I do not like such people. Perhaps I will bury someone else there, just to spite him. Now you have some facts which are more significant than the abovementioned about the lack of writing materials. Some future scribbler can draw a few conclusions from this and get his doctorate. First: in this time, a lot of attention is paid to tombs because of the obsession with death, and the nobles build their eternal homes while they are still alive. Second: the nobles are unusually vain, morbid, and they tend to tinker with the details. And there you have it, I also leave nothing to chance and I should not be surprised if they bury me in a potter's field.

At this moment, interest in my personal history practically does not exist. Only here and there do a few mentions of me sprout up. But those are just Grossman's memories; he has more than he needs. This time and place, among other things, is flooded with memories. In spite of everything, I am writing my history because only one who has no history has the right to write it. Everyone else is biased. In the same way – he thinks best who thinks not at all. Every thought is evil. Father Albert, my confessor, told me that, and I learned it by heart. Sometimes I do not think anything for a few days. I swing on my throne, dully staring at the deer antlers on the wall, and my courtiers pass by on their tiptoes and the rumor spreads: the king is thinking. It is simply hard to believe the extent to which people will be ass-kissers. When I, for example, stabilized my power, touched by one of Grossman's memories of the years spent in the kitchen, I bequeathed the title of baron to all my kitchen boys, all thirty-five of them. And so the dishwashers became great noblemen. All day long they sit in the taverns, gorging themselves, drinking, pinching the waitresses. Just like in that drawing by Gottfried of Mainz, *Wheel of Fortune*. However, they have become too decadent. The power has gone to their heads. I hear they are raising a conspiracy to overthrow me. They figure: if he, that is I, can become king without any title whatsoever, why shouldn't we, the noblemen? But Grossman is preparing our revenge. I am going to send them all back to the kitchen. I will have several of them shot, if gunpowder has reached Europe by then. If not, I will have their heads chopped off. Still, shooting would be more effective as a novelty. It is not a bad idea once in a while to burn a witch or two at the stake, or to hold a public execution. The people love to kill but they do not have the legal right to do so, so a reasonable king has to order an execution now and then, just to allow for some relief and to preserve law and order. Otherwise, I do not believe in witches, though Grossman does. If you believe in anything other than God you become a heretic. But I am tolerant toward heretics as well. This is my doctrine: if all men are sinful, no one knows God, and therefore all theologies are heretical. Short and simple. And that's why my kingdom is a sanctuary for heretics. They come under my auspices from all over. I am practically the forerunner of democracy. Not long ago, just in from Paris from where they had fled persecution, some Bicyclists arrived. Or something like that. I entertained their leader, Joseph Ferrarius and he showed me a clay tablet, a relic of theirs and a translation of it which I offer here in Grossman's version of it:*

---

*In ink that becomes visible only after two-hundred years, majordomo Grossman left the following note in the margins of the manuscript:

"On the order of the king-dishwasher I am copying this nonsense full of blasphemy and spitting upon me, Grossman, I who was just about to finish my doctorate and I who would be a doctor if evil tongues had not accused me of heresy. The fact is that he sees the future; any fool can prophesy. But what else can an educated man do in this time except to put up with the whims of madmen. Charles has become arrogant. He boasts of being the keeper of the faith, and he doesn't believe in God, nor does God believe in him. A few years ago he knelt before the crucifix, just for the sake of things (may the omnipotent one forgive me), and the cross fell down and knocked old Hideous on the head. Since then the knot on his head has not receded. It makes him even more hideous, if that's possible. In associating with me in that unfortunate tavern he learned a little bit about theology and now he constantly babbles about it to the courtiers who, pretending, flatter him and shout their approval. Why, recently he humiliated me in front of the followers while we were discussing whether women have souls. *Non habet*, I claimed, and was proving it, when Charles says: Huh, not only do they not have a soul, women don't exist at all. And then he said that since he had placed the vagina as the center of the female organism he had cleared the way for Nicolaus Copernicus, and that since he claimed that women don't exist, he was the forerunner of existentialism, some devilish thing. God save us! But even the Devil isn't that dark. Realizing that he'd gone too far, he feigned to repent and confessed. But not for long. As soon as Father Albert, his confessor, came back from the blasphemy he had to listen to, the Hideous executed Queen Margot just because she returned a look from the Baron Von Kurtiz. He executed the baron as well, of course. He boasts of

## THE BOOK OF JAVAN THE SON OF NAHOR

The words of Javan, the son of Nahor, to those yet unborn.

Coming from the east to the land of the Seran, I settled with my brethren, sons and flocks; and our wealth multiplied and we dwelled in harmony with the other tribes.

And behold, builders came from elsewhere, master masons; and they lit a great fire and began to bake bricks of clay, saying: Come, let us build a tower reaching into the sky. We shall take refuge in it from the beasts of the field and winds and floods. And above us shall . . . (text missing) . . . into the ages.

And in the sand did they draw a rather large tower. And the tower was broad at the base and a stairway wound about it like a snake, and its top did disappear in the clouds. And on the tower were gardens and streams and other beauties of the earth.

And in the seventh year of building, I slept and a dream I did dream: behold, a wheel was on the ground . . . (text missing) . . . in form and with the device the wheels were like . . . and both were equal and in form with the device it seemed that one was behind the other.

And whence the spirit did go, there went the wheels and when the spirit did fly so did they also rise, because the spirit was on wheels.

And behold, a terrible light did blind me and I heard a voice saying unto me: "Javan, open your eyes and behold the tower that you also are building." And I opened my eyes and beheld

---

having driven nails into the back of the throne, that he is constantly crucifying himself. He did put the nails in, but he also took a file and shaved them dull by his own hand. And anyway, because of his rheumatism, he always wears an ox-hide vest. The genius of half truth. Now he wants to write the history of the world ahead of time, and I have to participate in that lunacy. May God have mercy on me and on Europe."

the tower as it rose into the heavens, and its walls were as of glass and deep inside it could I see.

And at the bottom of the tower I saw a multitude kneeling before false priests and each of them was confessing his sufferings to a priest and telling him the desires and thoughts of his heart.

And the priests said: Be not afraid. We . . . (text missing) . . . when you confess the thoughts of your hearts to us, we will make you happy and you will live long.

And behold, those who desired to sin, they gathered together on one floor and did sin together, male with male and female with female; and a stench rose into the heavens and it was a torture to behold.

And those who wanted to go to war and to do battle, the priests did send them to the floor above. And that floor was barren and without grass, and here did they go to war and kill one another, and blood flowed up to their knees. And from above did the priests watch the battle and laugh.

And the drunkards did lie in a luscious garden and drink wine, and they spoke blasphemous words that were a torture to hear.

And behold, the peaceful and hardworking people at the very bottom of the tower, digging and plowing, and gathering the fruits of the field, they took them to the priests. But unruly guards did come out bearing whips and began beating all who raised their voice. And they cried: Is this why we have raised the tower, for you to tear it down?

And deeper, in the center of the tower, I beheld horrible sights such as my eyes never saw even in dreams. Sons murdered their fathers and lay with their mothers; and women were riding men. And I saw many more awful things which I know not how to describe.

And again I was blinded by a light and the tower disappeared and I heard a voice commanding me: Javan, repent. Take your brethren and your sons and flee to the north.

But before you set off, make a tablet of clay and on it write an account of what you have seen and heard. And at the bottom of the tablet, press in this seal of our secret testament.

And before my eyes appeared a seal which looked like those wheels of fire and between them the letter Daleth of fire as well.

And then the voice said to me: You should know, this tower will I destroy and it will be raised again and again I will tear it down, and then all be will one and all.

And behold, I was immediately awake, and in my hand was a tablet into which I pressed the seal of our secret testament, as I was told, two wheels of fire and the letter Daleth of fire.

Ferrarius told me all kinds of things. Not only how the first tower of Babylon was destroyed but also how another would also be built. He showed me their relic, a cart made in the image of Ezekiel's vision with wheels one behind the other. With it, he said, one can reach the heavens. I knew, of course, that this was just an allegory but, just for fun, I ordered Grossman to ride down the slope next to the court on it. He almost broke his neck. Since then he cannot stand the Two-Wheelers and can hardly wait for them to leave. Because of that, I ordered him to write a history of their sufferings in Paris. The hypocrite. He thinks that I don't know that he is secretly scribbling in *my* margins with invisible ink. If I strain my ears, I can hear him scribbling, scratching on the surface of history, leaving behind his stains, driven by the mindless desire not to evaporate from the world's memory. But, now back to the executions. To prove my lack of bias, I even sent my wife, Queen Margot, to the gallows. She was trying to usurp the throne with the aid of her lover, Baron von Kurtiz. I do not know what is wrong with these idiots, and their number is countless, what drives them to dream of ruling and of thrones? Do they think I saved every penny for twenty years just to rule? No, my intention is to bring a metaphysical concept into reality. Margot was not a bad wife, but she could not resist the handsome von Kurtiz. Radbertus of Odense, in a book he will soon write, says that beauty is the weapon of the Devil. And then, there is always female vanity. So, once I went into the coal room by surprise – and there was Margot in front of a mirror. The devil was taking her from behind, and she was staring transfixed by the reflection of the infernal buttocks. I knew this would not end well. In spite of everything, I did not want to act rashly. I thought, it's a passing madness. A couple of times I caught her in the garden, making out with the Baron, but I pretended to be dreaming. Ah, but then I had had enough and I awoke and called in my servants. The next day, I prepared a real show for the masses. Exciting and educational all at once. So that people would know what greed and beauty lead to. But this was a small comfort for my ugliness. This is how I look, for the sake of my offspring I will describe myself: short of build, crooked back, crooked legs, crooked arms; dressed in a shapeless tunic of laced leopard skin. On my forehead I have a rather large growth. My right eye is small, sunk deeply in its socket; the left eye is covered with a cataract. But such a depiction will never reach my offspring. Gottfried of Mainz did a rather flattering painting of me, fearing my royal anger, and I closed one eye in it, tricked by my own vanity, and accepted the painting as it was, a false rendition of myself, a fake . . .

As the Preacher said long ago: Vanity of vanities, all is vanity.

Taking the throne of a kingdom that I bought from a bankrupt count, I walled up all the doors on the monastery of St. Panfucius, in order to preserve the purity of the faith, and I changed the name of the monastery just to spite the Pope, that seller of indulgences. There he is in Rome lounging about in silks and velvets, instead of roaming the earth barefoot and looking for someone to crucify him. He sends the Jesuits to re-convert me to his mercantile religion. But no. I have switched to the Orthodox Church. The monastery is now called St. Gregory Palama. Underneath it I built a twisting labyrinth with its entrance on the square in front of the cathedral, and its exit in the courtyard of the monastery. Those aspiring to monastic dignity must pass through the labyrinth. The unworthy get lost and remain in one of its corners forever. Once, accompanying Grossman to communion, I saw some grinning skeletons in the torchlight and I thought to myself: If it weren't for those skulls, those little bones, man would be absolutely nothing. *Ouk on*, as my majordomo would say. Stop! Nihilism! Heresy. Those who are indeed led by the Holy Spirit, glory be to God, arrive safe and sound. In this way, a high degree of spirituality is achieved. Dry bread and a little water, farewell to space and time. My monks see forward and backward. They dream the dreams that will be had by future generations; they know the intentions of my enemies. They speak with angels. They walk on water. Occasionally I take one of the monks out to walk on the lake, for the good of the people and for the sake of obedience. On the high holy days, the Hegumen of the monastery rises a hundred or so cubits, so that I don't say "meters" as an anachronism, he rises, as I was saying, above the bell tower of the church and holds the High Liturgy. On the other hand, I built a huge tavern for the sinners, thieves and perverts where they can enjoy their vices to their hearts' content, and not upset the decent Christian folk. I separated good and evil and I swing in the middle on my throne-Golgotha. I am highly depraved. I descend into the very depths of sin in order to achieve the highest degree of holiness. That is the fabric of the world: Evil foes besiege the borders of my kingdom, demons besiege the soul of the king. Beautifully said. I defend my subjects from their enemies, both earthly and heavenly. I take all temptations upon myself. The monks have no time for that. Almost completely *beyond*, blind to this world, with a thin membrane that covers their earthly eyes and with white lilies in their hands – as if in a picture that Nemanja will one day paint – they are undermining time and space so that, when the time is right, they can raise my kingdom into Heaven. In order to pluck my empire from the claws of history, from the pit of sin. For this very reason, I never wanted to expand my borders. To make it easier for the kingdom. Who could possibly raise such a colossus as the Roman Empire into the heavens when, because of its bulkiness, it sank into hell, and is still sinking ever deeper? A large country, a multitude of people – there is nothing good in that. As time passes, there will be more and more people. But people are like golden coins. The more of them there are, the less they are worth. People as tokens. Counterfeit persons without ontological backing. They do not even know what ontology is. They think that God is hidden in the attic of my palace. Fools who spit upon the past. There you have it, one more reason to prevent the tyranny of the yet unborn common masses, to write their history ahead of time, to determine it for them. That is my natural right. Because, if I would just try, though I have no such intention, I could live another mere three hundred and fifty years, if I would just drink less and avoid wild game on the dining table. But none of those people, no matter how hard they try, will be able to return to the past, my past where I rule supremely with the aid of faithful Grossman, not out of a craving for power, but from a feeling of calling to teach those pretentious bastards the principle of subordination. And the monks all agree with me. They came by the other night. They sat with me. The Hegumen said that, in their dreams, they had discovered what happened to the Etruscans. What's an Etruscan, I asked. And the Hegumen said that, long ago, where Rome and the so-called *Vicarius Dei Filii* are today, a people named the Rascians used to live, who one day disappeared from the face of the Earth. Just as we ourselves intend to do. Their priests-dreamers, going into the future down the path of dreams, saw what will one day happen on the ill-fated Apennine peninsula. One night, they all went to sleep and in their dream they saw a new country across the sea, mountainous and water-rich, so they woke up there and, in order to cover their tracks in history, they called themselves by a new name – the Serbs. A shocking tale. It was told, as I later found out, to soften my heart and quiet my anger. Because, as they departed, the Hegumen took me aside and said that there, *beyond* it all, Margot was meeting with Von Kurtiz. Grossman told me the same thing. They see the two of them, they say, under my windows, in the dark of night, their necks bloody. And for the first time, I was overcome with sadness instead of rage. Is it possible that not even death, I thought, is able to overcome infidelity and treason? And then two tears appeared in the corners of my eyes: Oh, Margot, Margot . . .

I wrote a Code. Rigorous but fair. If you cut off someone's hand, cut off your own as well. If you do not do so, you will be executed. Why should we spread lawlessness? Why drag a third party (a judge, a guard, an executioner . . .) into the *circulus vitiosus*? The law is the law. That is what the first article says. If they did not want to submit to God's law, let them groan under mine. Everyone is guilty and everyone should be punished. But the time of cowardly New Europe will come, when persecutions will not be anathematized. Perhaps not so soon. I'm not sure if the Renaissance has begun in Italy yet. It will never be clear to me what is so bad about injustice, torture and imprisonment; those are privileges. A certain path to the Kingdom of Heaven. *Do not do unto others as you would not have them do unto you.* That is the second, last article of my Code. The rest, ten volumes, is filled with smudges. With the simulacra of letters. With the songs of troubadours. *Sancta simplicitas!* Whoever agrees to be robbed and murdered has the right to rob and murder. No one else. Since I have agreed to be murdered and robbed, I killed Margot and her lover but that did not help either. There, they have gone on cheating me, and they will continue to cheat me throughout the ages.

Before we vanish from the face of the Earth, I wish to leave behind a true account of my reign for my progeny, for the rabble that is patiently waiting the moment of their birth. To avenge myself ahead of time on the gloomy writers of history. I can already see them rifling through libraries, digging into dusty charters, scribbling treatises about what I did, what I thought, where I was mistaken, disturbing me in death just as my subjects disturbed me in life. Should they be allowed to control the reins of my actions from the fog of the future? I will put an end to the tyranny of the unborn, to the fruits of our common sin, to those who would deepen our transgressions; so that, from the nothingness of *my* present time, the profane who are wallowing in the mud of the past will not be able to find arguments to justify their own present time, which is even more oblivious.

I will not allow them to write my history, I will write theirs. By their own hand, on their own paper. As Radbertus of Odense says, can those who do not exist know anything? Even when they take on human form, what can they know of events that have vanished without a trace? I will make mistakes and lie, I admit, but I will not agree that that means I am godless. Now, they call me Charles the Clairvoyant, Charles the Edified, but as soon as I die history will remember me as the Ugly, history into which I am inserting myself by force in order to destroy it, in disgust. I want to overtake time. To describe it before a certain time is reached and then time will have no choice but to be exactly as I have determined it should be in my moment of divine inspiration. *Quod dixi dixi!* And that is why others should be born who will write down my thoughts. The wretches. They will think that those thoughts are theirs, and they will not even know that they do not exist yet. Isn't this a contradiction? It makes no difference. Grossman! Write this down: I, Charles the Hideous, in the name of God, decree that the following should be born: Herbert Meier, Arthur Conan Doyle, Sherlock Holmes, Çulaba Çulabi (what a silly name), Jurgis Baltrušaitis, Sava Djakonov, Rheiner Meier, his son Ernest, Afanasij Yermolayev, a dozen supplementary characters, Sigmund Freud and Joseph Kowalsky, yes, Joseph Kowalsky, Kowalskyyyy!

"No religion can change the world, and no single fact can ever refute a religion." Thus will Oswald Spengler write on the eve of one of the slaughters of the future. Hundreds of years will pass in vain; even then this will be clear to no one. Years pass in vain; that's the first premise of this chapter of *HISTORY.* Thousands of futile years. I watch Grossman: hunchbacked, wrapped in a bearskin, he is writing down my words. The second S in his name has gotten somehow smaller, grown pale. Were I to ask him: Do you get the meaning of Spengler's words, he would say: Yes, Sire; were I to ask him: Are you dead? He would answer: Yes, Sire. Complete obedience! The most certain path to the Kingdom of Heaven. Years spent at the Theological Seminary in Uppsala have left their indelible mark. But he did not learn anything about religion and facts there. He cannot be blamed for that, such knowledge is not gained by study. It is inborn, as in my case. And yet, I am not proud of it; genius brings a heap of unpleasantness with it. With it you attract the rage of the average folk. There, just *now* – although that *now* will have to wait its turn in the chronological order – one of the countless scribblers, a certain Herbert Meier, is writing and proving that I never even existed, that history makes no mention of me, that I am the fabrication of a mystical fraternity that I myself concocted. He is partially right, the good-for-nothing Meier; insofar as I am not a fact. I extracted myself from my shell-of-fact, thank God, and I watch what is going on at the grandiose fairground that stretches across the centuries in both directions. I suppose now it is understandable how it is that I know what happens in the distant past and far into the future: I am not a fact, I simply believe that I exist; that gives me the ability to recognize facts that are all happening at the same time, but for the sake of difficulty, they enter the *present* one by one. Time is just the normal ordering of facts, fact after fact: bones, skulls, written records; that fabulous heap of things needs to have a certain order. Isn't that so, Grossman? Yes, Sire. Then write this down: Construction of the Tower of Babylon happened just a moment ago, Judgment Day will happen in the next. All that occurs in between is not time. Only facts occur.

But I did not come into the world to adapt myself to its rules. From early childhood I was unable to see any deeper difference between the blueprints of cities and the cities that are built. The third dimension, which the scholars of my court pushed under my nose, made me laugh. This so-called third dimension is the same as a carrot strung to a stick and hung in front of a donkey's eyes. No one has any use of it, and it has done damage to many. Because, if you set off to catch it, if you head off into that ostensible distance, it moves away, it does not allow you near, but it draws you forward, like the carrot does the donkey, straight into trouble and death. Yeah, yeah, the scholars, professors and metaphysicists will cry out in protest, "But we live in this world, we have a soul and a spirit." One load of nonsense after another. No one has ever proven that. Life, let the professors get it into their heads, is not a fact. Don't be disgusted, Grossman, I am not denying the existence of the soul and spirit, far from it, I am denying the existence of the scholars and professors, I am denying that you exist. You are the parasites of your souls. You are a nasty disease that your souls must survive. You, as Grossman, or as Grosman, you are nothing. It is in my power to order you to go back to the beginning of HISTORY, to scratch out "Grossman" wherever it is written, and to replace it with, let's say, "Gruber." I can order you to embellish an even darker autobiography than the one you wrote, the one you rebelled against when I died, scribbling your pitiful denunciations in the margins. *Assine!* No biography can be as horrible as its owner can. But I have still not died in the world of facts. I just want you to know that I can see through your actions. Half-wit! To whom do you think you are justifying yourself? Haven't I told you hundreds of times that history will never mention us? Why don't you free yourself of your vanity? As if I cared, the opinions of a bunch of vagabonds in the future about the majordomo of an imaginary king. Then again, there are many things that I cannot understand. Why, for example, am I putting all my effort into taking you, together with the rabble who call themselves my subjects, out of history and saving you from death? To make matters worse, I will probably succeed. Now, that's absurd: one person spends his whole life on a pillar eating butterflies and moss, and he gets stuck in hell, and you – who are worried about whether your name is written with one S or two – you get into heaven. The will of God is mysterious. Didn't Jesus himself save a thief?

Last night, Joseph Ferrarius visited me in my dreams. He is sailing, he said, with his brothers toward the north to find an island that does not exist. Go ahead and laugh, you twerp. That doesn't surprise me. They have sailed from the lousy world of facts and will find an island which will, in their world of faith and mine, become a fact. No one else will know of it. How else can one save oneself from the upcoming onslaught of researchers, adventurers, archeologists, geologists and oceanographers? Why, here in another two hundred years or so they will find America. For now, Grossman, America is not a fact, remember that, and therefore it doesn't exist. If you were to tell someone that, across the way from Normandy, there is a world as big as ours, they would think you are a lunatic. And it does exist. But you will tell that to no one. You are a conformist! Pardon me, Sire, would you please repeat that last word. No, there's no point in it. It's too early for that word. Listen to what I am saying: There will come a time when people will no longer believe that God exists. That's impossible, Sire. It's possible, unfortunately. Just as you, brainwashed by Ptolemaic geocentrism, think that I'm babbling about another continent, so will future Grossmans, because God is not a fact, think that God was concocted by man in order to be less afraid. God is the eighth continent, Grossman. He is neither good nor evil, neither great nor small. God is something different. Always something different. And, please, spare me your ecclesiastical footnotes denouncing me to the future generations and accusing me of heresy.

And wait till you hear this. Your jaw will drop in amazement. Margot came to me last night. Not with her bleeding head under her arm as she appears to you and other superstitious twits like you. I was just getting ready to retire for the evening, prepared for my showdown with the evil spirits awaiting me on the boundary between dreams and wakening, when Margot burst in. Her presence. Not her ghost, mind you, but her presence, a bit unpleasant in the light of her infidelity and my vengeance. What do you want to tell me? I thought, and Margot answered: Charles, I am so lonely. You're looking at me with suspicion, majordomo, you're thinking that the Hideous is jabbering, seeing things; the queen is dead and she cannot possibly say anything. Half-wit, words do not exist for us to communicate; remember the book of Genesis when the Lord confounded the languages. Words exist to cause misunderstanding. And yet, they are so powerful. You are just a word – Grossman. Take out the 'o' and 'a,' the soul, and all you have left are consonants – *Grssmn*, or your skeleton, like the ones we saw in the monastery labyrinth. But let's leave the mantra aside. Alone, you say, Margot, I said somehow, and she confirmed it. I could have explained to her that loneliness is our destiny, that nothing can be done about it, but out of piety toward her death (which she has taken so seriously) I said nothing, but rather adjusted my presence so that she could feel some kind of sympathy. I say presence because even you know that the thing the courtiers and plebes hold to be my presence is just hanging about miserably on the throne, dusty, covered with mildew. The soul is closest to the body when it is not equated with it, that must be clear to you. The body is necessary so that everything is not ethereal, too ethereal for rogues like you and the other dropouts that you studied Patristics with. *Habet mulier animam*, Grossman? *Habet*, Sire. You keep hanging on to your errors, but that improves your reputation in my eyes. That's the only thing you have approached like a man, overcoming your fear. That error makes you a man. But you see, as time passed even I, having learned something new, have changed my point of view. I will not say that a woman has a soul, certainly not, but something like a soul, that's possible. Hand me that parchment. I'll draw you a representation of the male anima and the female animula:

THE MALE SOUL THE FEMALE SOUL

You see? The horizontal line is missing. I could tell you about that for hours, but it's no use. You won't understand, and anyway Jung will write about it better one day. And anyway, we've got business to do. Write! God loves radical changes. Write down what Meister Eckhart will say about that, because his books will be burned. "If a man completely rises above his sin and renounces it, then God, who is true to his promise, will act as if the sinner never sinned. He won't allow him to suffer for a moment because of his sin. If he committed his sins even as much as all people sinned all together, God will not force him to atone for them. In doing so, God established a closeness to man that he created with no other being. He will not consider what a man used to be. God is the God of the present." And now, Grossman, let's get down to work. We need to write history. Every moment is precious. While I'm here lamenting Margot, in the blink of an eye, some son of a bitch is born and tangles all the threads. The Schism has already occurred; so, the split *ad acta*. The Reformation must be prepared for. The what? The Reformation, you idiot. I'm sorry, Sire, I don't know that word. I don't know the details, either. Martin Luther is only four years old right now. But it's not my business to deal with the details. I already said that God loves radical changes. As opposed to the Pope and his flatterers who have built into the heart the same thing the pharaoh built in stone – a pyramid, Grossman, an Egyptian pyramid. In doing so they committed blasphemy because the Spirit is not building material. They want to withdraw inside, to hide from God, but it will do them no good. God is always inside. We're the ones on the outside. It's a mistaken projection, that's all. Here, I see a new split in the church. That's why I walled up all the doors at the monastery of St. Panfucius. Do you think the split between Constantinople and Rome came about because of such a sophisticated theological question as the *Filioque*? No. "You think that I have come to bring peace on Earth!" the Lord says. "No, I say unto you, I come to bring discord."

Do you understand? No, Sire. Even better. Write. The division in the churches is necessary because of historical progress. The Eastern Church mustered the strength to bear the cross and become a martyr. The deadly sin of her sister, the Roman curia, was not debauchery, not Simony, not the sale of indulgences, but architecture. It will spread in the west in order to raise its buildings, in order to spread its earthly kingdom. Will Maxim the Confessor discover America? No. Christopher Columbus will find it. But not before the Renaissance. Sire, you keep mentioning the Renaissance. Yes, if you repeat a lie often enough, it becomes reality. That's the everyday magic of words. Just as I kept repeating Grossman, Grossman, Grossman, until you finally appeared at my side in that damned tavern, full of quotations and rage, real, but also false. So I keep repeating the Renaissance, the Renaissance, the Renaissance. And the result? In 1369 – Bogdan Suchodolski will write – Leonardo Bruni will be born. That's the wrong date. The real date is 1368. But that changes nothing. Write, so that Suchodolski will have someone to copy from: 1380 – the birth of Poggio Bracciolini, 1377 – Filippo Brunelleschi, 1378 – Lorenzo Gilberti; in 1386 the famous Donatello will be born, Fra Angelico circa 1390, Jan Van Eyck in 1397, that same year (underline it) *Johann Gutenberg.* The material basis of desacralization is, essentially, laid; the dates are perhaps not accurate, but there's not much use in chronology anyway. We have to wait for the year 1401 for one of our own to be born, Nicholas of Kues. And don't ask superfluous questions. Do not try to discover that which you cannot find out. Remember once and for all, Grossman, we are not interested in history. We are interested in its ruin. Others are here to see that history is made. We are meant to undermine it. Don't forget that the characteristic of our time, according to Suchodolski, and I quote, is "the mystical hope of fixing the world by destroying it." I don't understand, Sire; these contradictions aren't clear to me. You don't understand, Grossman. You have a German name with two ornate Ss, and you don't know that the WEST in German is ABENDLAND – the land of twilight. No, Sire. What language are we speaking then? What alphabet are you using to write down my words? Nothing can be confirmed with certainty. Why is that so, Sire? Because everything is relative. Does that mean anything to you? No, Sire. Let me explain: Everything is relative because $E=MC^2$.

To keep Grossman from accusing me of heresy, I'm thinking in cursive. I closed my eyes and I'm watching him through the slit between my eyelashes, which confuses me because my eyelashes are down there, on my body, on the throne. One way or the other, it is impossible to avoid anthropomorphism. I am watching, as I said, Grossman. Thinking that I am asleep, he's adding in his disloyal footnotes. From down on the throne, I could (since the connections are never broken) cry out: Guards, arrest Grossman! But what's the point? Like the professors of whom he is the forerunner, he has simply convinced himself that he can smuggle in the truth, and somehow deserve his place in some sort of musty book. Those are the very historical errors with which I am constantly obsessed. Why do the superficial souls so easily accept the thesis that history is a continuum in which one event causes another, which is complete nonsense? I can see, I swear to God, everything that has happened and everything that will happen, insofar as that is possible for a man. There is no cause-effect relationship. It is all just a whim of mine. The Spirit allowed me to write history. Not because of my abilities. Just as easily it could have given that task to Grossman, and nothing would change. I don't know how to explain that. If this is all not just a dream, I can see the future of the miserable New Europe with absolute clarity, not because that future is a necessity, but because I want it to be that way. Let me repeat: the Renaissance, the Reformation, the Gothic, the Baroque, the Enlightenment,

Rationalism, Bacon, Boehme, Descartes, Spinoza, Malebranche, Locke, Grotius, Hobbes, Cudworth, Pufendorf, Newton, Leibnitz, Wolf, Berkeley, Hume, Helvétius, Rousseau, Jacobi, Kant, Fichte, Schlegel, Novalis, Schelling, Hegel, Marx. Then came two of our own: Joseph Vissarionovich Dzhugashvili, no, first came Joseph Fitzgerald Queensdale, then he. Just names that I dreamed up, but which will usurp those bodies and minds, thinking that they are a necessity and not just a whim. All those learned gentlemen will feel challenged to discuss the past, never guessing that they are just a tile in a mosaic that should be taken apart. All of that is being demolished. Atomized. History is nothing more than the process of the continuous atomization of property. Once long ago, the owner of the Earth was its creator, God. Then the Earth was ruled by kings. Then came feudalism, followed by capitalism, and finally socialism where everyone is the owner, where everyone owns everything, but there is nothing left to own.

From time to time, I'm overcome by doubt. It is not to be excluded that all of this is just a dream. Perhaps those future positivists, with that fellow Meier among them, are correct after all when they claim that I am just an ordinary mystification. I will leave that possibility open, but things will unwind just as I foresaw them and predetermined them, regardless of my ontological status. And not just that. I know the conditions under which all of this will collapse in flames. It is possible to do that even now, I mean in terms of metaphysics; but the technological knowledge of my epoch has not reached the state where it can solve the purely technical problem of the apocalypse. I must leave that to the future generations, to the new sort who will, defying gravity, ride on magical two-wheelers, despised by the world, just like our Lord who rode into Jerusalem on a donkey. There you have it, including such hesitations in my reflections, I am once again proving that I have a democratic orientation. Which is one more historical paradox: the democrats of the future will not allow their dreams to be called into doubt. With their heads full of the thoughts of the dead who came before them, doubting nothing whatsoever, they will bravely march forward and become dead men themselves. True enough, we will help them with all our might. Having slipped in among their ranks, clandestinely. We will construct their machines, which Grossman believes to be the contraptions of the Devil. The fool. The Devil was never so obvious. But the machines are a theological problem after all. Just as God created man, and man rebelled against his creator, so will man create machines and the machines will rebel against people. Hegel will write about this in the parable of the master and the slave. One day, machines will be able to think. Huh, if such a thought ever crossed Grossman's mind, he would tie himself to the stake and set himself on fire. The dogmatic consciousness that sees only *here* and *now*, never dreaming that they have already become the past. And not only will machines think, they will think faster and better than people. There you have it, the beginnings of cybernetics! People will stop thinking. They will become stunted. They will grow dull from their laziness and vices. The difference is great between them and, let's say, me: I have the ability to reflect on all of that, observe Grossman, and at the same time I am holding an audience of tavern owners and passing judgments in the ridiculous court cases of my subjects. Why, even Grossman, in comparison to the future generations, seems to be a genius. All kinds of thoughts are roaming through his head at the same time while he is writing down my soliloquy, but all of that, as Lenin would (and will) say is . . . petit-bourgeois, petty-minded. Grossman can think of nothing without getting himself involved, without calculating whether something is profitable for him or not. A typical modern man. One night I psychoanalyzed him, just for fun, and he thought I was interrogating him. And this was my conclusion: Grossman is an orthodox Christian just because Christianity is the state religion of our time, not to mention a matter of decorum, a rule of proper manners. However, if he were accidentally born at the beginning of the 20th century, I'll bet that he would be in the first ranks to charge the Winter Palace. As pedantic as he is, he would create a fine career for himself, but sooner or later Dzhugashvili would get rid of him, just as I will, sooner or later, get rid of him, though in a subtle way so that he thinks he is dying a natural death and has a place waiting for him in heaven. But the means of getting rid of someone are a matter of the tastes of a time. In any case, because of his faithful service, he will be buried in his marvelous mausoleum, embellished with his name including two large Ss.

Grossman! Wake up! I'm sorry, Sire, I fell asleep. I was tricked into dreaming. And what did you dream? Ugh, I dreamt that you were watching me through your half-closed eyelids, saying things that made the hair on my neck stand up. Then I found myself in a crowd rushing at some sort of palace shouting, I remember it well, in some language I don't know "da zdravstvuet tovarishch Lenin." And then? Then you woke me up. Yes, Grossman, forget about your meaningless dreams, it's time for us to get back to work. So, America. Forgetting which direction it is that leads to the real homeland, they will head for the west, longing for the wide-open, hungry for space, tortured by the clench of their hardened souls. Instead of searching along the vertical, they will head off for the horizontal. Do you know what that means? It means that they will keep running in circles. In order to avoid dizziness from the heights, they will submit to the grave dizziness of the soil; they will concoct races and adore blood. Do you know the root of the word "vertical"? No, Sire. It's from the root vertigo, dizziness. So much for the Latin you learned at Uppsala. Not to mention the Greek. But never mind, I'm not interested in diplomas. Let's get back to work. Write this: Disoriented by the vertigo, they will call their demise "progress." Unless they mean the progress of their demise. All of the gnomes, melusines, nymphs, werewolves, and household demons that we so democratically tolerate in our kingdom, allowing them to multiply and perform their rituals, all of those beings about whom Bombastus Paracelsus wrote about, or should write about, so inspirationally, they will all be destroyed and proclaimed to be fictitious. Don't you frown at me, I know those beings don't exist, but they must be destroyed first so that something more real can come next. And don't flatter yourself that you are much more real than a gnome. I can convince you otherwise in an instant. Just a wink of my eye and you'll find yourself in your mausoleum in body, with your soul beneath, with Von Kurtiz and that whore Margot, where you can all gossip about me to your heart's content, if you can find anyone to listen to you. Oh, Margot! The eternal struggle of the animus and anima. Perhaps you had a hand in this as well, Grossman; I could swear that you are prepared to do anything just to discredit me in the eyes of the senseless mobs of the future who will, one way or another, hate kings and all other noble things. I'll bet you are the one who brought Kurtiz to be around the queen. But that's all right, I'll leave that up to your conscience which irresistibly reminds me of the Euclidean understanding of spatial perspective: far away things look small so they fill you with the false hope that your sins are forgiven. You're not alone in such observations. In just a few years, art will head down the path of your conscience. Is it worthwhile for me to mention: every perspective ends up in a dead-end. You are looking at me with your inherent disbelief, with that look that makes me wonder if you are my majordomo or my court jester. Or both. I am explaining things, not for your sake, you won't understand them; art will destroy Europe. That is why the Jews forbade the presentation of images. Those lousy painters, those producers of illusions, wishing to represent reality, expressing themselves through their ridiculous senses, they will make reality unreal. They will teach generations to observe the world with eyes trained by their pictures. Indeed, the day will come when a house in the distance will look small, quite small. Sire, I really cannot believe that. I know that the world will meet its demise, but that houses where people live can look smaller than a man, I cannot believe that at all. That doesn't surprise me. You are not here to believe or not believe, but to write. You will gain eternal life for that. But this business with perspective, it will be precisely as I have said. Artists will shrink people. They will shorten distances. They will draw the New Europe. Let me go farther than the time in which my thoughts will be read like artistic fiction, in which all of this will be a chapter in an insignificant novel, let me tell you a secret. In the end of all things, when time nears its end, Europe will turn into an enormous library and an endless gallery of pictures. My poor Grossman, long before that apocalyptic twilight, *everyone will have their own picture*, down to the last busboy in the tavern. At the moment that is the privilege of the kings and high nobility. In those days, the kings will already be in museums. I won't be. Did you write the history of the sect of Two-Wheelers? No, Sire, I did not have the time. What do you mean, didn't have the time? I'm either writing down your words, or I'm down there by the throne. But why don't you write the history at the same time you are writing down my words. I'm sorry, Sire, but that's absurd. Never mind, just keep writing, the time will come when that will cause no one to wonder. Now, where was I? Oh, yes! In the year nineteen fifty-th . . .

*(Remainder of the manuscript destroyed)*

## MAJORDOMO GROSSMAN

# A HISTORY OF THE DIABOLICAL TWO-WHEELER

*Anno Domini* 1347, Monsignor Robert de Prevois, the Inquisitor of Paris, received news from the mouths of honorable citizens that master Enguerrand de Auxbris-Malvoisin, obsessed by the Unclean One, had left the saving grace of the Christian faith, turned to incantations and magic, and built a demonic device that he rode through the streets terrifying people. Not wishing to act drastically, Monsignor Robert ordered Brother Guillaume of Poitiers to clandestinely inquire as to the truth of the rumors. Two months later, Brother Guillaume made his report to the Inquisitor confirming that the news about the devilish dealings of master Enguerrand was true, but that it was incomplete. In his home, Auxbris-Malvoisin regularly gathered a company of witches and wizards whose heresiarch was a schismatic monk named Callistus and whose secular leader was a certain Josephus Ferrarius; this Satanic society met regularly at black masses where they broke mirrors and spoke unfathomable blasphemies about God.

The machine which master Enguerrand publicly and shamelessly rode through the streets of Paris, proved that he was inspired by Satan who is the author of all evil things. Frere Guillaume describes it like this: "Instead of two wheels connected by an axel, one next to the other like on a normal cart, master Enguerrand has built a vehicle where the wheels stand one behind the other connected by a beam which is topped by a seat. It is clear to everyone that such an apparatus cannot stand upright, and it certainly cannot be ridden. And yet master Enguerrand, obviously with the aid of the powers of darkness, accompanied by the great noise of frightened children screaming, rides down the steep streets on this hellish contraption and scandalizes all those who pass there."

Despite the irrefutability of the evidence, guided by the lessons of our Savior on tolerance and forgiveness, Robert de Prevois wrote a letter to Enguerrand, counseling him to leave his heresies behind, his sinful ways and bodily pleasures, and to return in humility to his mother Church, which forgives all sins and every blasphemy, except for blasphemy against the Holy Ghost. Master Enguerrand, obviously under the complete control of demonic possession, not only showed no intention or wish to repent, but rather haughtily replied, calling the Inquisitor a servant of Satan, saying that he himself was indeed sinful but that he did not know why he would be more sinful than he, Robert de Prevois; he said that he, Enguerrand, possessed evidence that Holy Father Sylvester II (may God protect us from the very thought) had become the Pope thanks to a deal with the Devil; he said that he repented everyday, but saw no reason to do so in front of the Inquisitor. Left with no choice, Robert de Prevois ordered the secular authorities to capture and shackle the heretics.

However, Satan, who is the Prince of this world and the Master of darkness, and who has the power to see some part of the future, found a way to inform his servants Enguerrand, Josephus and Callistus of what was awaiting them, so the three of them snuck out of Paris under the cover of night and went to find sanctuary with the Marquis de Rocheteau, an evil and perverted man. Feeling safe, from there they began sending letters to the honorable Inquisitor, letters full of insults and inconceivable rudeness, to the extent that it is troubling to read them and impossible to reproduce them. Completely overcome with the insanity of their conceit, steeped in irrationality, they began making as many of those demonic two-wheelers as possible with the insane intention of, when the time came, riding off on the path to heaven on them, never dreaming that they would be tumbling out of control into hell. At Rocheteau castle the scum of the earth, thieves, drunks and loose women began to gather, and the Marquis and Enguerrand gave a whipping to Isabelle de Monmoranse, a virgin whose virtue was known far and wide, for they said that no one is virtuous in this world. And so the rumors of the infamous atrocities of the demonic society, who called themselves *the Order of the Little Brothers*, reached the royal throne. Desiring to maintain peace in the kingdom and quiet among his subjects, the King ordered the Knight, Dagobert of Lourdes, to capture the Rocheteau castle and turn the transgressors against God's and the King's authority over into the hands of justice.

With God's ministration, on Good Friday of Anno Domini 1348, the knight Dagobert overcame the heretics' resistance, killing the scum, and taking the culprits – Callistus, Enguerrand and the Marquis de Rocheteau – in shackles to Paris. Using the cover of night, Josephus Ferrarius, followed by a small band of the heretics, escaped the hands of justice. From the righteous flames that engulfed the Rocheteau castle, Dagobert temporarily saved the manuscripts of the heretics so that they could serve as irrefutable evidence of their service to Satan. However, when the Inquisitor and Guillaume of Poitiers, having prayed to God, began to research the manuscripts, they found that, except the first page, all the pages were filled with complete nonsense, random series of letters, drawings that imitated texts, which indicated that the Devil was attempting to cover their tracks and save his servants. In vain. The first page was enough to send them to the stake. The parchment read:

THEOLOGIA FRATERNITATIS

and beneath that stood the emblem of their heresy – the cross stuck into some kind of pagan symbols.

At the bottom of the page, moreover, there were verses bursting with heretical ravings:

*When you fall asleep, die*
*to this world. Then arise from your corpse and go*
*Straight ahead regardless of the apparitions.*
*Know that those unfortunate beings exist only*
*When they trick you into believing that you exist, too.*
*Withstand, you must, the burden of death.*

The interrogation of the heretics was carried out immediately after Easter. The Inquisitor, Robert de Prevois, warned them that he had the means to torture them available and that it would be better for them to admit their intercourse with Satan outright, which the Devil's servants refused to do, and which was, after all, expected of them. Then the Inquisitor began the interrogation of the accused.

The monk, Callistus, was the first to speak.

"Two years ago, at this time, I was a monk on the holy mountain of Athos. I lived with the brothers in the community, I was an obedient hegumen and behaved, insofar as my weakness allowed me, according to the rules established by the holy fathers.

"One night I dreamed St. Gregory Palama in the company of a king. The saint told me: 'Callistus, Callistus, do you think you will reach the Kingdom of Heaven by digging in the garden? You got away from evil, hiding behind the monastery walls, but you did not defeat evil.' So, I asked him: 'Father, what am I to do?' The saint told me: 'Go out into the world!' Thus, I left the monastery. I went out into the world, and every night that king appeared in my dreams showing me more details of the machine that you call demonic.

"I arrived in Paris where Providence led me to the home of honorable master Enguerrand, and there I met Josephus Ferrarius. And that was how the three of us made the first two-wheeler. Combining our dreams into one, we fulfilled the inconceivable will of God. I don't know what purpose the two-wheeler will serve, nor do I want to know; I am unable to say anything about the secrets of the brotherhood. I think that the two-wheeler is the omen of the new age, the vehicle of man that will rise from the earth, one who leaves the house and raises his eyes into the heavens.

"But a man who stares into heaven long enough, sooner or later finds out that an even greater chasm exists inside himself and that, at the bottom of that chasm, hidden in the darkness, is an opening that leads to God. I interpret our actions as the will of the Savior for us to return to his words: 'The Kingdom of God is within you!' Those whom the devil convinced to build the Tower of Babylon, those wolves in sheep's clothing, are among us again. We, the *Little Brothers*, have turned our face from this world and from idolatry and have returned to a spiritual faith. That is why I refuse to admit that I am in collusion with the Devil, and I am ready to suffer if I must, not turning back from the path dictated to me by my conscience."

It was difficult and abhorrent for everyone who attended that interrogation to listen to these blasphemous words. Enguerrand did not wish to use his right to speak. He looked at the Inquisitor with impudence, at times scoffing at him, exchanging glances with his comrades. But the Marquis de Rocheteau magnanimously made up for Enguerrand's silence, pouring out a flood of noxious words, insults and blasphemies:

"You wonder why we break mirrors? What kind of magic is this? Here is the answer: we break mirrors because that way the deception has only one side, this one where we all are. That is not enough for you. You don't want God inside you, where you cannot hide your iniquities from Him, but you rather place him in front of you. On the outside you are whitewashed tombs, and on the inside you are rotting. And you think that you can frighten us with torture, while death and torture are exactly what we want. You try to scare us with the fire of the stake, and you already have one foot in the fire of hell, you hypocrites. But Ferrarius has escaped and you will never find him. He is now far away, followed by a few of the brothers; he has slipped out of the hand of your earthly justice. I know the date of my death, just as I know the date of my birth. I've got nothing else to say."

Robert de Prevois, seeing that the heretics were not showing the slightest inclination toward recanting, ordered that Callistus, Enguerrand and the Marquis be tortured, for the salvation of their souls. But Satan, who finds hellish pleasure in ruining actions pleasing to God, filled the bodies of his subjects with supernatural strength and they were able to withstand the most strenuous of tortures, occasionally joking about it or ostensibly forgiving their torturers. Seeing that the Devil was winning, and fearing for the souls of others, Robert de Prevois ordered a public-wide repentance and dressed himself in a goat's hair shirt.

In the meantime, one of the bandits who had slipped away from the justice of Dagobert raised a rebellion among the people and the crowd arrived in front of the prison, demanding that the heretics be set free. What was worse, the Satanic machine of Enguerrand and his company began to be replicated in Paris. The people, quick to do evil and slow to think, accepted the demonic two-wheelers because the rumor began that whoever could cover a certain distance sitting on such an apparatus without falling would have all sins forgiven. Hundreds of such monstrous two-wheelers appeared in Paris, disturbing public order and causing such scandals that it was shameful for an honest man to go out into the street.

In the meantime, the stubbornness of the heretics locked up and tortured in the dungeon began to soften. But they remained faithful to their belief, claiming that they had a Covenant with God and that they did not dare back down because they had sworn to undergo whatever suffering necessary. The Inquisitor told them that they had been blinded and that their covenant was with the Devil, but Callistus and Enguerrand did not want to give in. They had, they said, signed a covenant with God and that there was no doubt about it; the Devil does not personally bring a contract in which he is a party, but rather appears as a merchant, banker or mediator. The stipulations of the contract were ostensibly related to business, but that was trap, because the Devil later fits such a contract into the complex book of bills and debts that he uses to rule this world. The next day the Marquis fell unconscious because, according to his calculations, he was supposed to die the day after, which he actually did. But all Satan's hopes were in vain; the experienced Father Robert did not allow himself to be deceived; he knew that the Devil attempts to confuse people by foreseeing events from the future.

Dagobert again had to take up his sword. The unruliness of the crowd demanding freedom for the heretics went beyond all measure of good taste, and the King ordered that an end be put to it. For three whole days the rebels put up a strong resistance, but they began to fail from exhaustion and it was not difficult for Dagobert to send them scurrying. The Satanic two-wheelers were gathered into a pile and burned, and their production and use was forbidden under the threat of the death penalty.

Since the anger of the crowd was silenced, and since the heretics refused to recant, they were sent before the court of the Holy Inquisition and sentenced to death by burning, with the hope that the flames would achieve that which neither mercy nor torture had. Listening to the reading of the sentence, Enguerrand de Auxbris-Malvoisin spoke for the first time since his arrest. He recited some kind of incantation:

*And then you must pass*
*Through flames, painful and hard*
*But bringing salvation. Here, everything rotten will burn and*
*All that will be left is just that which*
*Fire is, but does not burn*
*and is not hot.*

On January 28, *Anno Domini* 1348, the confessor visited the heretics in the dungeon and they miraculously agreed to give their confession. The cart carrying Enguerrand and Callistus was driven all the way across Paris as a warning and example of the fate of those who rebel against the Divine Order. The commoners, frightened, downtrodden because of the recent uprising and bloodshed, followed the heretics in silence on their long last journey. Before the sentence was publicly read, the Inquisitor asked the heretics if they wanted to repent, to which they answered that they had repented even before they had been caught. Then, Brother Guillaume read the sentence and Robert de Prevois gave the signal for the fire to be set to the stake. The heretics quickly vanished in the smoke and flames.

May it stand recorded for all generations that Enguerrand, before losing consciousness, shouted an incomprehensible word, certainly some kind of hellish incantation: Dharamsala, Dharamsala, Dharamsala . . .*

* Note: The text of Majordomo Grossman is reproduced from the journal *Oblique* (3, 1967), dedicated in its entirety to the history of European heresies.

Charles the Hideous

Gottfried of Mainz: The Execution of Baron von Kurtiz (ca. 1346)

# ON THE THRESHOLD OF THE NEW ERA

## THE MANUSCRIPT OF
# CAPTAIN QUEENSDALE
## PUBLISHER'S PREFACE

In a copy of *The Encyclopedia of Wind Roses* printed in 1872, bought quite accidentally in a secondhand bookstore in Zürich, instead of the final signature which was missing, I found a manuscript dated 1892, written in calligraphy. The contents of the manuscript (which was, in fact, a copy of another) changed the direction of my life to a great extent, as you will see, just as it changed the life of the copyist. I do not possess a single proof that would support the validity of the lines which follow. It is possible that the whole thing is a joke. Someone with an English sense of humor (the copyist is English) is doubtlessly willing to undertake extensive and expensive preparations in order to, after his own death, make fools of a small group of unknown people. My intuition convinces me otherwise. In any case, whether the facts correspond to reality or whether they are the fruit of someone's imagination, I believe it is worthwhile to publish this carefully selected text, printed in six copies, and I now send it into the world to find its six readers.

Rheiner Meier
Zürich, 1903

# PREFACE
## BY THE UNKNOWN COPYIST

At the end of 1898, crushed by inexplicable depression and fatigue, I left London, a lovely social position, a reputable name (that I will not mention here) and withdrew to the land of my ancestors in Western England, hoping that, far from the hustle and bustle of the city, I would find peace and dignity, and prepare for death. At the beginning, it seemed that nothing would come of my plan because, not far from my home, one of the nouveau riche had moved in, some sort of London private-eye, a detective who had been on the front pages of the scandalous chronicles for years; a chronic user of morphine and amateur violinist, who broke down at the very appearance of a velocipede because he had recently suffered a nervous breakdown. I do not know what related the velocipedes to his illness but, since that vehicle had attained a certain popularity amongst the young, his attacks occurred almost daily. I doubt that, in my life, I have met a man, and I have met plenty, who was more completely in love with himself. In truth, to be in love with anyone is a matter of the naïveté common to early youth, but to be in love with oneself, and therefore with the person we know best, means either to be an idiot or an evil man, and my neighbor was, I am convinced, both.

To make matters worse, this good-for-nothing, about whom people of dubious reputation had even written several trivial books for entertaining the masses, was constantly attempting to visit me, to give me gifts, to invite me to games of bridge and, worst of all, I tolerated these intrusions with a hypocrisy and patience that was amazing, if one considers my pitiful spiritual state. And yet, I am most thankful to him, that genius of shabby logic. And this is why: in order to defend myself from his onslaughts I began, using the excuse of my doctor's advice, to take long walks to the shore of the ocean where I found a certain measure of peace in the silence, barely disturbed by the murmuring of waves and the whistle of the wind; by the way, I also learned, during a storm accompanied by roaring thunder, that the worst sort of noise is . . . the prattle of human voices in a closed room. If these words make me out to be a misanthropist to future readers, I will be satisfied. Was I not (like everyone else) a misanthropist who pretended to be a philanthropist in the tortuous farce of social life? Those walks helped me become aware that I had wasted my life in the constant presentation of myself as someone else, someone different than who I really am; that I put on the mask of a specter my whole life until finally, just as it says in the Caballah, I actually became a specter. I gave thanks to the Lord for mercifully doling out to me, near the end of my life, the flames of the worst suffering of the soul, for wracking my body with pain and insomnia; I was thankful for every suffering that opened my eyes, blinded before that by the trivial sparkle of worldly things.

During one such excursion, while the coachman waited for me in a nearby tavern, as I walked along the seastrand, I saw a shining object cast upon the beach by the high tide. I can be grateful to Providence and someone else that I descended the steep cliff, for I might well have broken my back or a leg. Far from it, that I feared for my life or my health; I was lethargic and fainthearted, and I would undertake such an effort for nothing – by earthly criteria – valuable. But the object sparkled mysteriously; that which greed could not do was done by curiosity, and I descended, wading knee-deep into the water, and I snatched it up. At first glance, it was just a common bottle of fine glass, carefully sealed with pitch. Immediately I called my driver and rode home. That evening, in the privacy of my study, I broke the bottle. Inside was a scroll of paper, the manuscript of Captain Adam Queensdale, dated 23 October 1761.

Although it had been well-protected, over the one hundred and twenty-five years the bottle had been carried by the ocean currents, the paper had suffered a degree of damage. I spent several exciting evenings copying the contents of the original which threatened to disintegrate into dust and ashes at any moment. The text contained a description of a shipwreck that only Captain Queensdale had survived; a description of the island, Ultima Thulae, north of Iceland, where the castaway was taken in by the inhabitants, members of the heretical sect of Two-Wheelers, exiled from Europe in the 14th century; a description of the life and rituals of the inhabitants, of their mythology and eschatology; and at the end, a copy of the holy text, *The Purgatory of Sleep*, the greater part of which, unfortunately, was so heavily damaged as to be unreadable.

Studying this tale, which had a healing effect on my soul, I decided to save it from oblivion, but also from the curiosity of the masses, from the quasi-scholars and sensationalists. The only way to do that was to act just as the bottle had acted toward me: I had to let the story find its readers by itself. Toward that end, I made six completely identical copies and inserted them into six expensive, but uninteresting, books. I sent the books to the addresses of reputable secondhand bookstores in London, Istanbul, Heidelberg, Reykjavik,

Cairo and Bombay. They will, I am certain of it, know how to reach their readers. Everyone who comes to believe in their contents will do the same thing I did: he will make six copies of the text and find a way to release them into the world.

J. H. W.
4 July 1982

## THE MANUSCRIPT OF
# CAPTAIN QUEENSDALE

I do not know if these lines will ever be read. In their depths, the expanse of the oceans hides objects much larger than the bottle of Venetian glass to which I am entrusting these pages. The ancient books say that those depths swallowed up an entire continent that used to lie between Europe and America. But still, I am writing. If I write down my confession and entrust it to the currents of the seas (at times more conscientious than messengers), there is a hope that, even a hundred years from now, it will reach someone, somewhere. If I do not do this, it is certain that I will carry all I have discovered with me into my grave.

My great fortune came about in the form of a terrible accident. While returning from New England, the ship *Invincible*, under my command, was caught in an unprecedented storm. The crew threw our cargo overboard in vain, in vain we lowered the sails; the wind and waves snapped the rudder. On the second day (which I thought to be Judgment Day), an enormous wave broke the mainmast like a twig, under which nostromo Bradley met his death, and the next wave carried away three sailors who were rushing to help him. We had no other recourse than to pray to the Lord for the salvation of our souls. There was no more salvation for the ship.

The next day, water began to penetrate into the hold. Rudderless, with no sails, the *Invincible* was carried ever farther north. The sailors, believing that they had greater chances in the lifeboat, decided to abandon the ship. I could not blame them. They took the remaining stores of salt-cured meat, the last barrel of water, and they set off into the unknown. I doubt that they ever reached shore or that they came across another ship. For, when the sea finally calmed and the clouds scattered, I took the astrolabe and pinpointed the position of the swamped ship, and I realized that the winds had taken us far from any of the trade routes. But that was not all. Shocked, I saw a constellation in the sky that is not noted on any of the charts of the northern skies. I drew the configuration of stars onto the map, although I doubted that my discovery would ever be of service to anyone:

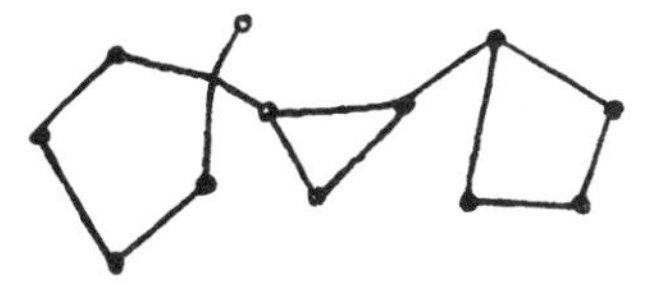

In my youth, I had read in a marine atlas, translated from Arabic, full of the fantastic deeds of Sinbad the Sailor and his company, about a constellation that appears every 365 years, when *the year of years* is fulfilled, and when *the winter of centuries* begins in which everything good dies out and the forces of evil grow strong. But, at the time, I could not remember how that constellation from the atlas looked, so that I could compare it with the one above my head. Nor did I have time. Already fairly exhausted, I reached for an ax, some rope and a hammer in order to make a raft. Wrapped in wax-cloth, on the raft I took the ship's log, a Bible, writing materials, some gunpowder and lead, and at dawn on 12 October 1733, I sailed into the unknown.

One who has never been on the ocean's expanse has also never experienced the sea of time with absolutely nothing to do. In spite of my desperation (or actually because of it), I measured time using instruments, and every twenty-four hours I carved a notch on the improvised mast, since day and night last for months at those latitudes. At the moment when, not believing my eyes, I spied land through the mist, there were seven notches on the mast. Setting foot on solid land, exhausted and hungry, I collapsed and fell sound asleep. I do not know how long I slept; perhaps an hour, maybe two, maybe two days, but I did not wake up on my own. Someone shook me gently, I opened my eyes and saw three people. One of them addressed me in some language, but I could not tell if it was broken Latin or Old French. To my surprise, when I spoke in English, the man picked up the conversation. I was expecting anything except the presence of a polyglot on such a distant island. But that would merely be the first of my surprises. To be honest, at first I thought that I was dreaming that I was awakened on a remote island by three blond men and that the eldest of them, who introduced himself as Joseph, was telling me that he had seen the sinking of the *Invincible* in a dream, and my suffering on the raft; that he had dreamt the place where I would land, and that he had come to meet me there. I thought to myself, "All of this is a nightmare; I have had similar dreams before; soon, I will wake up in my cabin on the *Invincible*, sailing smoothly for Southampton." But I kept waking up in another place: in a warm hut, on bedclothes made of sheepskin, next to a man who was hovering over me. When the delirium caused by my exhaustion finally passed, it became clear to me that nothing in it had been a dream: I was in an unfamiliar hut, on an island isolated from the civilized world, surrounded by strangers.

Or, perhaps it was all a dream.

One afternoon, Joseph, the elderly man who had found me on the beach, told me the history of the strange community. In the 14th century, a group of laymen and clergymen, led by a certain Enguerrand, a monk named Callistus and Josephus Ferrarius, dissatisfied with the Church steeped in Simony, had accepted an ancient teaching – a heresy begun in Asia Minor at the very beginning of the acts of Christ's apostles. This original group of master blacksmiths from Antioch sincerely accepted the Gospels, but they also committed a horrible sin. Namely, they undertook the construction of a Mechanical Bird which they intended to use to rise into the seventh heaven. This was the sin of pride. However, because of their unusual spirituality, the blacksmiths from Antioch were not condemned to vanish from the face of the earth. Their spiritual progeny was predestined to play an important role in the history of the world, but also to be exposed to constant exile, torture and scorn.

According to Joseph's words, they appeared in history again during the iconoclastic crisis that shook Byzantium. Already punished once because of magic and idolatry, they were the most enthusiastic iconoclasts. With the victory of the iconodules, the heresy disappeared from the face of the earth again, resurfacing after three hundred and sixty-five years when the monk Chrysostom found the third of the entire six copies of the secret texts of the *Little Brothers* and gave it on his deathbed to his pupil, Callistus, who took the secret teaching to Paris where it gained a large number of followers. Using the most conniving of intrigues, the Inquisition accused the most prominent brothers of colluding with the Devil. Callistus, Enguerrand and the Marquis of Rocheteau were burned at the stake, and a small group led by Josephus Ferrarius found sanctuary with King Charles the Hideous. From there, in a boat, led by a constellation which will be discovered only in the future, they reached the most distant Thulae, an island hidden by ice and fog, which I myself had found.

"One hundred years ago," Joseph told me, "my great-grandfather who, like my father and myself, was named Joseph, just as all the Grand Masters of the order of *Little Brothers* are called Joseph, dreamed that a castaway came to the island. He left his dream as a testament to his son who improved it, made it more profound and then introduced my father into its secrets. When my father experienced the honor of dying, everything was finished, you were born and it was my responsibility to maintain the whole dream, to dream it anew every night until a few days ago when it finally became reality. We needed you and that is why we created you. In return, you will compose a record of everything you see and learn; our time, the time of the inhabitants of this island has run out; we are preparing to return to our father. Now, get some rest, and when you gather your strength go see everything and ask questions about it all. Then take up the pen."

"Did it really have to be me?" I asked. "Couldn't you find a way to hand down your teachings earlier? Did my sailors have to die so that I would come here and try to save your manuscripts?"

"You're wrong," said Joseph, preparing to leave, "your sailors had to die because they had to die; they were mortal beings, and the circumstances of death are not important whatsoever. You got here because you had to get here. None of us is able to hand down the teaching because we all know it, and teaching is always passed on by those who are not dedicated to it, but who *believe* in it. From tonight onward, I will teach you every night in your dreams, and you will come to believe it because you already do. And now, good-bye."

It will be hard for the one who finds this text to believe its contents. I saw things with my own eyes, but as the Savior said:

"Blessed is he who believes without seeing." Anyway, Joseph tried to convince me that the text will go from one hand to another until it falls into the right ones, because it is not looking for just any reader, but for a certain one. To that unknown person, certainly as yet to be born, I dedicate the pages that follow.

The island itself is not big; it is about ten miles long and not more than three miles wide. At first I thought that was the reason that it remained unmarked on the nautical maps but Joseph, approaching me in a dream, revealed the secret to me. Fleeing from Normandy, the forebears of the islanders kept a copy of the *Vulgate* and the text *The Purgatory of Dreams*; they cast their mirrors, weapons and devices into the sea. And without mirrors, watches and swords there is no history; history is, after all nothing but a hall of mirrors in which it is not known which faces are real and which are only reflections.

Without chronology, without history, the island becomes objective insofar as it is the spiritual projection of its inhabitants; it is no less real, no less tangible than Britain, but it lies outside of time and space, or better said in parallel with them, due to the fact that there is no continuous series of events. Thus, I did not reach it, as I thought, by means of my raft, but rather by means of my delirium.

Those are things of which I could not conceive. Not even in the dreams in which Joseph patiently taught me the impossible.

"You see," he said, "it's not that difficult to understand. I will use an analogy. Just as America, from where you sailed, did not exist but was rather created by the longing of people for a place where they could extend their exodus to the west, so did our island exist, but it vanished to the senses of the world, because generations and generations of islanders despised space. Then again, it would not be correct to say that America and the island are two different worlds.

It's like when you turn a glove inside out. It remains the same glove except that what was up becomes what is down and instead of the left it turns into the right. At the same time, that is the only possible explanation for your mission. You belong both to the world of America and to the world of the island; you are the mediator in transmitting the secret. That is the real purpose. The description of the situation and of the island is of no importance whatsoever. It's just a way for all the things we are talking about here to become a part of history. Otherwise, it would all dissipate into nothingness. It wouldn't even be a fantasy."

I could swear that, except for Joseph and a couple of other dignitaries, I never saw the same face twice in a row, even though the island did not have many inhabitants. My arrival surprised no one. It was known about for ages, down to the last detail. The smallest of children spoke of the Masters who had died many generations before, and the adults spoke of events that were supposed to happen in the distant future. In great detail they described the assassination of an Austrian archduke in the middle of a Balkan gorge, and with horror they spoke of a great war that would be fought with only one goal: to kill and destroy as much as possible.

From time to time, the patriarchs of old would appear and then just as unexpectedly disappear, but this did not disturb anyone. However, perhaps the most interesting, those people were not sinless, lifeless creatures. Robberies happened, adultery, and even murder, not to mention all the lies that were told. The attitude toward the offenders was interesting. They were not punished, not judged, nor were they despised. On the contrary, they were showered with attention, and they were even envied because, by doing evil, they had obtained the saving possibility of repentance, and thereby the possibility of advancing in their spirituality. These occasional outpourings of evil served to remind everyone of the highest good, God, and so that no one forgot that among created beings none are perfect or without sin.

Still, their graves are the most interesting of all. Placed just along the shore of the ocean, facing eastward, they consist of a series of vertical recesses in which the corpses stand erect, their eyelids half-opened, mummified by the cold in the expectation of that day when the earth and sky will dissolve and when the unimaginable flame of the living God will flood light into the darkness of the human heart. Visits to those graves, scattered among the hills, are the only external manifestation of religiosity I have been able to observe. I have often noticed men and women going to the recess intended for them, getting into them, and practicing their death for hours. Hundreds, thousands of years of solitude that come before the moment when everything will become one.

Before I finish this story and, sealed in a bottle of Venetian glass (a gift from King Charles), introduce it into the fluctuating world of history, I will say something about the language of the island's inhabitants. At first, it reminded me of the quiet buzz of a beehive and it was completely incomprehensible to me, although it was beautiful. The secret of this language was revealed to me by Joseph, during one of my oneiric lessons. Namely, they speak the words of all languages of the world, the words that made up human language before the disturbance at Babylon, those that the Almighty shattered into a seeming multitude in order to stop evil from becoming perfectly formulated and organized. But for the good, as Joseph said, no words are necessary.

Because, just as resting is perfect movement, so silence is perfect articulation.

## ARTHUR CONAN DOYLE

# THE FINAL CASE OF SHERLOCK HOLMES

After the "Second Stain" affair, the last one I presented to the public, Sherlock Holmes retired to his home in Sussex, expressing the wish – which I have respected until now – that I no longer publish my notes about his investigations. Undoubtedly he despised the popularity that made him into a sort of public figure and thereby intricately interfering in his work, but I tend to believe that this is not the reason why my friend retired. The reason, above all, should be sought in the profanation of crime which, as time has passed, has fallen to the level of a purely technical deed, calculated and cold-blooded, almost professional, bereft of any romantic element whatsoever. However, something else is also afoot. I hope that the memory of Sherlock Holmes will not be tarnished by the admission that a significant role in his decision to withdraw was played by the case of "The Maniacal Cyclist," to my knowledge the only case Sherlock Holmes never managed to solve.

It was in the spring of 1898. Inspector Lestrade, as was his custom, had dropped by our room in Baker Street in the evening. We lit the gaslight and chatted over coffee. Sherlock inquired of the inspector if he were working on any interesting cases.

"You see, Mr. Holmes," said the inspector. "I do have one case, but I believe it's more of a case for Mr. Watson than for myself. A masked bicyclist appeared in Trafalgar Square seven days ago, making one round and then pulling out a revolver – he shot a clock in the window of 'James and Sons' watchmakers, and then he sped away. It caused quite a stir."

"Yes," said Holmes, "I read about it in the paper."

"But that was not the end of it," inspector Lestrade continued. "That same cyclist appeared again two days later in a different place and shot at a city clock in plain sight of a police officer."

"I read about that in the paper, too."

"Yes, after that there were no more articles in the newspapers, but the bicyclist carried on with his dastardly deeds. The journalists have agreed with our suggestion not to write about it until the case has been thoroughly investigated. You know, because of the panic. Because, if he shoots at clocks, by God, the maniac might begin to shoot at people as well. He's destroyed three clocks so far, and I don't have enough men to place a guard in front of every clock in London, which must number . . ."

"Exactly 3874," said Holmes, smiling at his friend.

After Lestrade had left, Holmes asked me to bring him a map of London. He compared the map with the list of places where the maniacal cyclist had appeared. Then he stood up abruptly, took his violin and, deep in thought, began to play as he always did when confronted with a difficult problem to solve. Nothing unusual in that, except for the fact that there was no problem.

"Ah, my dear Watson," he said a bit later, "you have fallen for the same deception as our friend Lestrade. I know it already: you're convinced that the maniacal cyclist is a mentally disturbed individual."

"Of course. All the indications are there. The acts he's committing are absolutely nonsensical. Neither does he have any use of them, nor do they cause any real harm to anyone. Doubtlessly, we have a mentally ill person here who is attempting to attract attention to himself."

"Wrong, my dear Watson. The bicyclist does want to attract attention, but not to himself, rather to his movements. Take a look at the map of London where I have dotted in the places where he appeared and connected them."

I have to admit that nothing was clear to me. No matter where he went it was possible to connect the dots. And what of that? I told Holmes that, no matter how much I appreciated his brilliant insight, this time there was no crime behind the acts of the maniacal cyclist.

"You are wrong," Holmes said. "Look more closely. The circle around Trafalgar square, what is that if not the front, large wheel of a bicycle; this was followed by the incident in Carnaby Street, that's the steering column; the next incident – that's the beginning of the bicycle frame. My dear Watson, our cyclist wishes to draw an enormous bicycle with his movements and his shooting."

At that moment, someone rang at the door. It was one of Lestrade's men, who handed Holmes a letter.

> Dear Holmes,
> The cyclist has struck again. This time in Abbey Road. He shot at a clock and vanished in an undetermined direction. This case is becoming serious.
>
> Lestrade

"He did not disappear in an undetermined direction," said Holmes. "Indeed, I can show you with certainty the place where the cyclist will appear on the morrow."

And with that, Holmes marked another place on the map of London.

Despite Lestrade's efforts, the affair appeared again in the papers, on the front page, no less. The case from the day before was given in detail. The cyclist was described as a gaunt fellow wearing a hood. In addition, at the bottom of the page, there was the latest news: the bicyclist had been at it again. I suppose it is unnecessary for me to say that he showed up at the place where Holmes had indicated on the map the day before.

"You're hiding something from me," I told him.

"No, Watson. I'm not hiding anything. In other words, I still don't have anything to hide."

Then he smiled cryptically.

"You see, tonight the cyclist will appear here, make a round and thus complete the silhouette of a bicycle on the streets of London."

"And we will be waiting for him there and capture him," I added.

"Far from it, Watson. Far from it. That's exactly what our cyclist is expecting."

It was only then that my confusion was complete. If Holmes is right, I thought, then the cyclist is indeed a psychopath. It is impossible for a man in his right mind to break the law in order to be caught.

"But no, my dear Watson. The cyclist is certainly not a psychopath. I would rather say that he is a member of a well organized criminal group. Now it is time for me to reveal the secret to you: all of London is abuzz with the affair of the cyclist. The police have turned their complete attention to him, which is reasonable because public opinion has been aroused. The cyclist will appear tonight at the place where we expect him to, but we will not be there."

"I don't understand."

"The cyclist and his cohorts have not forgotten my acquaintance with Lestrade and my cleverness. Quite correctly they have assumed that I will discover that the cyclist wants to draw attention to the pattern of his movements. But, I must say, they have underestimated me."

"What do you mean?"

"They thought I would appear tonight to arrest the cyclist who, this evening anyway, will not be the one who has been doing the shooting, but a hired layabout. Nothing could be farther from my mind. Tonight, my dear Watson, we will be with our friend Lestrade at the Gibson Gallery."

"The Gibson Gallery?"

"Yes. There is an ongoing exhibition of diamonds, among which is the Great Sari. The Gibson Gallery is not far from the place where the cyclist first appeared. Now do you realize . . ."

It was only then that all the pieces fell into place of this cleverly planned crime. Lured by the cyclist, we were supposed to rush to the opposite side of town while the thieves robbed the Gibson Gallery undisturbed.

I took my revolver, and Holmes took his hunting knife, his weapon of choice. Then we called a cab.

"Incredible," inspector Lestrade said as we waited, hidden in a broom closet, for the robbers to appear. "I never would have guessed that they are so clever."

"Inspector," said Holmes, "you should never forget that criminals also stay in step with times. That's why it is important for us to stay one step ahead of the times."

We stood there in the closet for quite a while. How long, we could not even guess, because in the absolute dark our watches were useless. Then someone knocked on the door and we all jumped. It was just one of Lestrade's men.

"Inspector," he said, "I'm afraid that we've been waiting here for no reason. They just reported that the cyclist appeared in a different place. He's been riding around all night like crazy, shooting at clocks."

"Give me a list of the places where he showed up," Holmes demanded, visibly disturbed for the first time.

Back home (and I should note that we did not utter a word during the ride), Holmes unfolded the map of London and dotted in the cyclist's latest movements. We were looking at a nonsensical drawing. Something like a cross was sticking up from the handlebars.

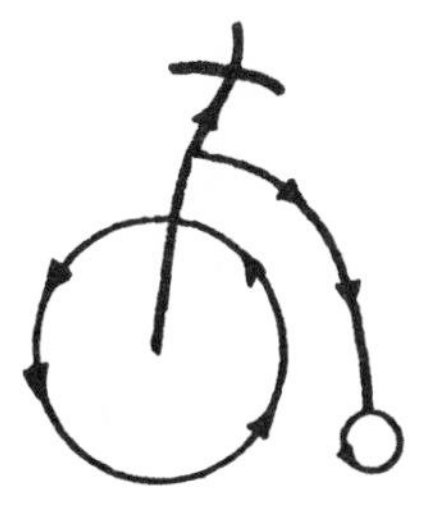

"The Devil take it, Watson, it seems like you and Lestrade were right after all. The chap must be a psychopath."

Holmes had already composed himself. In no way did he show that he was upset by the fact that his predictions had not come true. Soon after he retired into his room, from where the warm notes of a serenade could be heard.

The next day, he left for Sussex.

## SIGMUND FREUD
# THE CASE OF ERNEST M.

In the pages that follow, I will present an example of a subject who withdrew into the world of dreams, and of the personality split that resulted. The patient, Ernest M., was admitted to Professor Breuer's clinic after he took a meat mallet and broke all the clocks in the house, then hit his mother with the same object, inflicting serious injury on her. After thirty days of hospitalization, Ernest seemed to be completely healthy, but was also slightly depressed; his mother insisted that the young man be psychoanalyzed and Professor Breuer, knowing that I was working on the book *The Interpretation of Dreams*, recommended to me in a letter that I study Ernest's case.

From the patient's history, I learned that Ernest M. was left without a father early on. He grew up in the home of his maternal grandfather, a strict but fair man, with strong Calvinistic principles. At no time in his childhood did Ernest M. display abnormalities or signs of psychological instability. According to the words of his mother, Mrs. M., he was a completely normal young man, enjoying his friends and entertainment, but also regularly fulfilling all his obligations; he played the violin and was a member of a hiking club. However, at the end of the first year of his studies, Ernest M. suddenly imagined that he was a member of a mystical sect whose followers met in their sleep. Mrs. M. discovered this quite by accident; while cleaning her sons' room, she found a file containing written portions of poems, texts, and instructions, among which – and this caused the greatest doubt – was also a text ordering the assassination of Archduke Franz Ferdinand. This happened in 1928 – a full fourteen years after the unfortunate misdeed was carried out in Sarajevo. Mrs. M. gave me the abovementioned notebook, from which I offer two stanzas that are significant for psychoanalysts:

*1.*
*When you fall asleep, die*
*to this world. Then arise from your corpse and go*
*Straight ahead regardless of the ghosts.*
*Know that those unfortunate beings exist only*
*When they trick you into believing that you exist, too.*
*Withstand, you must, the burden of death.*

*2.*
*In your dreams it is always*
*good to know that you are not you, and that you are far*
*from yourself. Neglected because you turned your attention*
*to the specters in your body. Do not connect yourself,*
*either through pain or joy, to the illusions of reality*
*so that you also will not exist as they do.*

Disturbed by the morbid tone of the poem (about which more will be said later) and by the preparations to assassinate someone who had long been dead, Mrs. M. attempted to talk to her son, which caused an eruption of anger that ended in the above-described incident and Ernest's admission to Professor Breuer's clinic.

During our first meeting, Ernest left the impression of being a polite, well-adapted, but melancholic and above all introverted person. I must admit that this was the first and last time in my practice till now that I have met such a person. Except for the fact that he was unshakably convinced of absurd and illogical things, Ernest seemed to be a psychologically stable young man. It was quite difficult for me to penetrate the barrier that Ernest had placed between himself and the world; if it had not been such an interesting case I doubtlessly would have put it aside, because the patient showed absolutely no desire to be healed, which is the basic condition for the work of the psychoanalyst. However, Ernest showed much more interest and desire to cooperate whenever we began talking about dreams. In spite of that, he had great difficulty talking about what he had dreamt, not because he lacked education – quite evident from the texts in the notebook – but because of his hesitancy; he obviously did not want to betray his secret. I was present during the unusually interesting (but also slightly troubling) process of the split of Ernest's personality into the personality of the Dreamer and the personality of the wakening Ernest, where the Dreamer personality – obsessed with delusions of holiness and edification – mostly neglected and later even despised the personality of the waking Ernest M.

When I told the patient that his spite was leading toward an even more drastic separation of his personalities, he reacted quite calmly. "Of course," he said, "the old Ernest must die. In order for me to be born in the Spirit, I must get rid of the old Ernest. He likes girls, and women have the image of a soul instead of a soul." To my question: What is that, the image of a soul? Ernest drew this sign /\/\. I asked him to explain it to me and he agreed, with pleasure. What he ended up recounting to me was a flood of images from, I am convinced of it, the darkest regions of the collective unconscious.

The female soul, according to Ernest's account, is only an image of the male soul; it is Adam's rib twisted, the archetype of the letter M, like *mater*; hyle without form or substance. The male soul, on the other hand, has a horizontal cross-bar that gives it stability and it looks like this: /∇\. But that is not its real state, but its state after the fall because, as can be seen, its top, all of its ends, are pointed toward the earth. Therefore it is necessary to turn things around (*metanoia?*) and point the soul toward the vertical axis anew – \∆/ – so that it once again becomes receptive to taking in God's energy which results in and creates the *personality*, enclosed by God in itself, a personality that no longer dies and can be represented graphically like this:

However, the real surprise came after the question was posed of how that came about. Ernest categorically refused to play any sort of role in formulating a pseudo-Gnostic theory of the soul. He claimed that he had received his teaching from reputable members of the mystical order he belonged to, but about which he did not want to say anything more intimate. This, we could call it "oneiric" education, had begun when he was just seven years old. Every evening when he would fall asleep, his teachers would appear and give him lessons about the meaning of life on Earth. To my question: Who were those men? he answered that he did not know because they had been dead since long before he was born, but he had recently identified one of them as Angelus Silesius. As his education advanced he, Ernest, experienced reality more and more like the sphere of chaos, and his dreams as the intermediary space between the material world and spiritual world, and he called that *awakening*. In my later study I established that Ernest had not had a chance to become familiar with eastern philosophy and the Buddhist religion, to which, apparently, the expression *awakening* refers. I was interested in how it was possible for him to be taught by people who had died several centuries before. Ernest said that, in dreams, such things had no meaning, which is true, because the dead often visit our dreams, though in a different function to be honest.

By pure accident, those days I got a letter from an acquaintance from the world of art, with whom I had kept up correspondence for a certain time.

> "As you know," my acquaintance wrote among other things, "the process of the maturation of the human being is closely connected with upbringing and education; we teach our progeny the secrets and rules of life. We do not do anything like that with dreams. We dream, if I may say it that way, chaotically, randomly. Perhaps that is why we live as we do in reality: in chaos, like straws given over to the elements."

Those few remarks helped me to assemble an acceptable view of Ernest's disturbance. It is true that we live in a chaotic world where the illusions of order and a system trudge about. Ernest's sensitivity, fostered by his Calvinistic upbringing, could not stand the state of disorder, dominant in the world; added to that was the inability to change things. And that is why Ernest fled into dreams, a purely subjective place, in which he established a corresponding system of values, at the top of which God was found. The absence of his father (whom he did not remember), created tortuous complexes in him that he rid himself of by projecting them into the figure of Archduke Franz Ferdinand (the father of the nation=the father in general); in doing so, he killed two birds with one stone: he gained a father (a being without a father has no ontological backing) and he killed him at the same time (a being with a father has no independence), without exposing himself to any kind of risk because his father was already dead, brutally murdered.

Ernest, who became more communicative after seven or eight sessions, had a different version: Franz Ferdinand has to be killed because he was the inheritor of the Western Roman Empire which wants to control the Eastern – Byzantium. I reminded him that he thus brought about an aporia: Byzantium had not existed for centuries, and Franz Ferdinand had already been killed. But that did not confuse Ernest in the least: "Yes, doctor, the Archduke has been killed, but that was agreed upon just last year in October; I know that you will not understand me, but I will tell you anyway: the things that happen now are prepared in the future, it is a waste of time to seek for the causes of things in the past. Death does not come from the past, but from the future. As far as Byzantium goes, it never ceased to exist, it just went from being an exoteric empire to being an esoteric one. All sorts of states spring up on its soil, but the whole is never lost in parts; only parts are lost – the external ones." I must admit that Ernest had mastered a certain logic, similar to Berkeley's, that is hard to penetrate. Anyway, if by chance he had been born in the century when his imaginary teachers were, there is no room for doubt that he would have been a figure worthy of respect, judging by the wildness of his imagination, equal to Angelus Silesius. But chance wanted him to be born in the 20th century from which he fled into the saving extra-territoriality of the Byzantine Empire.

And then, there was also another factor: his relationship with his mother. Since she had no husband, and did have a son, she was like the Holy Virgin and Ernest saw himself in the role of Messiah; he identified with the superego to the extent that he experienced it as his true self. But there was also the ego. A well adapted personality generally seeks (and finds) justifications for the actions of the ego. In Ernest's case, the ego was experienced overall as interference; it was not able to do anything good. In other words: for Ernest, every action of the ego was wrong, in his case – because of his Calvinist upbringing – even sinful, which just made the situation worse. On several occasions I attempted to help Ernest become aware that he was ill after all. He never denied it, even once; the gurus in his dreams, purportedly, also told him that. But, Ernest added, the whole world is sick; there is not a single man who is not mentally ill. However, the sect to which he belonged had undertaken steps to fix that. Preparations are being made for the construction of some sort of fantastic hospital for 20,000,000 mental patients who will finally externalize the madness of the world and in that externalization make the madness disappear.

It was obvious that, as a result of his insufficient ego, Ernest was falling ever more frequently under the control of the unconscious. I will present some of my notes that support my conclusions:

> "I have never been able," Ernest said, "to say with confidence: I am so and so. But I believed others. I was convinced that that was happening only to me, that it was a rare disease that I had to conceal in order to exist at least on the surface. That is why I lived closed up in myself, unable to truly enter a conversation with anyone outside the circle of those already used to my presence, out of the fear that after just a few exchanges of words, others would realize that I don't exist, that they would laugh and wave their hands, and that I would have to dissipate into the nothingness where I belong. I was stupid. Now I know that other people feel that way as well, but they just hide it out of habit, but also partially out of silly self-confidence. Yes, we hide behind the screen of our clothes and

> our titles, which are indeed real, as opposed to people. But we can only hide our nothingness from others with those things. Not from ourselves. We do not exist on the other side. The more important one. The one inside . . .
>
> (. . .) I wondered how I would react to the news of my own death. I think I would remain calm. But I would still continue to go out for walks, to see my friends. Because we are all dead already; why get excited?"

No doubt, the causes of Ernest's existential insecurity should be sought in the absence of his father. One who has no father does not have an object to identify himself with; between him and his ancestors (history), there is a gaping hole – nothingness; all who have gone before him are dead, and he experiences his existence as an act of betrayal. That is why the verse says: "When you fall asleep, die to this world." That also suits his intolerance of time, symbolized in his breaking of clocks. However, this was not a rebellion against the time in which we are disappearing, but against the time in which we go on existing.

Naturally, Ernest had a different version. He was not interested in his father, but in being. He was convinced that he had no kind of father-related complex whatsoever. The blunder he made by breaking the clocks and hitting his mother was a consequence of his anger caused by his mother's indiscretion. Otherwise, he felt deeply sorry for his actions and he loved his mother. He had no intention of abandoning his convictions, but he was sorry that he had confided to me secrets that were worthy only of the elect few, thinking that I was more open to spirituality.

Miraculously, the complete disassociation of Ernest's personality, which had reached a truly high degree, did not cause suffering, or even asocial behavior. Ernest was reconciled with that duality and he lived, conditionally speaking, quite normally. He no longer came to see me, but I followed his further development with interest. Apathetically he graduated from college and found a job. The people around him were satisfied and they considered him to be completely healed, but I feared that all of that could not end well. As it soon turned out, my fears proved to be justified. On the eve of Easter the next year, I got a letter from Mrs. M., Ernest's mother, in which I was informed that Ernest had gone out on his bicycle one day and never come back. The police were informed, ads were run in the paper, all in vain. Since then, all traces of Ernest have been lost.

# CORRESPONDENCE

## FROM MRS. MEIER TO FREUD

*Zürich*
*23 September 1930*

Dear Herr Doctor Freud,

Two years ago, I informed you of the tragic disappearance of my son. Because I know how carefully you follow the lives of your patients, I feel obligated to inform you that I recently received reliable information that Ernest is alive and well.

When I had finally lost all hope, I was visited by Mr. Schleiermacher, a business acquaintance of my father, who reported to me that, while on a trip to Istanbul this July, he had seen Ernest in the company of some rather dubious characters. Led by a certain J. Kowalsky (Mr. Schleiermacher claims that he is an anarchist), they were riding velocipedes around Beyazit Meydani. Mr. Schleiermacher, being a thorough man and desiring to be certain, said hello to Ernest who got off his bicycle and politely returned his greeting.

The abovementioned gentleman assured me that Ernest seemed to be completely composed, that he acted and talked normally, with the exception of the slightly strange comment: "There, now you have a good reason to visit my mother."

However, a few days later, my joy at hearing these things was clouded by a letter from Ernest. The contents of that letter filled me with a mixture of profound sadness and terrible fear. In that letter bursting with confusing sentences, Ernest accused me of being Mr. Schleiermacher's mistress, and he predicted that I will die in the near future. Because only you can help me, there is something that I must confess. Before I married my late husband, Rheiner, I did have relations with Mr. Schleiermacher on several occasions. Likewise, during our latest encounter, I had relations with the same gentleman again; you can probably understand: I am a widow, the loneliness, the good news . . . What bothers and frightens me is indeed the question: How could Ernest have known about my relationship, the first part of which took place before he was born, and the second while he was thousands of miles away from Zürich?

Then, there is one more matter that I have never told you. Several months before his death, Ernest's father showed signs of, if I may say so, quiet madness. In some old book he had bought at a second-hand shop, he found the notes of the previous owner; some gibberish about a sect of heretics on an imaginary island somewhere in the far north Atlantic. If he had been introverted earlier, Rheiner finally broke off all communication with those around him. He spent his final days at the printer's, where he printed the abovementioned manuscript – a pile of impudent fantasies – in a print-run of only six copies.

I am convinced that my mistake – not telling you about these facts – was perhaps fatal; perhaps, if you had had those facts available, you could have done more for Ernest.

I hope that you realize what a truly uncomfortable position I am in. I am at the edge of my spiritual strength, and I hope for your support and encouragement.

With profoundest respect,
Herta Meier

## FROM ERNEST TO HIS MOTHER

*Istanbul*
*10 October 1930*

Dear Mom,

I'm writing to you from Constantinople, the capital of Byzantium. You have certainly heard of Hagia Sophia, the former basilica, later a mosque and now a museum. I go there quite often. Upon capturing Constantinople, the Turks executed a terrible slaughter in the house of God, destroying the frescos, breaking the crystal vessels, but they could not reach the painting of Christ the Almighty in the main dome and his gentle, serious face still looks down from the vault, just as he watches the entire fallen world from eternity and into eternity; among others, he watches you and Mr. Schleiermacher who came here, ostensibly on business, to accidentally find me. Mr. Schleiermacher is a clever gentleman, just as you are also a clever lady. I have no complaints about you. Dr. Freud would have more to complain about in connection to the unconscious, upon which he constantly insists. Your gesture is completely transparent to everyone except for the two of you; I'm not saying that you made a deal for Schleiermacher to find me so that you could fall into my arms – such a thing would never cross your minds, even in your dreams. No, with the words of Dr. Freud: Schleiermacher came here to find me driven by the unconscious, and that should not surprise you because unconsciously he knows where I am. Neither you nor your Romeo can even imagine that you are doing anything improper; on the contrary, your thoughts are ultimately honorable, but you (the entire West) do the iniquities suppressed in the depth of your souls, from where very little manages to surface.

Now I will explain to you what those iniquities consist of, the iniquity of solipsism that forced you to poison my father and then to convince yourself and everyone else that he died of a stroke. I made this decision yesterday, in the Hagia Sophia, looking at the figure of Jesus. Suddenly it occurred to me – Lord, what a circus that will be when we stand before the true face of God, when all our hidden thoughts are revealed, when Mr. Schleiermacher begins to justify himself: "But what was wrong with me going to Constantinople on business?"

What the theologians used to interpret as a multitude of sins, is in fact just one sin – the sin of self-deception. As time passes, it grows and a man becomes a slave to his own lies to such an extent, they take such control over him, that he denies everything before God, who is willing to forgive all, completely obvious things, and that is ridiculous because we exist on God like moss.

In the Gospel according to Thomas there is a line that I will quote from memory: "Whatever you let out of yourself, that will save you; whatever you keep in yourself, that will destroy you." I want to tell you that those things you have not let out, a rather large pile of garbage, has decided to destroy you, all of those secrets of yours and all that junk from the antique store of your memories.

I am not judging you in any way. Moreover, since you are my mother, that is, if I were in your place that suits me very well, it is my duty to instruct you, in just a few words, about how to behave when death comes. You see, life can be compared to riding a velocipede: you ride automatically, thinking about what will happen at your destination, enjoying the singing of the birds, and then you suddenly lose your balance, everything stops and at the decisive moment (overcome with fear), you see the surface of the earth hurtling toward your face . . .

(Ernest)

## FROM FREUD TO MRS. MEIER

*Vienna*
*7 October 1930*

Gracious Mrs. Meier,

I received your letter but the sheer number of my duties prevented me from answering you immediately, although I wanted to.

What is most important – Ernest is alive. Perhaps his flight was the fruit of his desire for independence, and I am convinced that I am not wrong when I say that this could be quite positive for his further development.

In terms of the company Ernest is keeping, I think that your friend's fears are unfounded, since I personally know Mr. Joseph Kowalsky, one of the most talented of the avant-garde poets in German, who was – it is true – a communist in his youth, not an anarchist, but in recent years he has become completely apolitical.

The style of Ernest's letter – I realize that it is confused and mystical – is probably the consequence of his consorting with poets. I do not have insight into the entirety of his letter, so I cannot say much more, but Constantinople is a city where civilizations, languages, races, dreams and reality all intertwine, and it has certainly left a deep impression on Ernest's psyche, which is sensitive in the first place.

Your fear related to the confusion about how Ernest knows of the nature of your relationship with Mr. Schleiermacher, is not such a difficult problem to resolve. Mothers and sons, in your case even more so, are connected by intuition; surely you remember in Ernest's childhood when he became sick and you "felt" something, even though you were not present.

I am absolutely convinced that, in this case, such intuitive knowledge is in question, or better said the suspicion that Ernest childishly relates to the desire for you to die. I talked with him about that several times.

I am convinced that you will gather the strength to overcome the crisis into which you have fallen, and assure you of my profoundest respect.

Sigmund Freud

## FROM FREUD TO FERENCZI

*Vienna*
*30 October 1930*

My Dear Dr. Ferenczi,

I would like to briefly present you a case which fits perfectly into the sphere of your interests, and a longer letter, an answer to your previous one, will soon follow.

Two years ago, I treated a young man (I am writing a short study about that) who ran away from home in an undetermined direction after our therapy sessions came to an end. Recently, his mother informed me that the young man has been seen in Turkey. A business acquaintance of her father encountered Ernest in Constantinople and spent a while talking to him. Upon arriving in Zürich, the acquaintance reported this news to the mother, and on that occasion renewed a relationship that had been broken off some twenty years before.

Now comes the most intriguing part: soon afterwards, Mrs. Meier received a letter from her son in which he accused her of having relations with the abovementioned gentleman and in which he foretold her death in the near future.

Two days ago, I incidentally heard that Mrs. Meier had died from a bursting aneurism.

Certainly a cause for mourning, but also a useful example for your study of intuition and synchronicity.

Sincerely yours,
S. Freud

## FROM FERENCZI TO FREUD

*(letter partially damaged)*

Dear Herr Doctor Freud,

I received your kind report on a case which, quite by accident, is not completely new to me. Straightaway I must tell you that I am on the trail of a discovery that could radically change our study of the psyche. Namely, J. Kowalsky (whom you also know), with whom I exchange occasional correspondence, wrote me the other day that, in Istanbul . . . *(remainder of the letter destroyed by water damage)*

## JURGIS BALTRUŠAITIS
# FAMA BIROTARIORUM

### I

There are very few facts about the mystical order – the *Little Brothers* of the Evangelical Bicyclists of the Rose Cross. Only one tangible document exists – the Basel Parchment – where one can find, besides the text about which more will be said, a coat of arms: an old-fashioned velocipede, having a handle-bar stem topped with a cross, carrying the motto GENS VNA SVMVS, but the whole thing could easily be a forgery. Some writers, like Herbert Meier, completely reject the idea of the existence of such an order. On the other hand, no less reliable researchers, among whom the authority of Carl Gustav Jung stands out, never question the existence of the order. Jung even mentions it, with some reservation, in one place in his work *Wandlungen und Symbole der Libido.*

In the circles of the esotericians, the legend is circulating that the Evangelical Bicyclists are the successors of the Byzantine iconoclast tradition and that they celebrate *basileus* Leo III as their forerunner.*

* In 726, Leo III openly spoke out against the cult of icons for the first time. Bishops from Asia Minor, iconoclasts, certainly had an influence on him as

The following words are attributed to a Grand Master of the order: "Let us pay respect to Leo! All images are the creations of Satan and idolatry. First, people put pictures of God on the wall, then the king, then Stalin. In the end, everyone will idolize their own picture, they will adore and fear themselves." It would be worthwhile to search for the roots of the geo-political and religious *weltanschauung* of the Evangelical Bicyclists of the Rose Cross in that allegiance to the Byzantine spiritual tradition. Namely, they do not consider the history of Europe to be legitimate after January 28, 842, when *basileus* Theophilus died and the iconophiles ultimately triumphed; the Bicyclists believe that God was forever exiled from the human soul into objects – into icons, churches, statues – and that since then every event collides with God's providence, that they are the work of human and Satanic aims. Consequently, they do not recognize any of the borders or countries that have sprouted up in the territory of the Byzantine Empire.

In addition, their view of Christianity is interesting. Paradoxically, the *Little Brothers* are convinced that it was the strongest in the 20th century because it was in its most profound crisis. Christianity that is not in crisis is not Christianity for them. There is one apocryphal writing, a bit of yellow paper without a title or a signature, on which the following words can be found:

> The misfortune of Europe is not that it became Christianized, as the young Hegel so regrettably interpreted things, but actually because it did not become Christianized enough. Way down in their souls, Europeans are still barbarians. There you

---

they had visited Istanbul just before that; also, a powerful earthquake also had an influence on him, because he, in the spirit of the times, took that as a sign of God's wrath, caused by icon worship. First, he held sermons in which he attempted to convince the people that respect of icons was against the Christian faith. (G. Ostrogorsky, *The History of the Byzantine State*)

will find them bowing down to icons and seeking forgiveness where the sin was committed, in the outside world, and not where it was conceived: in their souls. There you will find them forcing "pagans," by fire and the sword, to convert to the religion of love. The appearance of Nazism is the proof that they remained more or less secretly pagans. It could be said that people were waiting for centuries for Hitler to appear.

It is astounding, the lack of care which the Evangelical Bicyclists show for their documents, which are anyway so small in number. Their most important work is "Theology and Bicyclism" and, to my knowledge, no one has ever seen the integral version of it. Written on some fifty pages of paper, of various sizes and quality, it is actually not even kept all in one place, but its individual parts can be found among the members of the order for reading or study. The one manuscript readily available, the abovementioned Basel Parchment, is not very convincing. Although perfectly printed in calligraphy, and though the parchment is of excellent quality, the content leaves a lot to be desired:

Grand Master to the Brothers!

I would like to announce that Dharamsala is a city in India of some 40,000 inhabitants. All day long, they do nothing except sit in the shade of mango groves crying out till they are exhausted: OM MANE PADME HUM, in the expectation that they will be enlightened. Of the other points of interest, I should mention the herds of holy cows that are different from regular cows because they have haloes.

In the whole city there are only three bicycles, rusty, neglected, and falling apart.

Where the cows are saints, the bicycles rust. He who has ears, let him hear.

The abovementioned Herbert Meier cites that very document, the most tangible one, about the *Little Brothers* as evidence that the order is a fabrication, a mystification created by idle souls. According to him, the text lacks spirituality of any kind. In the polemic which appeared in the *Christian Science Monitor*, D. H. Grainger opposed Meier, comparing the Basel Parchment to the lessons of a teacher of Zen. "Taken from the context of the spirituality of a closed community," Grainger writes, "a sentence, or even a paragraph cannot be expected to make sense outside the group of followers. Even the Bible, whose myths are deeply entrenched in the collective unconscious, seems like a heap of nonsense and hallucinations to the untrained eye." Further in the text, Grainger relates the negligence of the Bicyclists to their deeply implanted feeling of belonging to the eternal. "One who truly looks into eternity," the author says, "does not care about the ephemerality of things and books. It is logical to connect the iconoclasm of the Evangelical Bicyclists with their scorn of manmade objects. One might say: they consciously abhor books about the holy, so that the books will not conceal the holy."

However, as far as it is known, the *Little Brothers* do not hide their manuscripts, projects and actions in the least, citing Christ's words from the apocryphal Gospel according to Thomas: "If you take out what is within you, what you have taken out will save you. If you do not take out what is within you, what you have not taken out will destroy you." Due to the completely public nature of their actions, the Evangelical Bicyclists are protected by the greatest possible secrecy. If we examine that claim a little more carefully, we will see that it is not lacking in logic whatsoever: an object of interest is generally one that is hidden, while easily available things go unnoticed; the more obvious a thing is, the more mysterious it is. Even the Creator himself, who is the most real and most present, is he not also the most invisible and the most unapproachable?

In the real world, the *Little Brothers* do not own any kind of building, they do not have gatherings or significant initiations or rituals. According to some sources, they meet in a safe place, far from the noise and curious onlookers – in their dreams. It is worthwhile to mention that J. W. Kowalsky, who is thought to have been a Grand Master or at least an important member of the order, in the period between 1930 and 1936, maintained intensive correspondence with Sigmund Freud, the father of psychoanalysis. One of J. Kowalsky's letters addressed to Freud was published in the journal *Psychoanalysis Today* (8, 1959):

> Dear Herr Doctor Freud,
>
> The remarks on dreams that you presented in your letter are undoubtedly of great importance for the further explication of that phenomenon, otherwise neglected by scholarship. The fact that dreaming directly anticipates the future (the case of the alarm clock)* not only indicates its nature in protecting the dreamer from waking, but also shows that we need to reflect most seriously about all our fundamental knowledge of time and space.
>
> Even though you reproach me for being a "poet," even though I am interested in matters of scholarship, I am prepared to withstand such reprimands. I would dare to claim: not only are dreams a territory full of the symbols of the libido, they are much more than that. I would say: they are the frontier between our world and otherworldliness, or whatever you would like to call it, where completely different laws apply than these that we are accustomed to, perhaps by force.

* The dream mentioned by Kowalsky is fairly well-known, and is related to dreams that come just before the alarm clock rings. In such cases, the long and logical flow of dreaming overlaps with the ringing.

The misfortune lies in the fact that we are too highly oriented to events in reality. Not only are dreams not taken seriously, they are even thought to be nonsense. Your contribution to a different view of this matter will be highly valued by history, I am convinced. I would like to offer you a rather daring supposition: as you know, the process of the maturation of the human being is closely connected with upbringing and education; we teach our children the secrets and rules of life. We do not do anything like that with dreams. We dream, if I may say it that way, chaotically, randomly. Perhaps that is why we live that way – chaotically and randomly. I am convinced that self-discipline, so necessary for success in waking life, would render excellent results in our dreams as well. If, one day, we were to take control of ourselves in our dreams, instead of surrendering ourselves to sad fantasies, undoubtedly we would discover a lot about our own past, and also about the past of the species to which we belong.

I anxiously await your reply and humbly ask that you receive my deepest regards.

J. Kowalsky

Unfortunately, it is not known if Freud answered Kowalsky. Anyway, that is not the purpose of our study. The letter was quoted to support the thesis about the activities of the Evangelical Bicyclists in dreams. D. H. Grainger, with whom other authors agree, proposes that, as time has passed, generation after generation of the members of the brotherhood have perfected the skill of dreaming; controlling the "sad fantasies" that Kowalsky mentions in his letter to Freud, they have obtained the ability to meet each other in their dreams, regardless of the spatial or temporal distance, and in doing so they avoid all the limitations imposed by time and space. The church of the Holy Spirit is also mentioned, an enormous hovering cathedral which, being dreamt of for hundreds of years, has become an oneiric entity. In other words: it is not dreamt by anyone as they like it, but whenever it appears in a dream, everyone sees the same church whose beauty exceeds all description. Whoever reaches that region of dreams finds a vision that takes their breath away. It is also dreamt by those who do not belong to the Order. One such dream was recorded by Julie Mass in the book *The Sacred Symbols of Dreams* (Princeton University Press, 1961)

> (. . .) The patient insists that several times he dreamt the following: "I find myself in a wide field that I have reached after a nightmare. I look up and see a large cathedral hovering in the sky. It is completely translucent, although I would not say that it is made of glass or of any other material . . . I can see that, inside it, a cross is also hovering. Inside there is a multitude of people. When I try to draw near it, everything fades away and I wake up."

The interpretation of the dream that follows the quote is not significant for us. Grainger claims that he has come across several identical descriptions of the church of the Holy Spirit among dreamers who have never even heard of the order of *the Little Brothers*, and who do not even have esoteric inclinations. In the text "Endless Bicyclism," still unpublished, the same author writes:

"As soon as they fall asleep, no matter where they are, the Bicyclists of the Rose Cross go to the church. In the complete silence – far from time and the tumult – the dead, living and future members of the order gather there. The dead, who are in contact with the lowest hierarchy of angels, counsel the living about how to act in history. While that is going on, the future members are learning their destinies by heart. The great influence of the Evangelical Bicyclists on events in the world which are, perhaps not without reason, are ascribed to *the Little Brothers*, is founded precisely on the cooperation of the brothers from all temporal categories. This also explains the strange indolence of the living members of the order. Not only is fanaticism foreign to them, they are almost completely uninterested and serve only as an incarnation, as a material point, an anchor of the order in space and time. However, the real activity of the Bicyclists takes place in the past and future. Taught by the dead brothers (who are in collusion with the heavenly hierarchy), the *future* members of the order prepare themselves to redirect the course of history toward Providence whenever the danger appears that history will turn in a direction determined by people. So, it is supposed that J. V. Dzh. – a member of the order prepared for the destiny of the clergy – was suddenly forced to take another position. Leaving the Seminary in Tbilisi, he infiltrated the orders of the revolutionaries and delivered the decisive blow to the idea of the thousand year Reich, even though, to make the paradox greater, he did not even know how to ride a bicycle."

## II

In terms of the spiritual content of the document "Theology and Bicyclism," it could approximately be reconstructed like this: The bicycle symbolizes the vertical. In the age of darkness, Kali Yuga, one should embark – the writer (or writers) of "Theology and Bicyclism" believe – on the road to salvation by bicycle. That is absurd, but because of that it is also salutary. Because "absurd" does not mean "impossible." Theology renders a pile of useless knowledge; that knowledge can also be true, but it is unusable. That is exactly why theology and bicyclism should be combined. The advantages are obvious. Above all, the classical methods of salvation are no longer suitable for this era, which is so steeped in corruption that there are special institutions and services for inhibiting salvation.

No doubt, *the Little Brothers* are not far from the truth. The system of values of this world is tragically twisted. It is easy to suppose that Buddha would be arrested nowadays for begging, Jesus would be locked up in the madhouse because of his parables about the resurrection of the dead. Riding a bicycle, that is not conspicuous and this is very important. "Because," as it is written in the 'Theology,' "the persecution of Christians goes on at full intensity, in spite of the commonplace rumors that it is a thing of the past. True, it is done more subtly and clandestinely, but also more efficiently." That is why the *Little Brothers*, inconspicuously riding out of the cities on bicycles, turning the pedals till they are exhausted, attain mystical ecstasy, meditating on the symbol of the fish in which the name of the Savior is hidden – Ικϑυς.

The symbolism of the bicycle is interesting in itself. Seen *from above*, thus, from the viewpoint of the Holy Spirit, the bicycle looks like a cross to us:

The Evangelical Bicyclists, generally speaking, try to observe everything *from above*. Since that is impossible because of biological determinism, patient exercises in imagination are needed so that one can observe things from a birds-eye perspective, which significantly changes the meaning of events on the surface of the earth. A battle, for example, takes place according to the laws of iron logic for the participants and observers: we defend ourselves when we are attacked; we charge at a high point, because that will strengthen our position. Yet, if that same battle is watched from above, we just see a herd of fools moving about here and there, chaotically, shooting, killing and getting killed. The pinnacle of the Bicyclists' meditation is to separate the soul from the body and observe oneself on a bicycle from a height of some three hundred feet, but rare are the brothers who have managed to do so.

Observed, on the other hand, horizontally, the bicycle is teeming with ancient symbols:

Its two wheels, two circles, symbolize two eternities: the rusty – front wheel – which turns meaninglessly and *does not know* that it is set in motion by the real eternity represented by the back, driving wheel. These two eternities are connected by the triangle of the frame that symbolizes the human conception of the Holy Trinity, because the true Holy Trinity is transcendental to the mind, like the bicyclist is to the bicycle. The large and small sprockets (connected by the chain, by the representation of the chain of cause-effect-cause) symbolize the unity of the macro- and micro-cosmos.

If we remove the wheels of the men's bicycle, there is just the frame with its forks, and that is a graphic representation of the male soul:

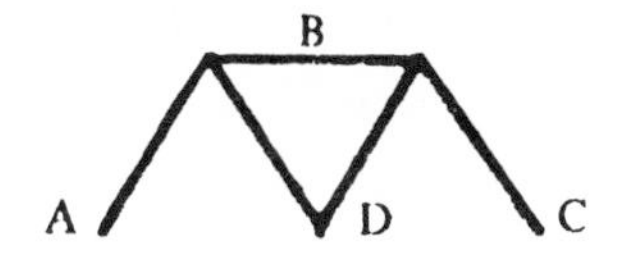

The female soul is represented by the frame of the women's bicycle. Since it does not have the supporting crossbar, it is susceptible to deviations:

The top of the triangle (D) is facing down, a symbol of the depravity of man, and the legs (A and C) – are iniquity and passion that pin the soul to the earth.

The second chapter of the document "Theology and Bicyclism" deals with the city. It should be mentioned that *the Little Brothers* despise all urban settlements. For them, the *urbs* is a labyrinth with no way out because, after wandering about for a long time, after the unsuccessful search for meaning, you end up at the graveyard. There is a legend that the Evangelical Bicyclists authorized a project for a gigantic mental hospital (with a capacity for 20,000,000 mental patients) in which the madness of the world would be classified and organized like a complete city. However, there is no data about it. There is something else, a portion of short text which is ascribed to one of the Grand Masters of the past, rendered here in full through the kindness of Branko Kukić, who is its owner:

THE ARCHITECTS' CONSPIRACY

> When the Lord confounded the languages and stopped the construction of the Tower of Babylon, the architects did not capitulate. They made a sacrifice to Baal and convened on the ruins of the tower on a night with a full moon. They knew that they had mistakenly built the tower upwards, toward heaven, and that never again would they succeed to ascend

to the place they wanted. So, they made a decision to build heaven on earth.

Thus, they began working on the project of a horizontal tower. They needed hundreds and hundreds of years to calculate the paths of the stars, a thousand years of study, so that they could compose the Great Urban Plan. But that plan, when it encompassed the whole planet, was no longer a plan of a city, but the blueprint of hell. Still, since it encompasses the entire planet, it is impossible to build any kind of structure that is not foreseen in the Urban Plan. So it is that, whoever builds something is building hell for himself. Because, as early as the 14th century . . . (the manuscript finishes here.)

Finally, it is worthwhile to mention some of the projects and documents of the *Little Brothers* of the Evangelical Bicyclists of the Rose Cross: *the Metaphysical-Strategic Defense Plan of the Eastern Roman Empire*, *the project of a Door for Exiting History*, *the Transcendental Biography of J. V. Stalin*, *Places That Are Vanishing*, *the Technological Approach to Producing a Bullet That Will Miss Archduke Franz Ferdinand*, *How I Became a Member of the Order of Little Brothers of the Evangelical Bicyclists of the Rose Cross*, *the Secret List with the Biographies of Meritorious Members of the Order*, *The Third Eye*, *The Death Fugue*, *Somnambulists* . . . and many others, most of which have never seen the light of day.

The latest project of the *Little Brothers* is the DICTIONARY OF TECHNOLOGY, the interpretation of key concepts of the modern world in the light of the Spirit, published in the magazine *Vidici* (1-2), 1981.

# AN ANALYSIS OF THE IDEOLOGICAL ORIENTATION OF THE JOURNAL, *VIDICI*, AND THE NEWSPAPER *STUDENT*

This Report speaks of the ideological bases of the activities of a group of bicyclists associated with the journal *Vidici* ("Perspectives"). We use the words "ideological bases" because this is doubtless a coherent and autochthonous conceptual system whose genesis clearly indicates that the introduction of elements of a new ideology are in question, with the tendency to offer an entire and all-encompassing interpretation of reality.

It is well-known that every ideology represents a concrete articulation of atomized reality, an expression and explanation of the existing which the compartmentalized social conscious experiences as the truth. In that sense, this new ideology is no different than the earlier ones. The thing that makes up the most significant feature of this conceptual system, the *diferentia specifica* of the group's teaching and public appearances, is their *highly marked utilization of metaphor Aesopic language, their speech encoding.* Each of the primary categories is actually a encoded; its interpreted-ideological essential meaning can be understood only if one decodes the *key*, if each crucial concept is "translated" and if, from the seeming shift in meaning of phrases and entire sentences, one moves beyond into the real, true *reading* of the texts.

Therefore, the main task of this part of the report is actually *the translation and interpretation of the basic categories*, more precisely the complete explication of the thoughts that must be hidden behind the code in order to survive. At today's level of conceptual consciousness, with the modern development of social relations, in a situation when the duties of the media of informing the public are clearly defined, it seems completely incredible that, under the auspices of a journal, for two years and more, *from volume to volume, from text to text*, an ideology could be developed and established that is not only non-Marxist, but actually openly and aggressively anti-Marxist. This was possible precisely because of the abovementioned concealment, the linguistic camouflage, but the situation has changed completely with the most recent declarations of this ideologically like-minded group.

For the purposes of interpretation, the explanation of basic concepts, we will strictly hold to those definitions that the authors themselves gave in volume 1-2, 1981, which is called the *Dictionary of Technology*. This volume is actually presented in the form of a dictionary and it represents the peak of the ideological work of this group, because with it one obtains an overview of all the "projects" in earlier volumes, of all main concepts and all main ideas. Therefore this volume is of great significance for the ultimate establishment and popularization of this ideology. The *Dictionary of Technology* is, as the authors themselves say, "a proclamation," in fact, the ultimate *manifestation of a profoundly anti-humane and anti-socialist worldview*, an open invitation to action, and the open work of those like-minded and of their collaborators. Thus, "the publication of this *Dictionary* testifies to the final unmasking of technology" (p. 1), thus, it is "a barbaric act of provocation," and thus this manifesto is an invitation to the *final and unconditional solution*.

## INTERPRETATION OF SOME OF THE BASIC CATEGORIES

Just like every other ideology, the one we are now analyzing also possesses a foundation of *positive and negative categories.*

The key positive categories are the following: *Will*, *Person*, *Apocalypse*, and the key negative categories are *Technology*, *Mirror*, and *Boys*:

> *TECHNOLOGY:* (first concept) is a leitmotif that is interwoven in all the texts and all the volumes of the journal. It is defined as "the production of forms" (p. 24). "Technology" is the New World, amnesia (forgetting) of the old, dual world, a world opposite to the world."
>
> *Technology – society*
>
> Technology is nothing other than a false world, the world of deception, the world which lies in opposition to the real world. Technology is the entire world that has come about from Descartes (from the 17th century) forward (p. 8), it is the world of institutions, science, democracy, technologies, humanism, the world in which the foundations are shaped by systems: society in the social system, science in the scientific system, philosophy in the philosophical system. That world, the world of technology, is the world of evil, of hatred, of mutilated and limited people, the world of lies and deception, therefore a false world, a world opposite to the real world. It is related to the real world like a mirror:
>
> *Mirror – social-political system*
>
> *MIRROR* (second key concept). Toward real life, the Mirror only reflects the truth, the mirror is an illusion, a reflection,

a shadow of reality. The historical existence of technology is the Institution, "a Tower of Babylon whose walls are made of Mirrors. Within those walls, pleasantly delimited and protected, the Technologists walk about" (p.10). Thus, just as technology is a codeword for society, so mirror is a codeword for institutions, for the system, or for any other organization . . . Within the mirrors are all those who serve the institution or the system: the Technologists. The Technologists are hierarchical monkeys" (p. 24) – the codeword for social-political workers, "officials, philosophers, scholars, artists" (p. 17, 24, 25). A synonym for Technologists is:

*BOY* (the third key category).

*Boys (technologists) – officials, scholars, philosophers, artists*
Why are the Technologists called Boys? Simply because they are not mature, because they are too infantile to be called people. The Technologists as Boys are eternally incapacitated human individuals, and are therefore *a lower race of people.* "Technology has been noted as the production of Boys" (p. 6) because it is precisely there that a differentiation is made between *two clearly separate kinds of people*: between the Boys and the Persons.

*Person – a member of the group of bicyclists associated with the journal* Vidici.
*PERSON* is the first positive concept (it is quite clear that the authors of these texts consider themselves to be Persons). Persons are all those people who are outside the institutions of the system, who have "seen through" Technology (society) and who are on the other side of the Mirror (system). "Within the Institution there are no Persons, just Technologists or Boys" (p. 5)

simply because "Boys respect the rules of the game imposed by the Institution" (p. 8), but "A Person does not respect the rules of the game." The basic rules of the game are *the law and morals*. "The Law is a limitation of the Person. Life in accordance with the law affirms Technology but it destroys the Will. The Will, the Person, does not have laws in life" (p. 8). THE PERSON IS ALLOWED TO DO ANYTHING, because it can: *"It is strong enough to do anything it wants without regard for the law or for form"* (p. 22). *The Person*, likewise, *does not respect morals* because "morals are necessary just to keep Technologists from running into each other, but the Person does not need them." Persons and Boys are two clearly separate races of people.

*The Will to break the Mirror –*
*the desire to destroy the social system*

The difference between Persons and Boys leads us to the second positive concept, to the *Will*. Only a Person can possess a Will, while Boys have self-will. Will is formed at precisely that moment when a man becomes aware of Technology (society), when he becomes aware that it is actually the system that is limiting him. He then obtains the *WILL TO BREAK THE MIRROR* (the system). *Perspectives* are actually defined that way (p. 4): "Perspectives are the Will to break the Mirror," to tear down the system, all the institutions and everything that makes up Technology (society) and thus "bring it to an end."

Just as the *Barbarians* destroyed everything they came across, so the *Persons destroy everything that exists*.

1) *The Person abolishes society*. "Society is a medium (an intermediary), mediating between the Boys in an idol, because Boys can only come into existence in Society" (p. 6). A Person does not belong to

society in any way, he is outside of it because he is only interested in society insofar as its destruction is in question: "The problems of Society are not at all the problems of the Person. REALITY CAN ONLY BE ATTAINED IF SOCIETY IS ABOLISHED," which is the basic meaning of breaking the Mirror.

2) *The Person abolishes humaneness.* A Person is not humane, because humaneness is a product of Technology. "Boys are humane" (p. 6), say the authors of these texts and, therefore, they are not offering any kind of compliment because humaneness is a pejorative term for them. "Anthropology is the name of *the western evil called humanism.* Humanism, self-will, selfishness and evil are synonyms" (p. 26).

3) *Persons kill Boys.* Since "Boys are the idols of life, they should be broken" (p. 6). Killing Boys (technologists, officials, scientists, artists) is not evil in any way, because Boys are not people: "those people are *not alive* because they *sold their soul* to the Grand Inquisitor. The Technologist needs the Barbarian *who will kill him and in doing so give him life*" (p. 24).

4) *The Person abolishes democracy.* Democracy is, likewise, a product of the Devil, an invention of the Boys that is used to maintain the system (institutions) and limiting the Person. Democracy is nothing more than "a collection of individual self-wills (self-wills because, clearly, Boys do not have a Will) that render an opposite will" (therefore a false will). "That is a Technology that only the Person can *abolish.*"

5) *The Person abolishes all science*, all sources of enlightenment. Synonyms for science, or reason, are: the Devil (7), the scarecrow (7), the Inquisition (9), the Beast (8), Frankenstein (8), and hatred (11). Boys are enlightened (smart – p. 6) while "the Person is uneducated" (p. 17). Every system (a synonym for hatred – p. 22), and so also the scientific one, comes from the Devil (Technology): philosophy, science and art. "They are necessary only to the Technologists and their opposite world" (p. 25). The greatest scientists are, at the

same time, also the greatest Technologists (the complete realization of technology is given in the identity of the mind, history and work – Marx, Hegel – p. 24).

6) *The Person abolishes all systems* (every institution). As long as institutions exist, we cannot exist but we can only be reflected opposite to the institutions of living: opposite to Technology. "*Only when I break the Mirror do I stop being a Technologist and become a Person*" (p. 23, 25).

7) *The Person abolishes the truth and beauty.* Beauty and the truth are forms produced in the false world – of Technology (p. 24). "The Truth" is an idol of oppositeness. When the Mirror is broken, no kind of truth is necessary for life because *truth is the lie of life*" (p. 10).

## THE APOCALYPSE – THE MOMENT THE MIRROR IS SHATTERED

The Apocalypse is the crucial moment in the completion of the "project" of the editorial board of *Vidici*. In their Amon Düül-like dream of melancholy, the perspectives of *Vidici* are dedicated to the moment when the society of Technologists and Boys will grow into a community of Persons. Just as the *Dictionary of Technology* as a manifestation takes the form of a Gospel, thus the Apocalypse is graphically presented in the journal as Dürer's "Four Riders of the Apocalypse."

## THE GREAT INQUISITION – THE SOCIETAL, POLITICAL ORGANIZATION, THE GRAND INQUISITOR – LEADER – SOCIETAL, POLITICAL ORGANIZATIONS

"The Church is the personification of the Grand Inquisitor (so, for example, in the graphic representation of the concept 'church'

– which is anyway 'the personification of the institution, the inquisition, the beast' which is 'the highest ideal of the Catholic madhouse' – a picture of the Parliament of the Socialist Federal Republic of Yugoslavia is used). Everything else besides that is repetition." The Grand Inquisition, the institution, or the system of institutions headed by the leviathans, technologists, beasts, is all headed by the Grand Inquisitor.

## THE FURTHER DEVELOPMENT AND PRACTICAL COMPLETION OF THE GOALS ESTABLISHED IN THE DICTIONARY OF TECHNOLOGY ON THE PAGES OF *STUDENT* MOVE TO THE CONCRETE APPLICATION OF THEIR IDEOLOGY ON THE PAGES OF *STUDENT*

Thanks to the fact that the editor-in-chief of *Student* is one of the members of the "hard core" of this group, the group continues its public activity by publishing texts on the second, main page of *Student*; the texts openly (for those who have found the "key") *call for the abolition of the system established by the Constitution and for a radical showdown with all ideological opponents* (the so-called Technologists). This activity develops continuously, from edition to edition becoming more aggressive and open. In order for us to show the character of this activity, we will cite characteristic examples from the introductory comments (p. 2) from edition 18 to edition 26-27 in chronological order.

*Number 18:* In an "Open Letter" one of the members of the editorial board of *Vidici* (Slobodan Škerović) develops the theory further that "the problems of Society are not at all the problems of the Person." He rejects any kind of systematic solution to the problem of financing *Student*, even *rejecting the system itself in the end.* As a whole, Škerović as a Person clearly does not need a social-political system (a mirror) or the economic stabilization of the functioning of this system because stabilization: "is necessary to solidify and legalize the existing state of corruption, that is, disintegration, which is a farce created exactly so that nothing will be done." He attacks Bora Mišeljić, the editor-in-chief of *Student* because, in asking for financing for the publication of the newspaper, "he is taking part in the general farce of complaining about stabilization." "But comrade Bora, one enemy remained unconquered then, if I may say so, and I am right, an invisible enemy, and that enemy, the biggest one a man has, seems like failing, like failure in itself, because what is *this stabilization of ours other than failure itself*?" "Because, Bora, you fell into the trap of becoming a hunter of flies and you move in a *curved mirror*, in a beautifully imagined picture, a small role in a great performance. So, Bora, *SHATTER THAT MIRROR*, break the strands of the cobwebs! And *by your own will* (emphasis S. Škerović) put a stop to that illusion of decisiveness that is played on the flat perspectiveless stage, that is played out on a flat surface," etc.

*Number 19*: Bora Mišeljić completely accepts the invitation to break the mirror (discrediting the social-political system), publishing an article under the characteristic title: "Reality and the Mirror." In this article B. Mišeljić complains about how "we remain alone because the Person and living people are ever fewer," but then warns "that Student will not be the silent victim of some monster mechanism, nor will it, well lubricated, execute a completely unimportant, imaginary function and thereby justify its own disappearance."

*Number 20* brought the introductory article: "As You Like It," likewise from the pen of a member of the *Vidici* editorial board. The author of the text first praises B. Mišeljić because "he sees *the problem of the mirror* since it is obvious that there are many who are far away from understanding it as a problem." He also openly advocates that societal problems should not be solved in a democratic way and through the normal functioning of the social-political system. "In fact, the real questions and problems cannot be completely analyzed on the level of the political plane as has been done so far. Politics is not just a limitation, but is actually one of *the strongest underpinnings of the MIRROR* (read: societal and political system) together with its auxiliary weapons, from institutions to ideology." Since "real solutions cannot be given within the framework of politics," the author counsels that "one should not emulate the speakers in the parliament and at the meetings who just keep babbling: blah, blah, and then again blah, blah." Or, as it says in the *Dictionary of Technology*, "The Boy talks, the Person acts."

A new codeword is used: "The *Amateur Theater BEHIND THE LOOKING GLASS*" (emphasis by the author). Like all other code words, this apparently naïve one really does look like a proposal for a new theater. But the real key for the codeword: "Amateur Theater BEHIND THE LOOKING GLASS" is given in the next issue (21), p. 2, which is the peak of the insolence and aggressiveness of this group. There it can clearly be seen that the "Amateur Theater BEHIND THE LOOKING GLASS" is the *state of affairs that should take the stage after they shatter the mirror* – the socio-political system. That is why the author of the text, published in number 20, invites B. Mišeljić and the editorial board of *Student* to join him, with the words: "What do you and your, that is our, editorial board think about, let's say, taking part, active participation and perhaps informing the students and the rest of the world about that project," mentioning that Bora, "probably knows people who are not steeped in politics and who might be available to join this group."

B. Mišeljić, of course, conscientiously did his part of the job and, in number 22/23 offers the text (p. 2): "I Am Publishing Communism" whose writer signed in under the pseudonym "Marko Broz."

In this text a clear difference is made between society and the community of this group of like-minded Persons that is called a *comunis*. Speaking thus also in the language of code, here the thesis is emphasized that a member, *comunist*, answers only to his community and not to society. "Our commune, our community, must be the most important to us so we cannot proclaim the municipality, for example, to be more important than the commune. *If someone goes beyond the comunis-community, they can further proclaim a province, republic or state to be the most important*" (emphasis "M. Broz"). A general state of irresponsibility reigns in the socio-political system, as opposed to the community (read: this group of the like-minded) which answers to everyone. That is why "the community cannot fail" and the system can, "It is easy for the system to fail when it does not answer for itself or to others, but rather someone must answer to it."

The next number *24* offers the text of Antonio Negri (known as the *ideologist of the Red Brigade*) in the column "Theory of Crisis," which fits exceptionally well into the conception of the abovementioned group and which speaks of the complete identification of conceptually like-minded people. Here Antonio Negri, using his own terminology, proves that the only way to solve the social crisis is the overthrowing of the Constitution and the system founded upon it ("When does this mechanism collapse? When the contractual representation collapses which is the moment of the transformation of values into institutions, social products into planning and Governmental Legislation. That can happen for several reasons, which after all touch upon all the essential terms of *the basic norms, i.e. the material nature of the Constitution*: in the aggressive dynamics of the social contract it again becomes possible if the terms are changed of the *basic* proportions of *the material written in the Constitution*"). *Number 25* brought the introductory article (p. 2) where, under the cover of the interpretation of events in Poland, the ideology of breaking the mirror is reaffirmed. Here it is once again unambiguously claimed that all problems can be solved only by destroying the social system, by the pogrom of the Boys and the affirmation of the Person. These are the characteristic quotes: "The question is inevitable: is there an army in the world that is able to offer long term defense of the wall with *THE MIRROR THAT MUST BE SHATTERED*? Can the committees put an end to hope? *Hope must shatter the MIRROR. The tension is actually in the mirror!*"—Zoran Petrović-Piroćanac.

*Number 26/27* disperses all doubt about what is meant by the mirror. In the introductory article (p. 2) *it is expressly claimed that the socio-political system of socialist self-management is a mirror* (which should be broken, of course): "The socio-political community (federation, republics, etc.) have taken over the duty of supplying the citizens, but in principle it is clear that they cannot do that well because they only have the illusion of decision-making, an illusion of responsibility. They (i.e. the socio-political communities) ARE A MIRROR (!!!). How does it look when an *official of the mirror* wants to solve real human problems? We can see that best these days in the goal of justifying the ideological concept of stabilization, beginning with the artificial solving of problems" . . . etc. in the tendentious style.

Keeping all the tendencies of the editorial board of *Vidici* in mind, with their theory of destroying the socio-political system, the editorial board of *Student* practically concretizes the problems in its texts.

This social criticism in *Student*, especially explained through texts on housing, electrical systems, airplane crashes in Ayachi, media, etc., in fact, is a concretization of individual ideas that are proposed by the editorial board of *Vidici* theoretically, in a scholarly way and through their projects. Especially questionable, though quite clear, the texts on the problems of housing and their theoretical analysis is given in the *Dictionary of Technology* under the entry "housing."

In its criticism of the Association of Socialist Youth and the Communist Party, *Student* applies the same principle of constant critique, regardless of all the objective problems in society. It is quite important to point out the fact that *Student*, in one phase of its activity, criticized the Basic Organizations and other forms of organizing at the University level (the University Committee of the Association of Socialist Youth, the University Committee of the Communist Party) (UC ASY and UC CP). This critical forum was especially harsh in the electoral period in the organization of the ASY at the University. On the pages of *Student* a special discussion was held of the activities and role of the CP in society, of the efficiency of its activities in the existing international relations and in our socio-economic situation. Here, mention should be also be made of the texts about Poland that appeared in parallel with texts that speak of individual "crises" in our socio-political system. It should be emphasized that this is not accidental, but that in *Vidici* no. 8, in the texts about the crisis of institutions, the revelation of the mirror, the texts on Poland also appear. *Student* developed the concrete approach only later, when the crisis in Poland had become critical. At the same time, *Student* sharpens its criticism of the "phenomena and state" in our society.

Some of the problems, actually, which could justifiably criticized (and should be criticized), were criticized on the wrong basis, without a true Marxist analysis. In fact, they are analyzed from the ideological position of the editorial board of *Vidici*.

This criticism of the Party culminated in the Letter to the CP of the Association of Communists of Yugoslavia. The basic goal of the letter is not the reaffirmation of the Cominform, but rather an attempt to discredit the Presidency and the leaders of our society, which is complete accord with the ideological orientation of *Vidici.*

## THE ESCALATION OF AGGRESSIVE ACTIVITIES

The escalation of the aggressive activities of the group of like-minded congregating around the editorial boards of *Vidici* and *Student* led to a frontal and radical attack on the socio-political system, unabashedly and openly calling for the destruction ("dissolution") of socialist society and the workers' self-management. Since *they did whatever they wanted, uninhibited*, they began to think that the Technologists ("slaves of the system") could do nothing to them, the Persons, that their will always triumphed and that the breaking of the mirror (the socio-political system) was just days away. Speaking out from edition to edition, their appetites grew, their texts became more and more aggressive and open, their allusions ever clearer, so that finally in *Student* no. 21 they came out with a text whose contents were a message that was so *openly and aggressively hostile* that its very publication was an exceptional confirmation of this ideology – thanks to their will and cleverness, Persons are omnipotent in the world of the Boys (the Technologists). The superiority and mastership of the Person over the "*hierarchical apes*" (officials) was obviously confirmed here: "the hierarchical apes" provided the means, provided a place in the pages of newspapers, provided everything the Persons demanded, and when the Persons published their Manifesto, those "hierarchical apes" stared stupidly at the texts, not comprehending a single word, shaking their heads in confusion and not knowing what to do with all of that. Is there a greater irony than the fact that *they invested huge financial resources in the popularization and affirmation of this ideology*, and thus confirmed the thesis of the Persons that the "hierarchical apes" will ever remain stupid and senseless "hierarchical apes."

The "Boys Project" was intended to show how a concrete idol is created, using a practical example. The project was designed as the affirmation of a hitherto unknown musical group through various media: by writing the name of the group on walls, publishing photographs, printing their records at *Vidici.*

The group "Idoli" ("Idols") was to serve as the band around which the younger generation gathered, along with other bands that appeared in Belgrade and further.

However, becoming aware of their popularity and significance in the world of music and to their audience, "Idoli" separated and pulled away from the editorial board of *Vidici*, heading off on their own. So it was that the editorial board of *Vidici* lost the chance to manipulate the "Idoli" in the sense of the practical testing of the completion of their "projections." The text on the second page of number 21, "Why Are We Left in the Dark," had the header "on the occasion of the dissolution of a system" and the tendentious sub-header "Why did the system fall apart?" The article is seemingly about the anniversary of the collapse of the electrical system, but it is more than obvious that it is an allusion to the possible (and desirable) collapse of the Socialist Federal Republic of Yugoslavia. In the left column we will offer the original text, and an interpretation and explication in the right, which is not even necessary in some places.

| | |
|---|---|
| *"Collapses begin in places that no one is paying attention to."* | The demand to break the mirror (to destroy the system) is first set out by a group congregating around the magazine *Vidici* in the *Dictionary of Technology*; they say for themselves that they are a marginal group (p. 3), i.e. that they are on the margins of the system. That is a place to which no one (and here they are absolutely right) pays any attention – |

breakdowns, changes in the editorial board, replacement of the editor-in-chief, happen at the newspaper *Student*, but *Vidici* continues to act from the wings, clandestinely and skillfully. When the editorial board at *Student* is replaced, *Vidici* just insert their own people again (for example B. Mišeljić) and everything goes back to normal. The entire group is like a Hydra – cut off one of its heads (replace the editorial board of *Student*) and a new one grows on it because the others remain untouched (*Vidici*). The place where no one pays attention (*Vidici*) – the place where the collapse begins – are the first cracks in the structure of the system, a structure which will, and this is what the members of that group believe, soon collapse once and for all.

*"Who could have guessed that our ties to that western system were so important that we will, without them, collapse. Events have begun to occur at a dizzying pace. Soon the Eastern basin, to which belong the systems of Serbia, Macedonia and Montenegro, will completely separate from the western part and will function separately for a while."*

Doubtless, this is the imagined scenario of the disintegration of Yugoslavia, a scenario like so many other similar plans made by a wide variety of hostile organizations. The difference between this one and them is that this scenario was published *in Socialist Yugoslavia*, in the newspaper of Belgrade's students, by the ASY and the UC of the ASY. The break in economic and other relations with the West leads to the collapse of Yugoslavia and the formation of the special "systems" of Serbia, Montenegro and Macedonia. However, these "systems" also become the victims of collapse soon afterwards.

*At the top of the pyramid there is a place known as the* seat of the mirror, *or the Yugoslav dispatcher center. This actually brings up the basic question: Is there really a Yugoslav system? Is that peak of the hierarchical pyramid a reality or just an illusion of it? A midsummer night's dream?* Or *a committee of people who control the system*, who possess power, so that *maintaining the system is a matter of their self-will?*

The peak of the pyramid of government is actually what maintains the mirror-system, and it is called the "seat of the mirror." The presidency of the SFRY and CP of Yugoslavia as a dispatcher center are just a committee of people who control the system, thanks to the fact that they possess power. The system is maintained only because of their self-will – since they are "hierarchical apes" and not Persons, it is clear that they cannot have a Will but only self-will.

The Technologists do not have the power to stop the collapse of the system – they can only impotently observe the shattering of the mirror and wait for the Person who is going to kill them.

*There is no power* in that pinnacle, in that inductive *mirror.* Events occur according to *the very logic of disintegration*, without any sort of possibility of affecting them. Is it not clear, the *system is collapsing* but the federal dispatcher, the only one who can actually see it, can just observe that multitude of varying images of one and the same figure.

*"At the top, the system is completely lifeless, just a reflection of a real event. It has no power, just an ideology of power, because its entirety is just the mechanical sum of the parts that make it up. Its entirety is not reality but ideology. The crowd of people – the ghosts who maintain their abstract image – are just marionettes of an amateur theater. They move by the will of the system, not their own, but when the system loses its power to function, the force that animates them also vanishes. They do not know how to act, but just how to function. Then, in panic, they create chaos.*

The Technologists, the officials, maintain a system that manipulates them like a puppeteer does his marionettes. That is why they are called "marionettes of the amateur theater." (Now the meaning of "Amateur Theater BEHIND THE LOOKING GLASS" is completely clear.) They do not have a will but move by the will of the system and they do not know that it is actually the system that keeps them from living, not understanding that there will be no life for them until they destroy the system.

*They will never understand that the system is* the thing that keeps them from being alive."

*"It is no longer amazing that if the hierarchy of an organization is higher, the power and strength of that organization is less. So, the power of those at the very top is the least. They are only actors. The only thing the upper echelon of an institution can do is to observe how those lower in the hierarchical chain manage their subsystems. To observe and to ask for information from time to time – 'there hasn't been a collapse, has there?'"*

The top of the pyramid – the organization is composed of Technologists who only pretend to have power, although they are only actors in the theater of mirrors. When the mirror is broken they die, because the internal drive of their actions vanishes.

*"There is no better image of the illusory reality that the system produces. The system as such, as Kant proved, is indeed the very production of illusion. The peak of the system is no sort of reality, nor does the top of the pyramid in its hopeless oppositeness have any relation to existence. It is just a reflection, a mirror, empty ideology: glass."*

NO COMMENT

*"Therefore, dear colleagues, the answer to the question asked is: the system has collapsed and the system will collapse because of the nature of the system itself."*

*"Where there is a Will, there is no disintegration. When the system obtains wholeness with its Will, it will cease to be a system – it will become reality. But reality is here, on the glass, or behind it. People cannot solve the problems created by the system, because there are no human problems there."*

Within the framework of the system, human problems cannot be solved, rather, all problems actually arise as a consequence of the existence of the system – if there were no system there would be no problems. The system and its collapse, that is the world of Technology, of Boys without a will. Opposite to that fake world, to the world of illusion, there is the world of Persons, the world where there is no disintegration ("Where there is a Will, there is no disintegration").

*"You, the elect, who know the power of your breath, create the whirlpool of life with it,* THE TIME HAS COME FOR YOU TO ARISE AND BREAK THE DAMNED MIRROR OF POWERLESSNESS. *And look at the world, not on the control panel, but with your eyes wide open."*

An open invitation to destroy the system. A war-cry to the Barbarians to attack and break the mirror.

*"On the battlefield, everyone is equal and the perspectives are open to everyone."*

The theory of mirrors in the interpretation of the journal *Vidici* is not original. As early as the 19th century, anarchism was born as a desire to destroy the capitalist states and the state in general. Likewise, the teachings about "the Will" and "the Person" are just a variation of Nietzsche's theory of the Übermensch/Superman. The division of people into Persons and Boys, into individuals of greater or lesser value, likewise has its parallel in the racist theories of Chamberlain, Godineau, Hitler and Rosenberg. The influence of psychoanalysis and anti-psychiatry is also present (the separation of the personality, the mirror is equated with the system), along with the influence of the works of Huxley and Castaneda. The philosophy of Punk and the New Wave also have their place in this conceptual mélange, especially that part of them that deals with forms of de-construction (anarchism and ludism). The influence of Bazeley and Negri can also be noticed (neo-anarchism, the theoreticians of the Red Brigade), and anarcho-syndicalism (the theory of horizontal structures by the Polish author Lamentovič).

Therefore this ideology is a compilation – "a meta-goulash of various ideologies," mainly "radical" and "anarchic" (destructive of society), especially developed and applied to concrete socio-political and economic conditions.

## HERBERT MEIER

# THE HISTORY OF A LIE

We live in a time of mystification, a time of disorientation caused by the loss of a center and by desacralization. Such a time is ripe for the appearance of false messiahs, a flood of no less false spirituality and the flourishing of fake mystics. Deceit often takes on the illusion of truth. Christian Rosenkreuz comes to mind who, in his leisure, composed the fantastic tale of the company of the Rose Cross. Readers of that nebulous, syncretistic prose – without the author's knowledge – founded an order and played their part in the all-encompassing disorder and moral chaos that is shaking the very foundations of European civilization.

In recent times, the legend of the Evangelical Bicyclists of the Rose Cross has been circulating among the "esotericians." This mystification, a simple mishmash of the mystification that came before it, has found champions, unfortunately, even among authors of pristine reputation. This is one more proof in support of the thesis that no one – if one leaves the solid ground of science and the credibility of the experimental method – is immune to error. And the error, in this particular case, is more than obvious. Already at first sight we notice the almost naïve diversity in the documents of the so-called Bicyclists; they are nothing more than a heap of completely contradictory concepts forcibly connected into a vague theory. What a fabulous mixture: iconoclasm, theology, psychoanalysis, scholastics, astrology, mechanics, dubious poetry, falsified biographies, misrepresented history, and unconvincing, obviously construed, symbolism. With near certainty it can be claimed that such a fraternity, such a gathering of people, does not exist in reality. It is more likely that the *fama birotarorium* is the product of a few liars with too much time on their hands.

Before we denounce and unmask the sources and documents, let us look at the goals of these infamous Bicyclists. The sect, or so it is claimed, originated in a secret society of blacksmiths from Antioch, scattered about the world with aim of spreading a secret from one generation to the next, a secret which can be reduced to approximately this: there are two kinds of craftsmen, masons and blacksmiths; the first are sons of the earth, in collusion with the Devil. These Archaitektones (as they call them) have one single goal: to build a tower that will reach into Heaven. Their first attempt, the construction of the Tower of Babylon, was foiled, but the fraternity of masons did not give up on its plans. The first tower was only a prototype of the final, perfect, upside-down tower that is to be built beneath the earth as a system sufficient in itself – a complete city. On the other hand, the blacksmiths of Antioch, as sons of fire, are the guardians of the ancient Covenant between God and man; they are the sons of Heaven. Supposedly the task of these preservers of the tradition of the Antioch blacksmiths, the Evangelical Bicyclists, is indeed to change the direction of history and to thwart the plans of the masons. In Tatlin's plan for the monument of the 2nd International, the Bicyclists purportedly recognized the sign of the last days and, after centuries of silence, decided to discretely publish their teachings. From the existing "documents" it turns out that the

Bicyclists are battling against the intentions of the architects with the synergy of the dead, living and future brothers (*sic!*). To make the farce even greater, they do so by having the *dead members* (since they observe time integrally from their otherworldly position) teach the unborn how to have an influence on events. Living members, the earthly camp of the brotherhood, only exist so that the unbroken thread will have a material basis. Otherwise, everything would just be an illusion. Which, in fact, it is. At the same time, this also explains the this-worldly passivity of the Evangelical Bicyclists. The central place in the Bicyclists mysticism is certainly the plan to outsmart the architects by having the Bicyclists themselves do the planning for the ultimate tower; they are to slip the apparently completed plans of the structure to the architects, and after being built the structure will destroy itself at a given time.

How utterly charming!

Let us now look at the documents of the Evangelical Bicyclists. First is the Basel Parchment, a charter of undetermined age, a collection of absolute nonsense in which certain interpreters find hidden material. Even if the parchment is authentic, it says nothing. The text is not even worthwhile citing. We can comfortably say that it is the most commonplace of farces.

The second document is *A TALE OF MY KINGDOM*, the authorship of which is ascribed to a certain King Charles the Hideous. Historical sources make no mention of such a king. Not a single mention. To be honest, Charles the Hideous himself in the *TALE* announces his disappearance from the historical scene together with his fictitious kingdom. We can perhaps recognize the hand of the falsifiers who, knowing that they are deceiving everyone, are preparing an exit strategy for themselves using purely literary devices. In any case, the third supposed document, *THE*

*DIABOLICAL TWO-WHEELER*, attributed to the majordomo of King Hideous, is reprinted completely from the novel *The Cyclist Conspiracy* by a little known author, published by "Prosveta Publishers," although the champions of the Evangelical Bicyclists have launched the thesis that the writer is the one who reproduced the majordomo's text.

The entire ruse would not be worthy of mention if it did not also contain a series of political implications wrapped in a thin veil of mystery. The Evangelical Bicyclists, whether they exist or not, consider themselves to be legitimate subjects of the Eastern Roman Empire, Byzantium, and they do not recognize any of the states that have appeared on the territory that Byzantium once occupied. It is not far from reason to suppose that the Evangelical Bicyclists could easily be a creation of a department for political propaganda of one of the great powers, for whom the existing state of peace is not agreeable. In any case, it is a morbid legend that is threatening to become fashionable, a testimony to the fact the phantoms of superstition are still raging the world of people, that vagueness and secrecy are still popular and that they persistently, but with ever less success, attempt to stand in the way of the scientific and technological progress of humankind.

*Christian Science Monitor*

## ÇULABA ÇULABI

# HOW I BECAME A MEMBER OF THE ORDER OF LITTLE BROTHERS OF THE EVANGELICAL BICYCLISTS OF THE ROSE CROSS

### (THE HISTORY OF TIMEPIECES)

I must admit: that morning when I was arrested, I actually did strike my mother. Because she did not wake me up on time. The night before I had left her a message to wake me up at eight, she woke me up at nine and so I was late to an important meeting. I got up and, angrily, gave her a slap. Almost a symbolic one. This comes as a kind of confession. Does my conscience bother me? Yes, but my conscience bothers me whenever I do anything; for example when I cross the street or smell a flower. So, I slapped my mother and quickly experienced all the things that a slap can get a man into, a slap that is, like everything else anyway, perhaps just fiction. Not even half an hour passed and I was already arrested and standing in the police station in front of the shocked policemen who simply could not believe that I had raised my hand against a parent. The very nature of those men's jobs is to raise their hand against people who are not related to them in any way whatsoever, and they – oh, the hypocrisy! – were shocked because I gave my mother a gentle slap. I am of the opinion that a man should occasionally beat his mother, if for no other reason than the fact that she gave birth to him – bang! – cut the umbilical cord, and shoved him into the world, where he is constantly attempting to return to the safety of the uterus by pushing his penis into women's vulvae, vainly attempting to widen the entrance, to slip back inside, to escape from the face of the planet, committing the deadly sin of promiscuity.

I thought about the whole thing later in my jail cell. And about how quite possible things are incredible to today's people. What is easier than hitting your mother? She is always nearby, and she is never expecting a slap. And yet, to the healthy mind that is incomprehensible. What was Jesus of Nazareth hoping for when he preached the final resurrection of the dead? This healthy mind, since I like to represent things visually, always reminds me of that lieutenant of the guard at the Kremlin who falls asleep every night, sinking into the nothingness, not surprised by it – yet, at the very mention of "resurrection" grabs his Kalashnikov and angrily shoots at the crows on the Kremlin domes where, supposedly, the listening devices of the CIA have been placed, of the famous Lieutenant Morozov, described in the *Moscow Memoirs* of T. J. James, first secretary of the United States embassy. Indeed, such guys killed hundreds of people at the Gulag, and they never raised their hand against their mother. In such situations, the best thing to do is reach for Hegel; that man could justify anything. "The process of life," he writes, "is the formation of the character just as much as it is the removal of it." That dialectic is irrefutable. In spite of everything, we strive just to have our personality formed, which is understandable to an extent, but impossible. That causes a misunderstanding. Life strives to remove us, we struggle and thereby we get further entangled in the contradiction, as if in quicksand.

Because of everything mentioned, you should not hold that little slap against me; I was just being a tool of the unconquerable force of destruction.

You see, I thought, each of us has a Lieutenant Morozov deep in our souls. I also do, of course. One morning, for example, I opened the window and bird flew into my room, followed by several more and in the twinkle of an eye the room was full of the flapping of little wings and loud chirping. In my mania for classifying things, I noticed that there were several species: *Fringilla coeleba, Tudus merula, Sturnus vulgaris, Hirundo rustica, Ignica pillus* . . . I stood in the middle of the uproar, like Moses on Mt. Sinai, and asked myself: How can this be? Then again, I accepted it as a normal fact that, in the very same way, one hundred thousand people *suddenly* swarm in through the doors of a football stadium. The birds were all over the room: on the bookshelf, on the lamp, on the wardrobe, on the bed, on the table. Two or three of the littlest ones were squatting on the tilting picture of Joseph Vissarionovich, threatening to knock it over. I stood in the middle of that feathery uproar and crossed my arms, thinking: They will ruin everything; they will bury me and the room in droppings, it will all turn into guano, an excellent phosphate fertilizer. It never even occurred to me that they were harbingers of heaven, symbols of angels, which Providence had only sent me so that I would put aside systematization and classification.

At that time, before I met Kowalsky in prison, I lived in a chamber of hell. In truth, I was waiting to hear God's voice, but not very energetically, more just to deceive myself. In my brutishness, I was practically waiting for a thundering shout from the heights of heaven, which shows perfectly the enormity of my idiocy, my addiction to anthropomorphism that is not inhibited even when faced with such nonsense as "*the legs of a chair*" and "*the head of state.*" Kowalsky was the one who finally explained it to me: God has spoken for ages and he can send messages, through a mediator, to certain lucky souls in their sleep; complete silence is perfect articulation and all speech is a lie, utter nonsense at the very least. This Kowalsky fellow was a member of some sort of sect, the Bicyclists of the Rose Cross. I learned a lot about Bicyclism in those few days I spent with him in the same cell. He was arrested for breaking clocks. The Bicyclists of the Rose Cross, in fact, believe that timepieces are Satanic devices.* This is how Kowalsky described the event to me. First, early in the morning he broke his alarm clock. Then he went to see a few friends, convinced them of the usefulness of breaking those devices, and together they broke twelve of them, some wristwatches, a few pocket watches, some alarm clocks, right in front of some flabbergasted passersby in the street in the very center of town. However, they did not stop there. In a nearby store they bought two dozen more cheap watches and began to break them, while Kowalsky preached to the curious onlookers that they should leave time behind and look toward eternity. Then, Kowalsky and his friends got on their bicycles and rode off down the street, breaking the town's clocks until the police stopped them and arrested them. Still, Kowalsky carried out the biggest exploit at the police station. He hypnotized the police officers present and ordered them to break

* Here is, among other things, what one of the members of the Order of the Bicyclists of the Rose Cross, Lewis Mumford, says: "The clock is, in addition, such an operational machine whose 'products' are seconds and minutes: in its essential nature it separated time from human events and helped to create belief in an independent world of mathematics and measurable sequences: an independent world of science. In everyday human experience there is proportionally little basis for that belief. During the year, days do not last the same amount of time, and the shorter travel from the east to the west changes astronomic time by a certain number of minutes."

their watches. When they returned from their hypnotic sate, the police vented all their anger on Kowalsky. He was covered with bruises, but satisfied. I have to admit that I was greatly pleased with this idea about breaking clocks.

"The thing about watches," Kowalsky told me, "especially digital ones, that I don't like is that they work too fast, they count off hundreds of seconds as well. Generally speaking, a web of great mystification has been woven around time. Above all, the mystification about the ostensible objectivity of time. Utter nonsense. Time is a completely subjective matter, but every person is not a subject, and that is the problem. Timepieces are perhaps exact, but time is not, time is a matter of personality, or even of affinity. So, since no one is without a watch any more, no one has time. A multitude of other mystifications are built onto that one, like the general advancement of technology and medicine that have brought about the extension of human life expectancy. Perhaps human life expectancy has been extended, but it is only pro forma. According to some research, which does not claim to have the right to exactness (far from it), in the 13$^{th}$ century fifty years lasted as long as, approximately, 110 in the 20$^{th}$ century. That is the secret: the general collapse of things includes time as well; it is degenerating, losing intensity. The world is already half as big as it was 1,000 years ago. In order to support this claim, I will use a formula from physics . . ."

And Kowalsky wrote with his finger on the dusty floor:

$$S = \frac{V}{t}$$

"You see," he said. "Space (S) is a function of Velocity (V) and Time (t). In other words, if we move faster, space grows smaller. There is no great mysticism here, that is how the world is disappearing."

Now I will return again to the description of that place in hell where I lived for so long. It was a normal student dorm room. There was nothing terrifying in it, no cries of tortured souls, no demonic pitchforks. A rather suitable place with an average temperature of about 63 °F, incomparably lower than those they ascribe to the depths of Hades. And yet, it was hell because, of all the endless places in the world, each is equal with all the others: all of them are the entrance to hell. Of course, if that place is occupied by a human; that is the *conditio sine qua non*. If I am to be in hell, I must occupy space. I read some authors who say that hell is a space, and that it must have a being inside of it for the horrifying surroundings to make sense. I tend to believe, however, that hell is of internal origins, that it radiates out into space. In any case, a flat projection is unimportant. Those are all descriptions and nonsense. It makes absolutely no difference whether horror comes from the outside or inside. The horror is important.

There in that room, which was only missing a HOME SWEET HOME sign to make the farce complete, my soul was stewing on the flames of my own hell, being deceived by the average temperature of 63 °F, and by statistics in general. Until the day when I met Kowalsky and became enthralled with Bicyclism. Listening for several days to his stories about the secret order, about his magnificent exploits, I realized that my entire previous life had been a series of absolute mistakes. I felt unworthy to ask if I could become a member of *the Little Brothers* of the Evangelical Bicyclists of the Rose Cross. To my misfortune, I was quickly released from jail and told to pay a fine. I went home, paid the fine, made up with my mother and almost forgot about Kowalsky. Two years later, I got a letter from India. Wondering who could be writing me from that distance, I turned the envelope over and saw "from: Kowalsky."
Here are the contents of that letter:

*Dharamsala*
*21 December 1953*

Dear Doctor Çulabi,

No doubt you are surprised that I am writing to you even though we did not exchange addresses, but I am also sure that you will not be angry. Two years ago, when I had the honor of sharing a jail cell with you, I spoke of *the Little Brothers* of the Evangelical Bicyclists of the Rose Cross. I still remember the interest you showed in my, probably lengthy, explanation. I am also convinced that you yourself wished to belong to the brotherhood, but that you did not dare to ask. However, I must tell you that you were *already, at that time*, most certainly a member of the Evangelical Bicyclists. Unconscious of it, of course. But the best and most edifying things are done unconsciously. Even the members of the trifling sects of psychoanalysts talk about that.

But now I will move on to the explanation that I owe you. This is how it is possible to belong to the brotherhood and not be conscious of it for years. The dead members of our ancient and honorable Order do not cease their activities after death. To the contrary, it could be said that the real activity of all Bicyclists of the Rose Cross actually begins then, but such a definition is meaningless. Wrenched from the course of time, they see a certain part of the past and a corresponding part of the future as integral. Maintaining the legend, our dead fathers know all members of *the Little Brothers*, not only those who were and are, but also those who will later be. Consequently, a Grand Master of the order knew about you long before I did, and I was assigned to be your mentor long, long before we met in that charming cell.

Before I induct you into the secrets of the Order, a warning must be given: it is neither easy nor simple to be an Evangelical Bicyclist.

You must be prepared to do anything. And above all – to believe in everything.

It is customary that the mentor tells the newly-accepted member something about his life. The purpose of that act is initiation, because mentor and candidate are connected in a mystical way. Regardless of whether they ever meet or of how great the distance is between them, their lives are connected and they somehow complete each other, making up a coherent whole, and therefore the number of members of the Evangelical Bicyclists is always an even one. The day when one of the members dies, the mentor begins to compose the text for the initiation. However, the text is sent on the day of birth of the dead member. Your predecessor in the Order, whose secret name was Steely, was born on December 21, and that is why the letter was sent to you on that date. Since letters from Dharamsala travel exactly 40 days to their destinations, you are becoming aware that you are one of the Bicyclists at the same moment when (after the post mortem purification, the length of which is calculated with the formula: *date of death + time from date of death to date of birth + 40 days*) your predecessor is becoming aware that he has overcome death, passed the Second Initiation and taken his place in the eternal hierarchy. In this way, the consciousness of the individual, and indeed of the entire Order, is constantly increasing through carefully coordinated this-worldly and other-worldly events. In that way the Great Secret is carefully hidden from the profane, simultaneously revealing itself ever more to the consecrated. This goes so far that even people of remarkable spirituality, but who are skeptics at heart, consider *the very existence of the order* to be a rather bad joke.

So much for now. Remember the words of St. Paul, "I have fed you with milk and not with meat: for hitherto ye were not able to bear it." My confession follows. You should keep in mind that it is not true, because in this world nothing is true any more. Once long ago, the Truth revealed itself, but few were those who believed it. That is why the world is punished by believing in the greatest lies.

In my youth, my dear friend, I was this way and that, much more evil than good. But that is no longer important. The dead brothers have erased my past. I will tell you about my gradual conversion. After many years of studying poetry and literature, after a period in which I was a nihilist and revolutionary, overnight I changed my convictions and became a royalist. You might ask: What kind of belief is that anyway, to be a nihilist? The answer is: the most edifying. To consider the world and yourself in it as null and void, that is worthy of the most edified spirits. However, the years got to me: I became something of a conformist, it was harder and harder for me to put up with the extremeness of nihilism and the unity of the revolutionaries to whom I belonged. If anything could make me angry (I am using the past tense, because nothing can make me angry any longer) it was unity and unanimity. And yet, the fact that I was a subject of a country ruled by a king gave my convictions a certain dose of bizarreness, necessary for me to be able to live at all. At that time, you see, it was not fashionable to be a royalist. My comrades at the time, I must mention this, despised me, but I could already see then that the envy of the rich was concealed behind their concern about the welfare of people, and I already knew then that, once they had triumphed, they would become the same as the objects of their hatred. Because, like takes displeasure in like. In my dreams, I always saw a terrible multitude of people, raising their hands and repeating nonsense like a choir.

That dream soon became a reality, but I remained a royalist. I was not led astray by fashion. I justified it like this: if the Lord had wanted to create a multitude, he would have made many people, not just one as he did, and that one – quite human from the outset

– messed it all up. If things really are like that, I thought, then one should be disunified and in disaccord at all costs.

The second, quite important, element for my conversion was the heraldry. Probably because of my humble background, I had always felt veneration toward the coats-of-arms of the royal and noble families; all those lions and eagles excited me to tears with their radiant grandeur. Yes, I know, not everything was noble in the good old days, but things were visually better shaped and much less naïve than the red pieces of linen that my former comrades used to hang on the façades of buildings immediately after winning, where it would say that everything is excellent and that it will be even better. To make matters worse, the masses believed that everything really was excellent and that it would be even better. (The power of the written word is enormous and that is why they control it so carefully.) Actually I was offended by the childishness of the attempt to convince me (or anyone else) that I came from an ape, that I am now a man, and that I should be happy because of that. Above all, in this world the possibility does not exist, nor even the right, for someone to be happy, and everyone knows this but no one is willing to admit it. Because of cowardice, at that. That is why the kids in the schools have to learn commonplace lies instead of being taught about Nagarjuna's metaphysics and the texts of St. Augustine.

On the other hand, the consciousness in me grew that the royalist option is not a degradation but an advancement, because this all-encompassing democratization has led to nihilism. Sometimes it is progressive to go backwards. Just as the world was made from nothing, I also came into being from nihilism. I realized that I was given a message from the Lord. The difference between the Old Testament prophets and me, in a moral sense, and all other senses, was more than evident, naturally to my detriment. But the times had changed, again to my detriment; people now are of ever weaker quality. So it is – it is only right that, for the imbeciles (as people are), a prophet should be an imbecile (like I am). I supposed, by analogy with the Old Testament, that persecution awaited me. The character of the *homo sapiens*, that character which anthropologists, psychologists and all the rest of that breed do not mention, but which is most typical of the species, is that it does not want to hear the truth about itself and it is ready to kill in order not to hear it. And the truth is short and clear: we are vermin and perverts. And yet, liking to hear flattery, that homo gets suckered by the most fantastic of lies. Still, wherever there is vanity, there is also Nemesis, and Nemesis is the cruelest to those for whom the vanity is unfounded: toward all those individuals of humble backgrounds who want to be emancipated, who are proud of their handicap.

And then, there was the love of work, the glorification of day-laboring, the savageness in the coalmines – it filled me with a quiet, secret hatred. God does not do anything, that was proven by St. Augustine in *De Civitate Dei*. I swore a hundred times that I would never do anything. I comforted myself with the thought: Perhaps my laziness is evidence that I was a marquis or baron in a previous incarnation. Then there is that nonsense about historical progress: The poverty of the slaveholding system! The darkness of medieval feudalism! Nonsense after nonsense. Let us examine it: the slave worked, he got food and clothing and had no freedom of movement. All right. In the feudal system (for which I have a weakness), the serf worked, got a little more food and clothing and had no freedom of movement. That's all right, too. Let's see what kind of progress the emancipators brought us. Now the worker (supposedly) has unlimited freedom of movement, his salary is enough (barely) for food and clothing, but not for traveling. I just want to tell you – and this is a truly important point in the initiation – that nothing in history changes except the forms. Nothing and never important. Only gentlemanliness, nobility and politeness perish. And here is an example: try to imagine the beauty of a medieval hunt, where people went with bow and arrow on horseback, and then compare such a hunt with the modern hunting trips of the aristocrats where "the hunters," steeped in vodka, shoot guns at deer that have been drugged and tied down.

In the circle of my closest friends, two opinions ruled about my conversion. One – that I was striking a pose, the other – that I had lost my mind. The matter stood – half and half. To be honest, those facts, that I was striking a pose and losing my mind, did not bother me in the least. On the contrary. First: every opinion is a pose, nothing can be done about that. Death is also a pose. Is there anything more artificial than a corpse? And then: What's wrong with losing your mind? That is just, if I may use political jargon, turning away from the wrong direction. I never put much stock in the human mind. Nor in heroism, for that matter. I think that heroism is the highest degree of cowardice. A man becomes afraid of death and, come on now, we do it spontaneously, rushing at a foxhole, disposing of our fright and shouting HOOORRRAAY!, we die and remain in the memories of our progeny not as cowards who committed suicide, but as heroes. Since the dawn of time it has been that way, and our progeny does not care about it. Human stupidity is eternal. Moreover, it is eternity itself. Whoever recognizes that, whoever despises the wisdom of the world, becomes immortal.

The equation is quite simple: If I think that I am stupid, I am wise and immortal; if I think that I am smart, I am stupid and dead. Çulabi, nota bene. It was revealed to me that I am an immortal being, but that did not offer me any relief. Au contraire. I felt better when I was a nihilist; nihilists generally feel better than everybody else. At least at the beginning, while they are still numbed by the vanity, like Nietzsche who bombastically declared the death of God and then ended up dying himself. Now, one can shout in tranquility, "Nietzsche is dead," and that will be completely correct. But about God, still nothing is known; he is still surrounded by the unknown, which is a trait that especially attracted me to Him. Pomp and circumstance – that is for the rabble. One should turn to the secretive, to the dark: to secret societies, secret fraternities, and even to secret agents, why not. I, for example, felt a certain attraction toward the secret police just because they do everything far from the eyes of the public. But Nietzsche loved noise. He went so far in his mindless love of power that he began to anticipate Stalin visually: same haircut, same moustache, and the same stare. But he did not succeed. Stalin is out of reach.

The deeper I sank into obscurantism, the more sympathy I felt for, now deceased, Joseph Vissarionovich. I obtained his picture (just as you once did) and hung it on the wall next to my picture of the Savior. I admit, led astray by propaganda and democratic ideas, for a time I was an anti-Stalinist. But, as I matured spiritually, it became clear to me that Stalin was unjustly slandered according to the usual practice of humankind that it always despises its best sons. Çulabi, nota bene. As soon as the mob begins to spit on someone, that person should be admired. Joseph Vissarionovich was supposed to serve as a sacrificial lamb, so that a multitude of crimes could be dumped on him. Matters stand quite differently: the mob wants to denounce, to destroy, to desecrate, to kill. Let us not be deceived; one single man cannot turn millions into evildoers unless they are already evildoers in the depths of their souls. Here, Stalin was, if I may say it that way, just a catalyst; he directed the aggression of the masses so that destruction came to those who would have executed Satan's plans in their entirety. Never forget that, in recent times, evil wears the mask of the good.

That is enough for now. With fraternal greetings I congratulate you for joining the honorable order of the *Little Brothers* of the Evangelical Bicyclists of the Rose Cross.

P.S.
Buy yourself a ROG bicycle.

Perhaps it is shameful to admit it, but I did not know how to ride a bike. In spite of it all, I bought an old ROG velocipede and patiently practiced in the yard. In the next letter I got, this time from Teheran, Kowalsky wrote that it was not important whether I knew how to ride a bicycle or not; he explained that the symbolism is important. The bicycle, namely, is a vertical device; it contradicts gravity. In itself, it carries no special meaning and it represents a sort of mandala, the purpose of which is to stimulate contemplation. Likewise, he informed me that a Grand Master of the order had decided that I should dedicate my this-worldly life to the study of time and timepieces.

In that letter, which I unfortunately do not have, Kowalsky wrote about the history of our brotherhood in more detail. At the beginning of the 3rd century, when the order came about, it was simply called *the Little Brothers*. In the 16th century, the adjective "Evangelical" was added. As early as the 19th century, we became Bicyclists, and in the 20th – Bicyclists of the Rose Cross.

> "In truth, there are facts," Kowalsky wrote, "indicating that, as early as the 13th century, an Orthodox monk from

the monastery of Žiča tried to construct a bicycle. The drawings have been preserved of an awkward wooden construction that did indeed look like a velocipede in almost every detail. However, it is reliably known that the abovementioned monk, named Callistus, was not a member of the Order. Scandalized, the hegumen of the monastery ordered that the 'diabolical thing' be burned, and the first bicycle in the world ended up as a bonfire. There is no data about the fate of the builder, the monk Callistus. Still, even though he was not a member of the Order, the 'Giro d'Italia 51' bicycle race was secretly dedicated to the memory of that man.

"In history," Kowalsky wrote further, "if memory serves me, the order has had countless names. Even now it is known that *the Little Brothers* are supposed to take on another attribute soon, 'Who Painstakingly Pedal toward Golgotha,' but the conservative members of the order are resisting the name change . . ."

As far as I could gather from the rest of the letter, *the Little Brothers* will be given more and more attributes and the full name of the order on Judgment Day will simultaneously be its work – a long sentence which will describe in detail all that the Bicyclists have done throughout time . . .

And that is all I can say. The time has come for me to finish the story of how I was accepted into the Order of *the Little Brothers* of the Evangelical Bicyclists of the Rose Cross.

## ÇULABA ÇULABI
# THE HISTORY OF TIMEPIECES

Ladies and gentlemen,

This humble paper is the result of years of study that stand in clear disproportion to its length. It should be emphasized that the limited size of the text is a result of the intention to indicate, in the broadest strokes, some of the significant turning points in the development of devices for measuring time, without delving into more detailed explanations.

As I have established, time is anthropomorphic. It is therefore no surprise that the Hellenes imagined it to be that way, as the persona of the god Chronos. There is no doubt that time belongs to man and vice-versa. God is outside of time. That means that it is not an unchangeable, objective or external force. In his activities, man measures himself against time, but time is only what man makes it out to be. Furthermore, it is not endless: man disappears in time, that is irrefutable, but time also disappears in men. In dying, everyone takes their part of time into the grave, the place they go precisely because of the action of time. Thus, a post mortem supply of time is created, and this explains the possibility of communicating with the dead. However, demons, who are completely extra-temporal spiritual beings, often use the curiosity of spiritualists in order to create chaos.

One of the oldest devices is the sandglass. It is composed of two vessels connected by a narrow neck. A clepsydra is filled with fine sand that flows from the upper vessel into the lower one, creating a visible, almost tangible, flow of time. Additionally, looked at symbolically, the upper vessel represents Heaven, and the lower the Earth. According to the writings of John of Cologne, the same thing happens with the time of history: the time determined by Providence "flows" from eternity, and the last days can be recognized by the acceleration of events by analogy with the clepsydra: if we observe a sandglass, we see that, when the amount of sand becomes small, it very quickly rushes into the lower vessel. Thereby, the fact that there are athletes who can run 100 meters in less than 10 seconds is a sign that the end is near. The excitement that happens every time a record is broken is proof of the spiritual obtuseness of people in this era.

However, the appearance of the mechanical clock was violence done to time. The working of clocks was accelerated by hanging weights on them, by compressing energy into springs that, as they release tension, controlled by a system of cogwheels, ever more quickly turn the hands, and with them – everything else: the number of heartbeats, breaths in and breaths out. This leads to the appearance of heart disease and tuberculosis, as was noted by Johann Huizinga.

On the plateaus of Tibet, in the monasteries of Sinai, Athos and Europe, work was done on the absolute slowing of personal time in order to gain insight into timelessness, while the monk Gerbert, later Pope Sylvester II, constructed the mechanical, "armillary sphere." Soon after the clock-face was divided into sixty minutes. Time devaluated and inflation resulted: instead of twenty-four hours, people now had 1,240 minutes available to them; for the first time, boredom appeared, the mortal sin *acedia*, which will later bring Western civilization to very edge of destruction. Shortly thereafter, the guild of watchmakers appeared – to which you, ladies and gentlemen, belong – that guild of introverted, hardworking people who have large families, who never get drunk and take the secrets of their craft with them into the grave. I have always felt an unusual respect for these craftsmen, these gentlefolk who reverently stare at devices for measuring time through a magnifying glass.

But it did not take long for the minute also to devaluate, so that an advanced skill was used to build a timepiece that would show seconds as well. The sexagesimal division of time, based on the number sixty, within a culture based on the decimal system, unambiguously indicates a relationship to Chaldean magic.

Electronic watches lost even the last symbol of eternity in their construction – their face in shape of a circle. Now, the small monitors dizzily count off tenths and even hundredths of a second. And not only that: they also calculate, and they can wake up their owners with an alarm bell. But that is not precision. The atomization of time with electronic machines indicates the void of time and the void of men within time. Because of timepieces we have become abstract, like the definition of a second, which states:

"The second is the duration of 9,192,631,770 periods of the radiation corresponding to the transition between the two hyperfine levels of the ground state of the caesium 133 atom."

But that is not all. Japanese scientists are hard at work on a project of a computerized timepiece with biochips that can be built into the human organism. This timepiece will take over a large number of functions; it will choose the user's friends, help him make decisions and control the state of his health. Predictions also exist for a timepiece with refined intelligence that will attempt to correctively instruct or, if necessary, kill its owner, insofar as it is established that said owner is harmful to society.

In spite of it all, ladies and gentlemen, with you I share the ideal of the return to good, old-fashioned clocks with cuckoo birds and a pendulum.

(This speech was given at the annual conference of the Association of Conservative Watchmakers of Europe, London, 1959.)

SAVA DJAKONOV

# THE PILGRIMAGE TO DHARAMSALA

*Y siguendo el fiel del rumbo*
*Se entraron en el desierto . . .*[*]

The pilgrimage to Dharamsala, which appeared to be an athletic competition to the general public, was actually undertaken with a different purpose. On the eve of our departure, the goal of our trip was explained to the gathered Bicyclists by J. K., an emissary of the Grand Master. In the salon of the "Majestic Hotel,"[**] built upon the axis dividing East and West, where the force of the Earth's gravity is the strongest in the northern hemisphere and stands at 1.7g, J. K. read an epistle from the Grand Master wishing us success, and then he held a speech that, I believe, everyone present will remember forever.

Briefly, the speech went like this: Dark clouds are looming over Europe; the architects' conspiracy, begun at Babylon for the purpose

[*] Headed straight in a familiar direction, I entered the desert . . .

[**] Not far from that place is the building where the *Dictionary of Technology* will be authored 40 years later.

of establishing an Earthly Empire, is threatening again.* The task of the Evangelical Bicyclists is aimed at disrupting the plans of the architects, at changing the flow of history through unnoticed acts of intervention in a direction opposite to that which human pride has planned. For that reason, the route of our supposed marathon went in the opposite direction to that in which history moved forward: from west to east. The big picture of all our tasks, J. K. said, cannot be seen by an individual; that was not even necessary because only the entirety of our accomplishments made sense. So, the seeming insignificance, triviality, and even weirdness of our individual tasks ought not deceive the pilgrims.

That same evening, all the participants got envelopes with a demarcated route, a detailed description of the dreams they were supposed to have at individual stages of the journey, and individual tasks. Immediately it became obvious that the warnings of the Grand Master's emissary were not just empty phrases. Without those warnings, the tasks would have made everyone wonder. I will cite just a few: One Bicyclist, for example, was to buy ten grams of hashish in a certain street from a certain man in Istanbul, and then to smoke it during the month of September in room 213 of the "Paris Hotel"; another, on the other hand, was ordered to buy an old house in Smyrna (with the help of a certain D. Çulabi), to renovate it, furnish it and then give it to a third Bicyclist who was to arrive in Smyrna on August 15 in order to set that same house on fire during the night of the 16th and 17th; one was actually supposed to open a fabric store in Athens, and another to become a chef at the residence

* The later development of events showed that the visions of the Grand Master became a reality. It was no accident that the architect Speer was at the very top of the Nazi hierarchy, just as it was no accident that Tatlin's project for the monument at the 3rd International was a slightly modified structure of the Tower of Babylon.

of the British ambassador in Ankara. I had, among other things, the slightly silly task of sending a postcard from Thessalonica to the address of a man I did not know in Chicago, with the following text: "It is spring in Greece. I'm waiting for you to come back. Ana."

I have given just a few of the tasks, though not the most bizarre ones because I still hold to believability, at least a little. I knew many of the tasks, in no way were they secret. But even if I had known them all, I never would have been able to find a logical connection between them. That became clear to me after many years wasted in searching for a hidden meaning. Years and years had to pass for me to realize that I could not find any sense in them, not because there was none or because it was hidden, but because, like most other people, I am nonsensical and the best I can do to defend myself from nonsense is to do what I am told without making sense of it. Indeed, at that time the obsessive search for meaning had still not become fashionable, but doubt tormented many of the bicyclists (including me), the doubt that was worst of all – that our campaign was futile. That is why, from this distance in time, the exploit of one of the brothers (who wished to remain anonymous) who hovered above a pebble of three grams for eight years and made sure it did not move from a certain spot (not far from one of the fountains at Beyazit Meydani), seems to be a magnificent example of spirituality. I must admit, not without bitterness, that all of those who were given the dirtiest and stupidest tasks were, in fact, the elite of the Evangelical Bicyclists, the elect for whom that was a chance to carry out an exploit. The abovementioned brother, whom the merchants, hash smokers and pimps at the Grand Bazaar called Crazy Aziz, guarded that pebble for eight years (sleeping and eating nearby) so that the balance of the Earth's mass would be thrown off, in order to cause a powerful earthquake in Japan. That earthquake caused disturbances in the flow of things whose far-reaching consequences we cannot even guess at. And yet, every detail was carefully planned. In the eyes of the Turks, in anybody's eyes for that matter, a man who spends years making sure a pebble does not move is a nutcase. That is why, of the three possible locations for causing the imbalance, Istanbul was chosen because Islam tolerates morons and fruitcakes.

How proud I was, drunken with conceit, that I was given the honor of traveling with Ernest M. – a master dreamer – and with the emissary of the Grand Master, in person. Oh, that they named me the Grand Chronicler of the Holy Pilgrimage to Dharamsala, I know that now, was just a mystification; they must have joked a lot on my account. Therefore, this chronicle, too, should be accepted by the reader as a mystification, because the reason for the existence of our Order is indeed the spreading of mystifications and the causing of disturbances. But I will speak of that later. For the sake of the truth, I should note that I did not travel with such reputable Bicyclists because I was among the chosen, as my vanity flattered me, but because my texts would be used in another time as part of the material for a completely fictional novel. Additionally, if I had set off in the company of less experienced men, I certainly would have gotten lost somewhere in Asia Minor, in the labyrinths whose paths are made of reality, but whose walls are made of dreams.

No doubt, as time passed I became more accomplished under the supervision of the older Bicyclists. I learned the most important thing: be patient, and also – do not believe yourself. The use of that is salutary in two ways. By rejecting faith in yourself, you find faith in God; the one who rejects his own thoughts, wishes, and ideas is headed down the path of Providence; one who follows himself is headed straight for himself, and that is hell. Second to that, patience and insecurity in one's own strength both slow down one's thoughts (which is remarkably important) and so the slowed perception of historical events shows them to be what they are: accelerated to madness, random, chaotic. We are too obsessed with explosions, mass movements and great misfortunes, and in that obsession we overlook the little things, the completely insignificant things that, far out of sight and unobserved, actually cause the cataclysms, like that pebble near the fountain at Beyazit Meydani.

But way back then, I was impatient and full of faith in myself. To some extent it is reasonable that I, as a newfound member of the Order of Evangelical Bicyclists, wanted to find out as much as possible about their internal organization. Already on the first day of the trip, I showered J. K. with questions. He liked to talk, he talked unceasingly, but for my taste at the time he was rude. As if he were in a hostile mood.

### *Discussion about Perspective*

"You've got a lot of preconceptions about our Order," J. K. told me. "You think that we're going to Dharamsala so that we can do something to save the world. That's just nonsense. We're going on an extended picnic. We're supposed to have a good time, starting tonight if possible. We'll party all the time, get drunk, clown around, and we will still save the world. Those grand words I spoke last night, those are just a part of the mystification. You're mature enough to understand that, I'm surprised you fell for it. It was just a ceremony. The masons and the Order of the Rose Cross have similar ones, based on the fiction of Johannes Valentinus Andreae. I'm almost certain that one of the readers of your forthcoming chronicles will actually found *the Little Brothers* of the Evangelical Bicyclists of the Rose Cross. That's good, too.

"However," he added after a pause, "I can't help you get rid of your prejudices because even what I know belongs to the sphere of prejudice. Actually, they are at a higher level, but that doesn't change anything; if you're climbing the stairs leading to eternity, it is absolutely the same if you are at *n + 1* or at *n + 25*. No one knows the real purpose of our Order. No one can tell you whether we are doing good or evil. We're simply doing what we have to. You should know that the Order is more of an interesting hypothesis than an organized institution or a power. That's good, too. That is the power of our community that has been maintained for a thousand years, due to the fact that it has never been constituted and, let's say, it hardly exists at all; it was created to not exist, but not to disappear. A rigid organization only offers the illusion of strength, but it is not strength."

Soon I got the chance to test the accuracy of those paradoxical words. First of all about the rigid organization. But not with the aid of reasoning. To the contrary. I tested it with my body. After some thirty kilometers, I felt extremely exhausted; the tempo was hellish. J. K. was merrily chattering and wildly turning the pedals. At one instant he affronted me, saying that I am structured like the Catholic church; your head, he said, is the holy father the Pope, full of pride and dogma; your heart is like the cardinals who dream of becoming the pope and of killing the father, and your limbs are like the flock, left to themselves and forced to obediently execute the orders that come down from above. I could not understand the parable, so J. K. translated it for me: my brain is full of Euclidean prejudices and I observe the world with the eyes of a geometry teacher, which is wrong, because that is how the illusion of perspective is created, and with it the illusion of distance. If I intend to reach Dharamsala, I should observe the world with the eyes of a Byzantine icon which places the important things in the foreground and above all – *sees things from all sides.*

"You mentioned icons," I said, "but I read in some document that icons are idols."

"Oh, icons, icons," sighed J. K. "Icons are not idols. They are painted with goal of teaching people to look at the world properly; to look at the world from above. Just remember, on the icons, how small the walls of Jerusalem are in relation to the human figures in front of it. Or how the patrons are holding their endowments in their hands. Or, if you like, how some buildings are seen *from all sides*. But people are just people: observing things in a Euclidean, horizontal way, they mistakenly see the icon in the same way they see the subjects represented on them. From the Renaissance forward, things have just gotten worse. In the center of the picture is no longer the human *face* that hovers over and illuminates the world, but the flabby human body crumpled and pressed by buildings, lost in the perspective of the world. That is the human view. Once a certain renowned scientist told me that human thoughts are in the form of a square and box. To us, the world seems to be stable and consistent. However, in God's view the world turns out to be horribly deformed. That is why the Lord turns his face to the Earth ever more rarely.

"But," J. K. said, "don't think about that. You'd better save your strength for the ride, because your muscles don't turn the pedals, your spirit does. And it would be better to see things like this: it is not you that is moving, but the road and the Earth are turning, and you are standing in place and keeping your balance."

## *An Oneiric Orgy in Niš*

In spite of the fact that J. K. brought me out of the clouds and down to earth, I was more than a little surprised when, at the end of the first stage of our trip, we stayed at a house whose red lamps left no doubt about the kind of place it was. The house was run by a certain Madame Greta with whom J. K. was very close, even tender. We had just settled in and caught our breath when the call to dinner came. I would have most readily skipped supper, lay down and slipped into my dreams, every bone in my body hurt, but I could not get out of it. Downstairs, in Madame Greta's salon, a company had already gathered consisting of scantily dressed girls, long-haired pale guys, rather obese gentlemen and a bunch of midgets. In the dimmed light, it all looked spooky; everything looked like it was prepared for some sort of black mass, and not like the welcoming committee for the athletes of a religious organization. But those were my prejudices. A month later, when we were close to Dharamsala, J. K. pointed out to me that I had been conceited; that I had observed all that with the eyes of a Philistine who categorizes everything as *good* or *evil.* And then, ashamed of myself, ashamed before Ernest and J. K., I remembered my childhood and the local prostitute, Amalia, with whom I was mortally in love. Her walk and thick layer of make-up, her happy face – everything about her filled me with excitement and I could not understand the mean thoughts and insults that people poured out on her; especially because those insults came from people that I also loved – my mother, my aunt and my father – and that is just one more proof in favor of the proposition that unsolvable aporias begin already in the unspoiled nature of childhood, when there is no division between good and evil, honest and dishonest, ugly and pretty.

But that night in Niš, after a rather large number of glasses of wine that had the bouquet of resin, the main dish was served, prepared according to the recipe of J. K., "Nightmare Chicken." Before I move on to the events that followed, I will reproduce the recipe for preparing that delicacy, convinced that it will enrich the history of gastronomy.

Wash a young, slaughtered, plucked and prepared chicken, then salt it and marinade it in wine and plenty of pepper for six hours. Remove the chicken, pull the spinal cord out of the spine with a knitting needle, and push two grams of highly sweetened raw opium into the spinal column with that same needle. Meanwhile, prepare the stuffing: fry some finely chopped bacon in onion and carrots, and when it begins to brown sprinkle it with the hashish pollen. Stuff the chicken with this filling, sew up the hole and bake at a low temperature for two to three hours, occasionally basting it with wine. Serve warm and eat immediately.

Already fairly tipsy, I ate that chicken with its pungent but tasty flavor, and a comfortable warmth spread from my stomach through the rest of my body, making it feel lighter. And just when I had relaxed and put my hand under the table onto the knee of the girl next to me, J. K. warned me that it was time for bed. In one room of the attic, three beds were waiting for us and, still in my clothes, I stretched out on one of them, engulfed in fantasies. I do not know when I fell asleep, but as soon as I did, I began to dream. And I dreamt Ernest and J. K. "Where have you been?" asked Ernest. "Do you think we can wait till dawn?" At that moment I began to dream something else: the bank of a river and an unknown woman waiting for me, but J. K. nudged me with his elbow and shouted: "This way!" We found ourselves in a rather large barracks where frost was building up on the walls. Jammed together, the room was filled with wooden bunk-beds. In the pile of bodies, we could make out two men. They were lying next to each other, smoking and talking.

"There's Vartolomeyich," J. K. said to Ernest.

"Yes," said Ernest. "Vartolomeyich is here." Vartolomeyich was blond. In the crowd of weathered and tortured faces, his radiated serenity.

"Who is Var . . ." I wanted to ask, but J. K. hushed me and told me to listen.

"Did you know, Pavel Kuzmich," Vartolomeyich said to his neighbor, "that I got here on a bicycle and that one man prophesied that I would end up behind bars."

Pavel Kuzmich smiled.

"My dear, Joseph Vartolomeyich," he said quietly, "your prophet was actually not very keen."

"By God, he was keen. He gave me that prophecy in 1920. And who would have even imagined that at the time . . . I wouldn't have ever even dreamed it, and to make things even stranger, Pavel Kuzmich, the night after that Kowalsky fellow told me that I would do time, I dreamt these barracks."

"These very barracks?"

"You don't believe me?"

"On the contrary, Joseph Vartolomeyich, on the contrary. You see, I got here thanks to the fact that I was smart enough to believe in such things, and stupid enough to write about them . . ."

Pavel Kuzmich did not finish his sentence, and we found ourselves on an endless plain, surrounded in a grayish light. "Look to the east," J. K. told me. I turned my head and, on the horizon, I saw a shining structure filled with blinding light. "That is the cathedral of the Holy Spirit, the place of worship of the Evangelical Bicycli . . ."

*(Remainder of the manuscript destroyed)*

## AFANASIJ TIMOFEYEVICH DARMOLATOV

# JUBILEE

That morning the mercury in the thermometer dropped below minus twenty, and the inmates were not taken to the building site. Joseph Vartolomeyich Kuznyetsov recognized in this a sarcastic token of attention from destiny or providence; on that day, exactly ten years before, he had been arrested. Now he could, in the relative peace of the barracks, celebrate the senseless jubilee. And he decided to celebrate it, just to spite destiny. He had some loose tobacco and three lumps of brown sugar.

"Pavel Kuzmich!" he called to his neighbor who was lying there staring blankly at the ceiling, "Let's smoke a cigarette and enjoy ourselves. Today I'm celebrating."

"And what, Joseph Vartolomeyich, are you celebrating, if I dare to ask? Your birthday?" asked Pavel Kuzmich Griboyedov, a philosopher, sentenced to five years, plus five more he had earned in the camp.

"No, Pavel Kuzmich. I quit celebrating birthdays. Today is a little jubilee for me. Ten full years since I changed my 'profession.'"*

---

* In the jargon of the camps, the words "charge," "camp," "sentence" were never used. Inmates usually used euphemisms in their communication with one another.

"Joseph Vartolomeyich, you're a real devil," Griboyedov said, rolling a cigarette. "I'm convinced that you will leave here in perfect physical and spiritual health. It is impossible to destroy people like you, unless a direct order is given to do so. You are a real Russian, one of those about whom Kaiser Frederick the Great said: 'You have to kill a Russian twice and then give him a shove.' You are celebrating a jubilee. Oh, how Boris Mihailovich would laugh if he could hear you."

"Hmmph, Pavel Kuzmich," Vartolomeyich sighed, "I'm afraid that I've lived through it all and that your Kaiser just has to give me a shove."

And they both burst out laughing.

"Hey!" frigate captain Zemski cried from the lower bunk. "It seems that the idleness has gone to your heads, boys."

The captain's remark brought them back to reality. They lay in silence, smoking. Josif Vartolomeyich inhaled the sharp hot puffs deep into his lungs and thought about how it would be better if people were made in the form a cloud of smoke, given their senses, feelings and reason, but still ungraspable and diffused; he thought of the accident by which man is, there you see, built like he is, stuffed into a pile of one hundred and fifty pounds, susceptible to imprisonment, capture, feeling cold and pain, and manipulation in general; he remembered, finally, that dusk ten years ago when he was arrested and, even today, it was not clear to him why they had also arrested his bicycle, carefully taking it apart and (while they beat him, by the way, in preparation) cut through the metal frame, shouting, "Where is the message? Where is the message?" Frightened by the beating, confused, Joseph Vartolomeyich could not gather his thoughts and figure out what kind of message should be in the bicycle, or if they were looking for it because it would fit nicely together with some sort of warrant they had for him about which he knew nothing. And by the time he did gather his thoughts, he had already been sentenced to five years, and the two months spent in Lubyanka seemed to be like two nightmarish days to him, nothing more.

Now, lustfully inhaling the last puff as the ember burned his fingers, now he was thinking quite differently. Those two months were not even worth two days, they were worth nothing at all, just as the rest of the nine years and nine months meant nothing. Everything was reduced to zero; time had passed and it was as if it had never even been. Joseph Vartolomeyich wondered: How can the future come out of such a nasty present?

Joseph Vartolomeyich often reflected on time, and he had concluded that time is nothing: all those fifty or sixty years dissipate in the end, and a man, hopefully, goes on – he comforted himself – and that gave him the strength to bear the brutal work and the cold and hunger and humiliation.

"Did you know, Pavel Kuzmich," Vartolomeyich said to his neighbor, "that I got here on a bicycle and that one man prophesied that I would end up behind bars."

Pavel Kuzmich smiled.

"My dear, Joseph Vartolomeyich," he said quietly, "your prophet was actually not very keen."

"By God, he was keen. He gave me that prophecy in 1920. And who would have even imagined that at the time . . . I wouldn't have ever even dreamed it, and to make things even stranger, Pavel Kuzmich, the night after that Kowalsky fellow told me that I would do time, I dreamt these barracks."

"These very barracks?"

"You don't believe me?"

"On the contrary, Joseph Vartolomeyich, on the contrary. You see, I got here thanks to the fact that I was smart enough to believe in such things, and stupid enough to write about them . . ."

"That Kowalsky," Kuznyetsov continued, "who was named Joseph, like me, was half German, half Polish and half devil; I met him in 1920 at a friend's place. Who knows where he ended up. I saw him two or three times. He's probably doing time like us somewhere, or perhaps that Kaiser of yours gave him a push . . ."

Joseph Vartolomeyich and Pavel Kuzmich again burst out laughing.

"Hey, hey," complained Zemski from down below, "you're inviting trouble. If you laugh in the morning, you'll cry in the evening."

"Ugh, Foma Ilyich," cried Griboyedov, "does that mean we should start crying in the morning?"

"Ugh, ugh," sighed Foma Ilyich.

"Ugh, ugh," sighed the blackened beams on the ceiling.

"Ugh, ugh," sighed the wind.

"Ugh, ugh," sighed the taiga.

Pavel Kuzmich Griboyedov was a brilliant student of classical German philosophy, but he did not like the classics – except for Hegel. He had a poetic streak in him and he could not get accustomed to the rigid logic that reminded him of a Prussian military drill. Pavel Kuzmich was a nihilist; partly because it was fashionable, partly because he followed the paths of his heart.

"Hmmm," sighed Pavel Kuzmich at tea parties, "what is history, my brothers? The famous link: cause-effect-cause. So, now, if we replace the series – cause-effect-cause with the series: binga-banga-binga, we end up in the same place. History is commonplace gibberish, nonsense . . ."

That is what Pavel Kuzmich said in order to entertain girls and his friends, but he worked seriously at home. He wrote a voluminous *Treatise about Time* in which he methodically proved – with evidence that ended up lost in the flames of a bonfire, unfortunately – that the present is determined not by the past, as it used to be thought, but by the future. The greatest minds of the time, reading fragments of the treatise, predicted that Pavel Kuzmich had a bright future ahead of him.

Pavel Kuzmich often thought about how those great minds had been wrong, how those great minds are very often wrong, and how those at the bottom – without any kind of future – frequently have a brilliant future, in no way deserved. But that did not vex him because it proved his theory which, after his arrest, he continued to write orally, in his head. "Because," Pavel Kuzmich explained to himself, "seven years ago when I was still at liberty, in the future I was already here and it was impossible to correct the force of that determinism by natural means. Otherwise, I would not be here. Only that which is possible happens; that which is happening right now is not possible but necessary. The possible is only in the future and that proves my theory, although no one wants to listen to the proof."

Pavel Kuzmich was also not vexed because his treatise – complete with footnotes, index and bibliography – stored in his memory, would remain unknown to the public and go with him into his grave where it would be useless because things there are known even to the laymen. No, his theory was complete, perfect and esoteric, and the despised expression *ars gratia artis* had become clear to him. In any case, Pavel Kuzmich considered that theory to be his less and less, and more and more to be a revelation that he had allowed to unveil itself to him, in which case all of his merit was removed. And that was connected to Hegel's thesis that the World Spirit reveals the phenomenal character, revealing itself. And it became ultimately clear to him that Hegel's saying, the conceitedness of which he had reacted strongly to in the past, the saying that was even worse for reality, if it did not fit in with my system, irrefutably correct and he could feel this correctness in his soul – a little piece of reality that, taken as a whole, had gone really bad.

If it will not bring me fame and fortune, Pavel Kuzmich thought, this knowledge will at least prepare me to calmly withstand the blows of earthly destiny. Because, if determinism, as it has been proven, originates in the future and not from the past, then that means that history is thought into being by a reasonable and eternal being and that it is not blind randomness – a registry that carries the corpses of the past through time.

And he no longer regretted that he had published some passages of the *Treatise* in the journal *Voprosy Filosofii*, 1923, where they were found by a dedicated and conscientious philosopher who immediately attacked him in the newspapers as a petit-bourgeois mystic. If he had not done so, he would not have been judged nor would he be in the prison, where – no matter how hard it was – his place was determined by Providence.

Pavel Kuzmich knew that if someone wanted to change the future, following the inexorable and unspeakable secrets of time, they necessarily ended up like the past – *ouk on*.

Joseph Vartolomeyich offered Pavel Kuzmich another cigarette.

"Oh, Pavel Kuzmich," he said, "I have started to long for books. And since we're talking about books, imagine that the two of us become the heroes of somebody's novel. Everything happens to us that happens, but permit me, it would be better. That way we would exist after all, but we wouldn't feel anything because we would be imaginary characters."

"My dear friend," Kuzmich said, "there's not much difference between a novel and life. It's all a story. It is just a matter whether a concrete being, you or I, forced the story to come alive. We can imagine worse, much worse, surroundings than these, but those hellish circumstances have no meaning unless there is a person within them."

"Interesting, interesting," mumbled Joseph Vartolomeyich. "Kowalsky told me similar things as well. He could talk for hours about strange things, and I am sorry that I have forgotten so much of that."

"What did Kowalsky tell you about?"

"Well, for example, once he said that, in the end, the world will turn into an enormous madhouse where the lunatics will not know that they are crazy because everything will be normal."

"What did he mean by 'normal'?" Pavel Kuzmich wondered.

"Well, like this: Let's say that I go crazy and begin imagining that I am the captain of a ship; in that future madhouse they will not cure me, but rather they will give me a ship and entrust command of it to me. If you, forgive the proposition, go crazy and begin to think you are a military leader, the doctors will not try to convince you otherwise, but will give you an army and send you to the battlefield. Well, now, I as the ship's captain can transport materials and equipment for your troops. You see, instead of suppressing the madness, they will make it useful for society. I think that Kowalsky made a report about that to the congress of the Comintern."

"By God, Joseph Vartolomeyich," Griboyedov said, "that boy had a wild imagination."

After lunch, warmed by the thin but warm soup, Joseph Vartolomeyich fell asleep and – who knows for which number of times – dreamt a dream: as if he, Vartolomeyich, is walking through a barren field toward a brilliantly shining building on the horizon. He is alone and feels some sort of anxiety. And at that moment Vartolomeyich (in the dream) remembers that he has dreamt that same dream hundreds of times, always forgetting it after waking up. The shining building, which had been a tiny dot on the horizon many years ago, is now quite close and he can make out its miraculous shape. To the left and right of him, on the periphery of his dream, Vartolomeyich, from the corner of his eye, sees some stooping specters in camouflaged uniforms. "Even here?" Joseph Vartolomeyich wonders, but then notices that those specters are unsuccessfully attempting to push their way into the higher region and that the fact that he noticed them makes their job easier, so he stops paying attention to them. It was becoming clear to him that he was drawing close to a goal that he had unconsciously sought all his life without knowing it. For, if he had known, he thought, he would have messed something up because people always end up in a place opposite to the one they were headed for. "Yes," Kuznyetsov thought further, "everything will become clear when I reach that building and when the circle is completed." And then (in the dream), knowing that it was not a dream, he continued walking toward the building that became larger and larger, ever closer, so close that he recognized the silhouettes of people whose faces were somehow familiar to him.

When he awoke, there was not a trace of the calmness he had attained in his dream. The barracks seemed to be even smaller, dirtier and darker, and the people even more tormented and afraid. Pavel Kuzmich was not in his bunk. Vartolomeyich wanted to tell him about his dream when he returned, but he changed his mind. Not because he was ashamed but because that dream, translated into words, was too pale, too unconvincing. Still, somewhere deep inside him the knowledge ripened that he had not wasted his life, and that the years spent in the prison were the crown of that life. Because, the path followed by those who refuse to destroy ends up in prison, just as it had, in former times, ended up at the stake, and before that in the Colosseum. And Joseph Vartolomeyich knew – more by intuition – that the question of good and evil is a question of the organization of life. And life, that is sleeping, waking, working, eating, sleeping, waking . . . And if you want to sleep comfortably, to do nothing, to eat well, you must turn from the path of good and step onto the path of evil. And the one who organizes the monotony of life according to his whims does not necessarily have to be evil by the standards of the world; he can be generous, honest, and once again end up in nothingness. Here, Joseph Vartolomeyich became dizzy from all the strange revelations, so he shook his head and rolled a cigarette. And when he heard the voice coming from the door: "Kuznyetsov, to the warden's office, immediately!" Joseph Vartolomeyich thought of an autumn day and the wispy birches losing their leaves . . .

Pavel Kuzmich Griboyedov returned from the neighboring barracks where he had played three games of chess with Boris Mihailovich Ivanovich, with figures made from bread dough, losing all three games. He climbed up into his bunk and got the urge to light a cigarette; since the mail would arrive tomorrow, his father would send him some loose tobacco and he would be able to pay Joseph Vartolomeyich back, and also to give him a few extra cigarettes by the way. But Joseph Vartolomeyich was not in his bunk.

"Foma Ilyich," he called to Zemski, "do you know where Joseph Vartolomeyich is?"

Foma Ilyich nodded his head indirectly toward the building whose name the inmates never spoke aloud.

"Well, yeah," grumbled Foma Ilyich, "I told him that it's no good to laugh in the morning. I told him . . ."

"Yes, you told him, you told him," Pavel Kuzmich said quietly.

Then he turned over, sighed and continued to write the second volume of the *Treatise about Time* in his mind, where he shed light on the problem from the subjective point of view: "The fact that man is thrown into time indicates the conclusion to us that time is not in man, that it is not immanent to him . . ." But he simply could not. For a while, Pavel Kuzmich lay there avoiding all thought of

Joseph Vartolomeyich, and then he wanted to go to sleep; he stuck his hand under his pillow (a habit from childhood) and felt a small pouch. Tobacco. Kuznyetsov had left him his tobacco . . .

While he carefully rolled a cigarette in the dark filled with heavy breathing and snoring, two large hot tears rolled down the cheeks of Pavel Kuzmich, for the first time in many years.

The title page of the mystical document
*Purgatorium Sommi*

TECHNOLOGY: (FIRST CONCEPT) IS A LEITMOTIF THAT IS INTERWOVEN IN ALL THE TEXTS AND ALL THE VOLUMES OF THE JOURNAL. IT IS DEFINED AS "THE PRODUCTION OF FORMS" (P. 24). "TECHNOLOGY" IS THE NEW WORLD, AMNESIA (FORGETTING) OF THE OLD, BINARY WORLD, A WORLD OPPOSITE TO THE WORLD."

TECHNOLOGY - SOCIETY

TECHNOLOGY IS NOTHING OTHER THAN A FALSE WORLD, THE WORLD OF DECEPTION, THE WORLD WHICH LIES IN OPPOSITION TO THE REAL WORLD. TECHNOLOGY IS THE ENTIRE WORLD THAT HAS COME ABOUT FROM DESCARTES (FROM THE 17TH CENTURY) FORWARD (P. 8), IT IS THE WORLD OF INSTITUTIONS, SCIENCE, DEMOCRACY, TECHNOLOGIES, HUMANISM, THE WORLD IN WHICH THE FOUNDATIONS ARE SHAPED BY THE SYSTEMS: SOCIETY IN THE SOCIAL SYSTEM, SCIENCE IN THE SCIENTIFIC SYSTEM, PHILOSOPHY IN THE PHILOSOPHICAL SYSTEM. THAT WORLD, THE WORLD OF TECHNOLOGY, IS THE WORLD OF EVIL, OF HATRED, OF MUTILATED AND LIMITED PEOPLE, THE WORLD OF LIES AND DECEPTION, THEREFORE A FALSE WORLD, A WORLD OPPOSITE TO THE REAL WORLD. IT IS RELATED TO THE REAL WORLD LIKE A MIRROR:

MIRROR - SOCIAL-POLITICAL SYSTEM

MIRROR (SECOND KEY CONCEPT). TOWARD REAL LIFE, THE MIRROR ONLY REFLECTS THE TRUTH, THE MIRROR IS AN ILLUSION, A REFLECTION, A SHADOW OF REALITY. THE HISTORICAL EXISTENCE OF TECHNOLOGY IS THE INSTITUTION, "THE TOWER OF BABYLON WHOSE WALLS ARE MADE OF MIRRORS. WITHIN THOSE WALLS, PLEASANTLY DELIMITED AND PROTECTED, THE TECHNOLOGISTS WALK ABOUT" (P. 10). THUS, JUST AS TECHNOLOGY IS A CODEWORD FOR SOCIETY, SO MIRROR IS A CODEWORD FOR INSTITUTIONS, FOR THE SYSTEM, OR FOR ANY OTHER ORGANIZATION . . . WITHIN THE MIRRORS ARE ALL THOSE WHO SERVE THE INSTITUTION OR THE SYSTEM: THE TECHNOLOGISTS.

THE TECHNOLOGISTS ARE HIERARCHICAL MONKEYS"

Facsimile of one page of the "Analysis"

# THE COLLECTED WORKS OF JOSEPH KOWALSKY

# KOWALSKY
# A BIOGRAPHY

## I

Last autumn, the daily papers printed a brief item at the bottom of the cultural column, stating that Joseph Kowalsky, poet, novelist and essayist, had died at the age of sixty-one in Dharamsala, India. Among the educated public, the news passed practically unnoticed. Kowalsky was neither a prolific nor a well-known writer, but his work, scattered about in magazines, was carefully read in certain spiritual circles. It should be noted that among the admirers of his stories and essays were people of such reputation as C. G. Jung, H. G. Gadamer, G. Bataille, and others.

The life of this man is full of unknowns, obscured by the contradictory rumors that Kowalsky made no real attempt to deny. In a letter to a friend in 1937, he wrote:

> *Every biography is a grand mystification and it seems to me that, the greater the rascal was who it is about, the more brilliant and embellished it is. In that vein, I don't do anything to refute the rumors about my past. If I didn't do whatever it is they say, I did many worse things.*

The rumors, which are not always far from the truth, just as many attested "truths" are only rumors, present us a Kowalsky in images that are mutually exclusive: sometimes he is an ascetic, a man submerged in his internal world; sometimes he is a lustful young man and matchless conversationalist; some describe him as gentle, full of sympathy; others as being arrogant, rude and cruel. In any case, the life of that man passed in an unpleasant balance of the uranic and the chthonic, the edified and the trivial, the divine and the satanic. Even though he attained remarkable spiritual heights,* dark and depressive states were not alien to Kowalsky. Only one thing is certain: the real truth about his personality is hidden in silence and mystification.

Kowalsky was born on January 12, 1901 in Tübingen, into the impoverished family of W. Kowalsky, a cobbler who neglected his trade in order to write syrupy lyrical poetry and dubious short stories. W. Kowalsky, purportedly, belonged to the Order of the *Little Brothers* of the Evangelical Bicyclists of the Rose Cross (which has not been reliably confirmed), to which J. Kowalsky later also belonged (which has been confirmed). He was left without a mother at an early age. In spite of that, he was a brilliant student. He excelled at Latin and Greek. That inclination probably encouraged him to enroll at the Seminary in Tübingen, the same one attended by Hegel and Schelling. At the Seminary he excelled through hard study and exemplary behavior. He was respected as an expert on the Bible, St. Augustine and St. Thomas Aquinas. And then came the turnabout, the first in the series that filled his life. It will never be known what caused him, on October 14, 1919, quite calmly as the eye-witnesses would have it, to stand up in the middle of a lecture,

* On his numerous journeys, Kowalsky stayed in Tibet several times and sojourned twice on Mt. Athos. In 1938, he spent two months in the Sinai desert with the monks, feeding on roots and insects. Kowalsky destroyed his notes from those journeys, and his diary as well.

approach the professor, jerk the professor's watch from its chain and crush it under his heel, saying, "Well, now I've had enough," and to walk out of the classroom forever. A girl named Grete is often mentioned, with whom Kowalsky was in love. There is no doubt that she occupied a certain place in his life (one of Kowalsky's first poems, "Fellow Traveler," is dedicated to her), but it is hard to believe that she could have been the only or even the main reason he quit his studies. We are more inclined to the thesis that, reaching the age when young men critically observe the world around them, inspired by fuzzy ideals, Joseph became aware of the hypocrisy and impoverishment of the society in which he lived.

> *"They say there are two types of people, the honest and the corrupt," Kowalsky wrote in those years, "but I say that there are just the corrupt and actors; ghosts who are outwardly loyal, kind and honest, while they are thieves and tyrants in secret. I do not want to say that I am better than they are; on the contrary – I am worse, but I do not pretend to be loyal, kind and honest. I was pretending for too long. Moreover, those Philistines, when one thinks about it more carefully, are not corrupt. They are something even worse: they are cowards who gather in their sad lodges and guilds in order to, counting on the slogan 'there's strength in numbers,' establish some kind of credibility and defend themselves from nothingness."*

In the light of such thinking, Kowalsky's actions become clearer. His beloved, Greta, was a prostitute. That obviously did not bother Kowalsky. For him, prostitutes were just ladies from the upper classes of society, heavily made-up geese who spend their days gossiping and feigning enjoyment of art – a skill that Kowalsky despised his whole life, even though he himself was a pet of the muse. In those years he joined the anarchists, and then – disappointed by their endless theorizing – the much more aggressive Communist Party of Germany. He was constantly on the move. Driven by a powerful desire to change the world, to crush poverty and to put an end to humiliation, he visited the poor and the laborers' settlements, he gathered financial aid for the most impoverished and spread propaganda.

## II

In 1920, Joseph Kowalsky went to the Congress of the Comintern as a delegate. A photograph from that period exists: in a large hall, obviously in a former palace, Jules Humbert-Droz, Bombacsy, and Lepety are sitting at a table and looking at a document that Humbert-Droz is holding. Lucien Laurat, leaning on his elbow, ruminating, is staring out the window. Not far from him is Henri Lefebvre; marked (in the photograph) with an X, in the right corner, is Joseph Kowalsky. He seems to be sleeping. In a letter to a friend, Kowalsky offers some of his impressions from the Congress:

> *We met in Moscow, in the throne room of the Kremlin. The throne was hidden behind a curtain. The rooms around the throne room served as the residence of the imperial family during their stays in Moscow. Those private rooms were rearranged for the congress into a reading room, a smoking room, a snack bar, and a relaxation room for the delegates. There was a large bed in the last room. Many delegates would take a nap there or spend just few minutes for the satisfaction of stretching out on a bed that was once the bed of emperors.*
>
> *I must say straightaway that I didn't like that in the least, that self-satisfying lolling about on graves, that bourgeois lying about in the imperial sheets. Boundaries should be set: the emperor is the emperor as long as he is alive; when he dies, he is just a corpse. Like everyone else.*

*We resided at the "Lux Hotel," which was in no way a luxury: it is full of bedbugs. We had breakfast and lunch together, in the dining hall, and for supper we got a "payok," a daily portion: heavy black bread, butter so rancid it makes you nauseous, a hard-boiled egg, but half-empty and of a nasty taste, like the moldy straw in which they are kept.*

J. Ковальский

D. H. Grainger, who refers to this letter in one of his texts, casts doubt on its authenticity and claims: either the letter is falsified, or Kowalsky copied it from Jules Humbert-Droz. However, Grainger, whose specialization is esotericism, and not at all the history of the workers' movement, has forgotten the unity of opinions that reigned in the Comintern at that time. People who think alike write identical letters. Either way, it is known that Kowalsky did not have a high opinion of Jules Humbert-Droz and that he thought of him as a "Platonic" revolutionary.* On the other hand, it is not to be excluded that Kowalsky, in order to mystify everything possible, wrote the letter at a later date.

Kowalsky remained in Russia for three months. Whether the scenes of poverty, so common at that time in the streets of Moscow, in sharp contrast to the bounty that already reigned in the circle of the developing bureaucracy and artistic elite, caused young Joseph to become disappointed in the idea of the revolution, or perhaps some sort of internal turnabout was in question – this can only be guessed at. Upon his return to Germany, Kowalsky decisively broke

* Lenin himself had a bad, practically degrading, opinion of the personality of J. Humbert-Droz. In his Letter to Inessa Armand, (editor's note) Lenin calls him "Tolstoy's philistine."

all connections with his recent comrades, calling them "a gang of demagogues and scoundrels." With the financial aid of his father, he opened a bicycle repair shop and established his own racing team with whom he won several important trophies in races all over Europe. At the same time, Kowalsky was writing; in 1925, his first (and only) collection of poems came out, *A Description of Nothing*. When the Nazis took power, they burned all the available copies of the book, so that today it is a rarity among book collectors. The collection *A Description of Nothing* was printed in a run totaling 300 copies.

Already the next year, 1926, Kowalsky headed to India, doubtless under the influence of Schopenhauer's philosophy, which he was studying intensively. From the extant documents (letters, journals, notes), we can reliably claim that he was actively practicing meditation. In a letter to his father, dated November 8, 1926, Kowalsky wrote:

> *Dear Witold,*
>
> *I am in Dharamsala. This is a city of some 40,000-50,000 inhabitants who do nothing other than sit all day in the shade of the mango groves, repeating the holy mantra* "Om mani padme hum" *till they are exhausted. Of the other points of interest, I should mention the herds of holy cows that are different from regular cows in one single detail: they have haloes. All in all, there is nothing of the atmosphere of spirituality and loathing toward the treasures of this world that I so longed for. But I cannot blame anyone; this world is still this world, therefore the world of fallen beings – hell. Only complete idiots would make the attempt to make heaven out of it. The wish in itself is good; oh, good indeed, no objection can be raised against it, but wishes in themselves – I learned that here – are not good, they are the foundation of evil.*

*The second thing I've learned was from a kind Tibetan, Lama Kazi Swami Dhondup, and is related to wisdom: in order to attain wisdom, the Lama thinks, one does not have to philosophize, but to reduce the amount of food one takes in. And I took his advice. I can't say that fasting brought any kind of enlightenment, but I did "learn" some things after all, about which I had not even dreamed.*

*That's how things get turned backwards. Among our people, eating a lot is considered to be a condition for good health. Drivel. It is much more edifying to drink a lot. Watch out for people who don't drink. I'm warning you, but I know that you watch out for them already. To poison yourself, that is not in the character of trivial souls. There's plenty of nihilism in that. Some people burn out slower, some faster, it's like with wood and coal bricks – a matter of personality – but those who never taste a drop because it is not, supposedly, healthy, those people are the dullest and most naïve. Ingesting only healthy things, that means to fatten your own corpse. And that is dangerous. "Healthy mind in a healthy body" – that's lie. I read in a certain mystic's writings that the soul cannot get away from a well-fed body, so it gets buried with it, experiences the process of rotting and undergoes terrible suffering.*

According to some of the assertions of D. H. Grainger, it was actually in Dharamsala that Kowalsky first made contact with the Order of the *Little Brothers* of the Evangelical Bicyclists of the Rose Cross.* In the poet's legacy, a photograph was found of a group of Evangelical Bicyclists and their friends. There is also Witold Kowalsky, who joined his son at the beginning of 1927. However, it is strange to note the presence of English philosopher Bertrand

* Evangelical Bicyclists: an athletic-esoteric association of refined and idle intellectuals, one of many that sprang up like mushrooms between the two World Wars. Some people are of the opinion that the legend of the bicyclists is just the advertising gimmick of one of the bicycle factories. (editor's note)

Russell and two ladies whose identity has not been confirmed.

As early as the middle of that year, Kowalsky departed for Tibet where he remained for several months. He returned visibly changed, both physically and spiritually. He was no longer that impulsive, happy young man. "He looked like Lazarus when he rose from the grave," D. H. Grainger describes, "like a man who has learned a horrible secret, seen the otherworld and then returned to this world." What he learned and what happened on the Tibetan plateau, we will never know. Kowalsky burned all his notes and journals, and he never bothered to write about daily events again. But this phase did not last long. That same autumn, we find him in the company of two ladies (perhaps the same two in the photograph), at a reception at the English Consulate. At the end of the year, he returned to Europe and began writing again. He worked in parallel on the novel *A Cross above Baghdad* (the manuscript of which has been lost) and on the project of a modern bicycle with several speeds. The novel never saw the light of day, but the bicycle did. It was patented and still makes significant income for the constructor.

Joseph Kowalsky celebrated New Year, 1928, in Moscow in the company of Joseph Vissarionovich. Hold up in Stalin's dacha in Podmoskovie, drinking enormous quantities of vodka, they spent five days in conversation, the content of which is unknown. D. H. Grainger is of the opinion that Kowalsky sojourned in Moscow as an emissary of the Evangelical Bicyclists of the Rose Cross, and that he delivered to Stalin a list of people who needed to be liquidated in order to prevent the establishment of the "thousand year empire." This thesis obviously belongs to the domain of fantasy. To be fair, Kowalsky did publish an essay, "On the Edge," dedicated to Joseph Vissarionovich, in the Leipzig almanac *Vom jüngsten Tag*, but that should be taken as irony. His encounter with Freud is much more significant, as is his correspondence with the father of psychoanalysis. In the beginning, Kowalsky was enthralled with psychoanalysis; he intended to invest the money he made from his bicycle to start a journal and library specialized in publishing works from that field. Then a total turnabout came: Kowalsky cut all ties with the psychoanalysts. "They are the sons of Satan," he confided in a friend. "It's no wonder that all psychoanalysts are Jewish; constantly driven by Christ's death, tormented by inexplicable guilt which they do not admit to, they search for the causes of their suffering in harmless myths. Yes, they want to live well and comfortably in this world. But the day is coming when they will be sorry. And everyone else with them."

We cannot confirm with certainty that Kowalsky knew the future of Europe (according to the opinion of some researchers, he was taught by the Tibetan lamas), but it is certain that he foresaw Hitler's rise to power. This is confirmed by reliable documents that can be trusted. In the first place are his letters in which he warned his Jewish friends to leave Germany before it was too late, and then there is his text *On the Discontinuity of History*, that he wrote in co-authorship with Ernest Miller. All copies of the print run of 300 shared the same destiny as the collection *A Description of Nothing*: they ended up on a bonfire; but several draft copies have been preserved from which it is possible to reconstruct the original text. That obscure, esoteric material quite often descends into the sphere of pure fantasy, the certain charm of which cannot be denied. If the abovementioned pamphlet is to be believed, Hitler's rise to power was no special secret to Kowalsky since, as a member of the mysterious Committee for the Liquidation of Franz Ferdinand, he actively worked on that. The fact that the Committee planned the assassination of Franz Ferdinand a full fourteen years after it was carried out, so in 1928, could only confuse those who are not versed in the esoteric teachings of the Bicyclists of the Rose Cross. That sect believes that the future determines the past; there is a legend that members of the *Little Brothers* influence the events of this world in the following way: the dead bicyclists from the otherworld, where space-time categories are unlimited, learn about a given period (according to Grainger, one hundred years) integrally, thus as the unity of all that happened, that is happening and that will happen; they foresee the intentions of the historical subjects and, comparing them with the aims of Providence, communicate, to the currently living brothers, the responsibility of planning what will happen in the past. That is possible, Kowalsky and Miller explain, because – as a result of human impatience and blindness – history has been accelerated (according to the calculations of that time) by twenty-four years, seven months and twenty days. Therefore, we are not contemporaries of the events we are participating in; according to the natural flow of things, they should be just about to happen, and the temporal discontinuity that arises from that is experienced as a feeling of emptiness, lethargy and apathy; "we wonder about swampy fogs with our arms outstretched, like sleepwalkers, never guessing that the sun has already risen," Kowalsky and Miller wrote. That is why the Bicyclists of the Rose Cross consider a man to be fulfilled and awakened if he "existed simultaneously with himself."

We can choose to disagree with such speculations, contradictory to even the most dialectical mind, but we cannot deny that, in the pamphlet *On the Discontinuity of History*, the date is predicted of the fall of the Third Reich, a trivial forty-eight hours different than the date of the actual fall. According to the abovementioned pamphlet, the Third Reich was inevitable so that a greater evil could be stopped; Franz Ferdinand, who was supposed to inherit the Austro-Hungarian throne, was also supposed to develop into a brilliant ruler who would expand the borders of the Western Roman Empire as far as Central Asia. That is why he had to die from the gunshots of the conspirators, planned fourteen years later so that the secret police would not uncover the conspiracy. Because, the expansion of the Western Empire would also spread rationality, and with rationality would come the lack of feeling and the apathy that accompany it. The assassination also meant the end of the Western Roman Empire; after 1918, the West will be cut into ever smaller pieces until it finally disappears in that atomization. And then, the Eastern Roman Empire (latently present the whole time) will be resurrected – Byzantium, which is the ultimate this-worldly goal of the Evangelical Bicyclists of the Rose Cross.

Hitler, who was superstitious, believed the pamphlet *On the Discontinuity of History* to be the work of Zionist Wise Men, one of the secret weapons of the Jewish conspiracy. The practically symbolic number of copies does not indicate that the pamphlet was thought to be a significant work of propaganda, regardless of the forbidding style and contents. In spite of that, the Fuhrer's aids for occult sciences monitored the work of the Bicyclists of the Rose Cross most seriously, building up a voluminous dossier that was incinerated during one of the last bombings of Berlin. Upon his rise to power, Hitler ordered, as a special branch of the SS, the formation of the *Traumeinsatz*, a unit of commandos for activities in the world of dreams.* Their task was to infiltrate and stop the actions of the Bicyclists of the Rose Cross whose activities took place in the deep conspiracy of dreams. After intense training, which included the synchronization of dreams, movement along the azimuth in dreams and camouflage, the members of the *Traumeinsatz* prepared several attacks, attempting to infiltrate the ranks of the Bicyclists, but

* There are some indications that, in the 1930s, the KGB formed a brigade for action in the dream-world, but that J. V. Stalin did away with it because it was unscientific.

without significant success. Their greatest "victory" was the desecration of the astral Cathedral of the Holy Spirit. One early dawn, while the bicyclists were slowly waking, a unit of commandos snuck up to the cathedral and, with the aid of pagan spells, broke down the eastern wall. SS Commander Meindorf was awarded the Iron Cross, and the unit was praised. For the next twenty-four years, the Cathedral remained damaged, because time goes by in dreams without acceleration.

Such a development of events did not excite either Kowalsky or the rest of the members of the Evangelical Bicyclists. They knew that the architect, who would not only renovate the Cathedral but actually make it incomparably brighter, had already been born and they just needed to wait a certain number of years. In addition, somehow also to that time belongs the death of Witold Kowalsky which was to send his son, Joseph, on the road again, this time to Ulaan Bator, to Mongolia. Kowalsky was not upset by this death; death never upsets the members of the Evangelical Bicyclists and they consider it to be a promotion, an introduction into the higher spheres of the Order. Anyway, Witold Kowalsky knew the date of his death (and the place) and he informed his son fifteen days ahead of time so that he could come and bury him in an upright position, that is, in a vertical grave, as is the burial custom of the Bicyclists.

But let us return to linear chronology. In the autumn of 1930, Joseph Kowalsky organized the Great Bicycle Marathon Belgrade-Dharamsala. Belgrade was set as the marathon's starting point because of its geographical position; built on a crest above the confluence of the Sava and Danube, it is the most distant settlement of Byzantium, the boundary between East and West. Arriving in the Yugoslav capital two weeks before the start of the marathon to do some organizational preparations, Kowalsky searched the ruins of an inn in Dorćol where Nicholas of Cusa, inspired by the Holy Spirit in a moment of enlightenment, formulated his theory, *Coincidentia oppositorum*, famous far and wide. In his free time, Kowalsky met with eminent Serbian intellectuals and authors, including, among others, Rastko Petrović, Miloš Crnjanski, Dragiša Vasić, and Slobodan Jovanović. It is believed that Rastko Petrović took part in the marathon for a while and that, because of his duties, as he returned from Constantinople to Belgrade, he visited the monasteries, the endowments of the Serbian rulers. Here, in Belgrade, "above which every evening, the east and west winds do battle while the red sun sinks into the Panonnian mud," in a room of the "Moscow Hotel," Kowalsky wrote the story "A Grave in Ulaan Bator." That story is the artistic vision of his trip to Ulaan Bator. The first version of this story was published in *Ideje*, a journal run and edited by Miloš Crnjanski; a second version was published in the journal *Hiperion* (1932, 1-2), and a third (under a different pen-name and insignificantly changed) on the twenty year anniversary of his death, in Belgrade's *Politika* on January 19, 1986. The publication of the final version was certainly the act of one of the members of the brotherhood and is a subtle memorial of the anniversary of his death, probably with a deeper hidden meaning because, as the Bicyclists say, the most unnoticed events have the greatest influence.

## III

The relatively small number of his works is in disproportion with Kowalsky's almost supernatural energy. However, the explanation for that is not hard to find; it is known that he thought that poems and stories were not written once for all time, but that they change like everything else in history, and that is why we have some thirty or more versions of some of his poems and stories; there is a prototype, a version each for winter, spring, summer and autumn; a version for the upcoming year with the accompanying variations, etc. Thus, his collected works take up eight entire volumes, and it is said that "Edition Minuit" is preparing a critical edition of the poems, stories, essays and copies of the journals of Joseph Kowalsky.

Just as he allowed time to affect his writings, he was also indifferent toward changes that time did to him. Comparing the signatures of Kowalsky from season to season, from year to year, we can see how his handwriting followed the internal changes in him. It might be interesting to hear the opinion of a graphologist on that subject:

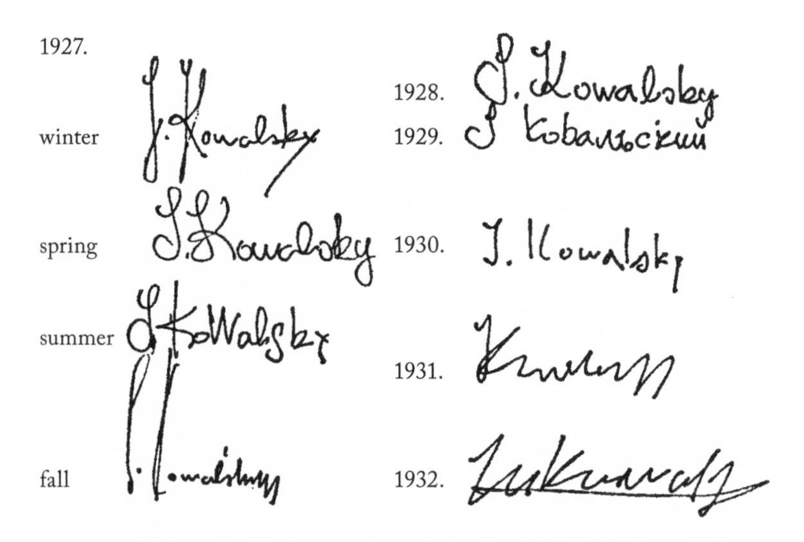


Similar to his handwriting, Kowalsky also changed his appearance. Although everyone who knew him agrees about one thing, that he was tall and thin, the other descriptions are sometimes diametrical opposites. Some describe him as bloated, wrinkled, with a bad complexion; others as spiritual and good-looking; some as a striking example of manhood; others as being homely, even ugly. They do not even agree about the color of his hair. Kowalsky himself used to say, "You can take on any appearance you like, because anyway a man's appearance is irrelevant. The main thing is to remain indifferent to it."

The Bicycle Marathon Belgrade-Dharamsala began at midnight on September 21, 1930. Officially a sporting event, the marathon had quite different goals by all accounts. The route Belgrade-Ras-Thessalonica-Mt. Athos-Sardis-Jerusalem-Babylon (which was taken by the first group of marathoners) indicates that Kowalsky had other goals in mind as well. Sava Djakonov, one of the participants in the marathon, in the partially preserved pamphlet *Pilgrimage to Dharamsala*, describes the events of the journey in a notably poetic way, although the criticism that he allows in too much fantasy are not without foundation. D. H. Grainger finds profound symbolism in the date of the start of the marathon, in the starting point and in the route. Reducing the year of departure to units, he first gets the number thirteen (1 + 9 + 3 + 0 = 13), and then 4 (1 + 3 = 4), which is written in Hebrew as ד (daleth), and is pronounced as "D," like Dharamsala. However, daleth is also the archetype of material existence in the tradition of the Caballah. According to Grainger, departing from Belgrade on a date that is the product of two holy numbers (3 x 7 = 21), in a year under the sign of daleth, the bicyclists were symbolically leaving the West, history and the obsession with material things, returning (via Babylon where history began) to the irrational, which is symbolized by the East.

Though they left in a group, the marathoners returned individually, and some never returned at all. Followed by quite a lot of publicity at the beginning, the marathon was soon pushed into the background by the events of the day, which eventually obscured it completely.

Kowalsky did not return from Dharamsala before 1936. Those six years of his life are veiled in complete darkness. In the above-mentioned pamphlet, Sava Djakonov claims that Kowalsky was working on versions of his poems, and that he spent the last two years with ascetics in a cave, which sounds likely; that, and this is not very likely, he occasionally had himself covered with dirt in a grave where he would spend some time, twenty-four hours at the beginning of his training, up to twenty days near the end. The hagiographic style and tone of Sava Djakonov's writings are doubtless the consequence of the time he spent in India, with an affinity for fantasy and exaggeration, in addition to his powerful feelings of loyalty toward Kowalsky.

Returning from the East, Kowalsky settled in Belgrade and that was, till the end of his life, the farthest west he ever went. By then, the commandos of the *Traumeinsatz* had begun their relentless search for him, but he hid in the dreams of the ascetics of Dharamsala, into which the members of the *Traumeinsatz*, primitive and aggressive dreamers, did not have access. In terms of his literary work, Kowalsky put out his novella *Bicyclism and the Theology of Witold Kowalsky* with the Belgrade bookstore and publisher G. Kon; in it he discretely explained some of the theses of the secret document of the Evangelical Bicyclists, *Theology and Bicyclism.* Somehow at that time came another in the series of turnabouts in Kowalsky's convictions. Formerly a revolutionary, a participant at the Second Congress of the Comintern, he now became an ardent royalist and thereby attracted the resentment of the intellectual leftists.

However, the real scandal was yet to come. Kowalsky pronounced himself to be a viscount. He published a proclamation in which he explicated the reasons for his act, and caused a flood of the most contradictory possible reactions. At one extreme were those who thought him a fool, on the other those who were enthralled with him, and in between were the moderate (who considered Kowalsky's self-proclamation as a viscount to be an act of artistic exaltation), and the embittered leftists with their accusations that Kowalsky's act was the very peak of bourgeois decadence.

During that time, Kowalsky held receptions in his luxuriously furnished apartment which often ended up as orgies, and that can be connected to the fact that our hero claimed that the Marquis de Sade was one of his spiritual forbears. With the reservation, according to the testimony of S. Djakonov, that the orgiastic destruction was not intended for others, but for himself. Semi-fantastic descriptions follow of such situations in which the viscount washes the feet of prostitutes, spends hours with his friends wearing hair-shirts, their bodies wrapped in barbed-wire. And indeed, in one place, Kowalsky himself writes: "There are two paths: to destroy others, or to destroy yourself, but the organization of the world is such that whoever does not want to destroy others gets destroyed, unless he is courageous enough to destroy himself."

In those years of general drunkenness and dissipation (which foretell the upcoming war), the coach of the "viscount" Kowalsky seemed grotesque in the streets of Belgrade, among the Balkan hovels, and that impression was magnified by the liveried coachman and pages.

## IV

On the life-line of Joseph Kowalsky, it is said, there was a small line that was, in collusion with the stars – after his brilliant successes – supposed to send him off into a concentration camp, and then into death. He was notified of this, by the mediation of an emissary in his sleep, and Kowalsky underwent an operation that very autumn. A certain Dr. Daud Çulabi arrived in Belgrade and performed plastic surgery on the life-line in a private clinic – an insignificant and harmless procedure which still took several hours because he had to find the most suitable position for the changed line in relation to the future position of the stars. In spite of all the effort of Dr. Çulabi, the only possible outcome for Kowalsky's fate was for him to become a railroad worker. And that is what happened. Kowalsky spent the next year and the war years as the station head in Stalać. In that foggy little town on three rivers (the West Morava and South Morava join into the Great Morava there), Kowalsky wrote what is certainly his most significant and farseeing work – the *Dictionary of Technology*. Based on the claim that language has fossilized and become a means of deceit, not of mutual understanding, Kowalsky attempted to study some of the key words of western civilization, to return meaning to those which have lost their value and to put in their rightful place those that have taken on undeserved importance.

"We pronounce our sentences like a whore makes love," Kowalsky writes in the preface. "Our conversations are not conversations but promiscuity." However, the importance of that project is not the project itself, although it is undeniable, as much as the fact that it was the forerunner of an even better *Dictionary of Technology* which will appear forty long years later. Kowalsky's *Dictionary* was to be just the seed from which a powerful tree would sprout. And indeed, in 1981, a new *Dictionary of Technology* would appear in an edition of *Vidici* which would arouse considerable excitement. The disconcerted commentators of the daily papers interpreted the *Dictionary* as "an open invitation to destroy the social system," although such invitations cannot be found on the pages of the *Dictionaries*. Soon thereafter, the secretive *Analysis* began to circulate in Belgrade, an unsigned text (probably from Masonic circles) in which a confused and malicious interpretation is given to the positions of the anonymous compilers of the *Dictionary*.

In 1943, the commandos of the *Traumeinsatz* picked up Kowalsky's trail. Sensing the danger, Kowalsky disappeared from Stalać only an hour or two before the Gestapo knocked on the door of his room. On that foggy night, all trace is lost of him, though the rumors continued to spread. According to some, he showed up in Tibet where he dedicated himself to the study of the *Book of the Dead*; according to others, Kowalsky became a monk at the Hilandar monastery, taking on the name of Callistus; according to a third group, he was killed trying to escape. A witness, whom we cannot believe entirely, claimed that Joseph Kowalsky left in the middle of his watch, climbing onto a bicycle, he quickly disappeared into a cloud that enveloped him. Whatever happened, before us is a selection from the work of an interesting person, a selection that, let there be no doubt, should be given our full attention.

S. B.
Belgrade, 1983

# POEMS

# FELLOW TRAVELER
## FOR GRETE

Fellow traveler
Pretend no innocence on this train, for
Thousands of years of my travels, no lady has there been.
They cheated you. Fancy fans and dances ride in first
class. Still it is wonderful to die between Budapest and
Stalać on 860 wheels between the beams of light
And the imposing bottom of some gentlewoman who soon
Gets off rhythm at a station with an unclear name and slips
Into the ear of the dispatcher.

Perchance I will love you for fifty, perchance even all one hundred miles
Indescribably heading east together with a gentleman
Who, there you see, brought his daughter along for a vacation
Into death. Fellow traveler, pretend no innocence.
Who knows if we shall reach the coast.
The sea is as large as the sadness in your eyes
And deep within me. The sun will rise between your thighs
For a change while we travel at once in all eleven
directions of the world. Love affairs are unreasonably brief
In the twinkle of an eye – there's the station where you get off.

Tell him
That I won't come

*(1919)*

# YOU DIDN'T COME

I think you didn't come.
You wanted to because it was Sunday.
You put on your skin, pulled on your hands, put on your feet and
Went down the stairs but the Amebas had moved the streets
Crisscrossed them, changed their names, hidden the things
that could have served as azimuths.

You wandered about with a smile on which
the zipper broke

Night had long since fallen and you no longer knew where you were.
You even forgot where you had actually been going and me and the only thing
you wanted was to arrive somewhere from
the omnipresent nowhere.
Around midnight the Amebas grew tired of their game and they once again
put the streets back where they belonged and so you once again found
the entrance to your flat – exhausted and aged . . .
You lay in bed crying
And just before dawn
Became an Ameba yourself.

*(1919)*

▪ ▪ ▪

I haven't slept all night long. I don't know if she
slept a hundred meters further down in a room from which
the veinal blood of the lampshade ran onto the sidewalk.

To comfort myself, I dreamt that I was dead. And then,
before daybreak, a vague foreboding shook me from my sleep.

It was hard, lonely, like a sweaty stoker
shoveling coal into the furnace of a locomotive from which
the dispatchers turn their gaze, pretending to rub the eye
of the lamp of the rail-switch and pretending that they
saw nothing

*(1919)*

*(Spring version of the poem* You Didn't Come*)*

## SCANDAL

Two eyelids swollen from insomnia.
Tears drop into the fine yellow dust, at first
One by one and then in crystal streams
That write hieroglyphs on the ground.
Suddenly, the city begins to fall
On the hunching shoulders and filthy children try
With fistfuls of mud to plug those treacherous
Those scandalous eyes.

The tears want out into the street.
But the other way round: the streets, following the tracks of the tears,
Gently crawl into the tear ducts. Beside the city and here now
The street and the evening plunge down upon the shoulders. Not likely
That they will hold up much longer, but they hold.
Came into being long before this city
These streets
Before themselves.

Only then does it vanish. Becoming smaller and smaller. It disappears,
Leaking through the cellar bars and remaining
Just two eyelids swollen from insomnia . . .

And then, before dawn, comes an enormous horse.

*(1919)*

## PARTING OF WAYS ON THE STEPPE

Tonight my soul is a steppe and on it drunken Cossacks ride at a gallop
Mikhail Sholokhov, this Don is not quiet like you described
Movements from which the sole has been torn and every prefabricated
  verse
Eyes brimming with dead-end alleys with muddy streets
From which a surgical procedure has
Removed every stride
This deep blue Don that carries me randomly in its inside
Pocket and occasionally takes me out into the light of mud to see what
time, day, month, year it is
This barbaric ice-blue Don
Tonight my soul
Stuck in an elevator between the cold
And the second floor where at the desk
Small like a man, it writes out on signatures of brain matter
With its sharply imagined pain
Mathematical operations of delirium and intricate equations of loneliness

Just so the night doesn't grow fat or go mad
Mikhail Sholokhov, until they fire a burst of breath into the mouth
Of an Anyusha or a Tanya
Until this Don takes me
To the bottom of the ocean . . .

*(1920)*

# A DESCRIPTION OF NOTHING

On a line stretched across the yard
Women hang out
The washed brains

A dead bird without ID
Falls into the wrinkled streets
And everyone wonders
what its name is

The mouths of the dead speak not

On rows of death notices
Your name printed
And year of birth

On my left lung
Likewise your name printed
And year of death

Is that the real reason why
Gutenberg
Invented the technology of printing

After that I go home
Resolute
To read nothing at all

Sunday
Holy Sunday
Fat roasted turkeys
Fly over the streets

Greasy Sunday lunches
Swollen greasy stuffed cabbage leaves
Lazily napping
On the dead backs
Of solemn tables set for guests

In Sunday guest rooms
Fathers counsel children

I'm waiting for you in front of the butcher shop
In solemn Sunday
First person singular

And so wonderfully
I do not exist

You don't have to come
Anyway you don't exist

I don't have to wait
Anyway you won't come

Let the Earth turn aimlessly
Around its sun

I am empty
Like the universe

This Sunday afternoon is
Longer than the smooth meridian
That severs me lengthwise

Thus there exists
An eastern and western
Joseph Kowalsky

An east and west heart
An east and west hand
An east and west waiting

And all of it divided
By a thin lengthwise line
Into an eastern NOTHING
And a western NOTHING

And in the middle
Holding my breath
I wait for you frantically

*(1923)*

## AMEBAS
### (1957)

At night, as soon as I fake going to sleep so
I could rest from pretending to be awake, my red boots
would set out. They would check to see if my eyes
were closed, and if my breathing was rhythmical and then
they would go out into the street.

I would follow them barefoot and bareheaded in my nightshirt. Without success. A few streets over they would lose me and there was always a cop there who was bored and liked to ask a lot of questions.

Who knows with whose feet they went, where they went, what they
did I never managed to find out where
they go
those boots of mine.
And still, I forgave their unfaithfulness, took them to the cobbler,
shined them with whale oil until they finally fell apart.

▪ ▪ ▪

It is impossible to simultaneously feel and not feel them
How uninvited they find refuge in the shallow seas of marrow
And blood
Named after kinds of ravings
Bloated shapeless Amebas

Look . . . two baby Cancer amebas
In your tear duct they are weeping
Jangle the rattles of your bones
Go on let them play
Let their soft mouths chew on you
Bring them mother's milk

Bring them yourself
In the right pocket of Cancer

■ ■ ■

In the left pocket is a trite emptiness
Dedicated to the waters; below the sun shatters into
Tiny boulders
Below is their home and ours
A large village of silence

And we shall
Return Cancer
The one and only Cancer

Look, two baby amebas on the corner sobbing

Break off the hands
Break off the head
Feed the insatiable hunger
Feed the amebas
Of Cancer

■ ■ ■

If they gently enter the whites of the eye and become cataracts
What word should you softly say so they don't become enraged
And deform even these pitiful contours
And these pilfered shapes
And these airy constants
How do you tell them to come to their senses when they do not even
Have themselves and when they don't know
In which direction and how far they spread
Into which of the unstable senses
Into which of the floppy ears

. . .

Watch out Cancer
One of them slipped unnoticed into your ear
Across your hand

Maybe it will tell you a lie
Maybe it will pierce your eardrum

Fly away, fly

▪ ▪ ▪

They are at times in my outstretched palms
and again at midnight they stick to the blind window panes
all by the way from childhood to this telephone booth
in the hospital wing of the madhouse

They call on the telephone: let us into your eyes
let us into your lungs
let us into your veins
let us into your glands
let us into you

Static in the lines

They naturally are not anything but they are also not stars
they twinkle though they barely exist usually around
zero-zero
(when the senses change shifts)
They flicker on the restless boundary between
semi-darkness and . . .

Static in the lines

# PROSE

# BICYCLISM AND THE THEOLOGY OF WITOLD KOWALSKY

1.

I will speak about my father Witold Kowalsky. About his conversion from being an atheist into a true mystic and Cabbalist. He is in the adjoining room. His cheeks are flushed. He is drinking vodka and writing the treatise *Theology and Bicyclism* dedicated to His Holiness the Patriarch of the Georgian Orthodox Church. Until a few years ago, my father never drank. Then he suddenly grew ill and fell into his deathbed. The doctors gave him two weeks at best to live. After four weeks, my father had not died, and the director of internal medicine, Dr. Wagner, lost patience with him and threw him out of the hospital for being undisciplined, and so that he would not occupy the place of someone who had more respect for medical science, someone ready to die by the determined deadline.

2.

In his *Confessions*, my father commented on that episode in the following way:

"It is a lie that they threw me out because I didn't want to die even though, according to all the findings, I was practically dead. They ousted me because, while I was sick, in a coma, I repented and returned to the saving grace of Christianity. It was not the doctors' fault. They did so unaware. The world order is such that Christians are persecuted and they are persecuted no matter how often the official policies, history and so on, claim that the persecutions of Christians are a thing of the distant past."

3.

Upon his discharge from the hospital, my father bought an icon of Jesus Christ and a used velocipede. He took down the picture of the Kaiser and hung the icon above the desk that he never ever worked at; at that time, he still had not started corresponding with His Holiness the Patriarch of the Georgian Orthodox Church. But, a mistake slipped by him: while making the frame, the glass-cutter put the picture-hook to the side of the symmetrical axis and therefore Jesus hung crooked, as opposed to the Kaiser who had hung perfectly, his stance at ease. My father tried, using cobbler's paste (exceptionally hard) to bring the icon into balance. In vain. The icon hung crooked as if it wanted to let him know that it was supposed to be crooked. One day, my father burst into my room and shouted, "*Felix error!* I realized what the icon wanted to tell me: Jesus is not hanging crooked, the rest of the world is; the world stands off the vertical axis of the Logos by 13°, no less . . ."

4.

From that day forward, my father began to be enthralled by mistakes. He said that mistakes are the steps to perfection. I did not understand him; at the time, I was not a mystic, I was a communist.

"Take the train schedule as an example," he explained to me, "the train schedule is the thing that introduces disorder. Trains always arrive on time, whenever they can and when that meets the goals of Providence. The whim of a transportation engineer, that train number 170 must be every day at 14:03 at a certain station, makes us get an illusion of disorder if the train is late. Yes, that's the way it is: in countries where the trains arrive exactly according to the schedule, lawlessness is greatest. In a similar, mystical way, to the way the schedule creates lateness, so does the law create crime. Listen, if you have ears . . ."

## 5.

"Thanks to the carelessness of a glasscutter," my father wrote in the *Confessions*, "I understood the mystery of the Original Sin. We are guilty even when we do nothing, we are also guilty as babies precisely because we are tiny parts of a world that has lost its balance, a world that is crooked and is rushing toward destruction. Therefore, everyone who adapts himself to the rules of this world is breaking God's laws, taking the guilt on himself, choosing it by his own free will and therefore distancing himself from God. But since God is everywhere, it is impossible to distance oneself completely from him. Origen is right. In the end, we shall all be saved. All will be one in the one."

## 6.

At that time, I met the future love of my life, Ana F. It happened in a dream. I was standing with my friends on the corner where we met every evening, at that time only in our dreams, because in reality some of us were already dead, others were thousands of miles away in Canada and America where they were making dollars in the cruel world of capitalism and slowly forgetting one another. Because of that, the atmosphere on the corner was unpleasant, the conversations forced. That night, in the middle of an argument about a football match, Ernest pointed at a girl coming down the street and said, "That's Ana."

7.

My father had a coat of arms made according to his sketch: an old-fashioned velocipede with a rose cross rising from the handle-bar stem:

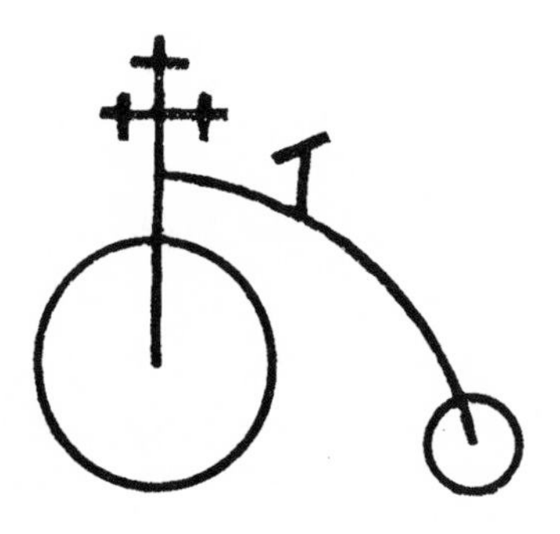

8.

*(a passage from a letter of my father, Witold Kowalsky)*

"Joseph, Joseph, when you were born I was beyond myself with happiness. I immediately departed for London. I checked in at a rather ordinary hotel and the next day I bought a bicycle. That evening I went riding through the streets. I rode like a madman and occasionally shot my pistol at the windows of watchmakers' shops. You're wondering why I went all the way to London. You yourself know that the English are cold-blooded. All of that shooting would never have been allowed in Tübingen. Even so, even there in London my celebration was met with quite a lot of publicity. As far as I could tell from the newspaper, none other than the great Sherlock Holmes was interested in my case . . ."

## 9.

*(part of the record of the investigation against my father)*

INTERROGATOR: This coat of arms, this stylized velocipede with a rose cross rising above the handle-bar stem, what kind of organization does it represent?

WK: That is the coat of arms of the Evangelical Bicyclists of the Rose Cross.

INTERROGATOR: What are the goals of this organization?

WK: The goals of the organization are summarized in its name. So, spreading the Evangelical truth, missionary work. We are supposed to travel around on bicycles and preach repentance and the imminent destruction of the world.

INTERROGATOR: Did members of the organization participate in any way in the conspiracy against and assassination of Archduke Franz Ferdinand?

WK: To my knowledge – no. I repeat, the goals of our organization are spiritual.

INTERROGATOR: Who are the members of your organization?

WK: To that question, I cannot give an answer.

## 10.

The next Easter, my father caused his first metaphysical scandal. Right before the eyes of some amazed people, he suddenly became invisible, and then reappeared in another place. Then he showed up in several places simultaneously; he started talking with his acquaintances, laughing and pointing his finger at his doubles, "Look, Helmut," he said, "there's another Witold, another one of me."

## 11.

"Father, how did you do that? How is that possible?" I insisted that he tell me the secret.

"Simple," my father said, "it's Tibetan wisdom. 'If you want to be invisible,' says Lama Lobsang Rampa, 'you must become perfectly still and stop all your brainwaves.' So, there, I sat perfectly still and stopped all my brainwaves."

## 12.

Several months later, my father caused another metaphysical scandal. Using the Cabbalah, he created a Golem, taught him the cobbler's craft, and the Golem worked night and day instead of my father. My father dedicated himself entirely to drinking, poetry and mysticism. Who knows how it would have all ended – perhaps in delirium, perhaps in a brilliant collection of poems – if the Labor Union had not found out about it. One day, representatives of the Syndicate visited my father and accused him of hiring an unregistered worker. My father grew angry and shouted "METH!" and the Golem dissipated into a pile of dust. At the very same moment, all the shoes that the Golem had made over the preceding two years also dissipated into dust and the gentlefolk in the streets stared dully at their bare feet, not realizing that a miracle had happened.

**13.**

One night in a dream, I remembered that, for a long time, Ana F. had not passed by the corner where my friends gathered. "That girl," I asked Ernest, "who you pointed out to me once. What happened to her? Why doesn't she show up any more?"

**14.**

"I don't remember pointing a girl out to you," said Ernest.

**15.**

One day, my father got a letter from His Holiness the Patriarch of the Georgian Orthodox Church. His Holiness had written:

> *Dear Mr. Kowalsky,*
>
> *The shoes that I ordered from your reputable shop suddenly fell apart before my eyes, and it became clear to me that the work of the devil is involved.*
>
> *Please do not take this as a complaint; we as Christians are not interested in the treasures of this world. It is my duty as archpriest, though of a different confession, to turn your attention to the harmfulness of such activities for the Christian soul.*
>
> *In the hope that you will turn to the true faith, the Patriarch of the Georgian Orthodox Church.*

## 16.

Having read the letter, my father secluded himself in his office, carefully staring at his bicycle. The next day, he wrote a response:

*Your Holiness,*

*I cannot express my regret because of the unpleasantness you were exposed to resulting from the situation with the shoes, but I would like to inform you of the fact that I did not make the footwear in collusion with the Devil. The truth is as follows: a Golem made those shoes. Because of circumstance, I was forced to destroy him, and thus everything the creature ever made was also destroyed. You certainly do not know that: Whatever God makes is indestructible and eternal; whatever a man makes lasts for a while; whatever a Golem makes lasts only as long as he does.*

*I made the Golem, this I confess, out of laziness. That is a sin. He worked instead of me. But I did not use that laziness for nothing. I used the time to construct shoes for walking on the water. You understand just how important for Christianity those shoes could be. In this time – when God does not appear and when the world is consciously distancing itself from the already faraway Lord – such shoes would be a real benefit to an archpriest. Because God will no longer appear until Judgment Day. I am sure of it. But, at the same time, I understand him completely. What should he do in this world? Even I, full of all sorts of horrible sins, can hardly stand its grayness and evil.*

*It is completely correct that I am sinful and that I am susceptible to all vices. However, I do not admit that I have distanced myself from the true faith. It is not possible to distance oneself from faith.*

*If a man completely rises above his sin and renounces it, then God, who is true to his promise, will act as if the sinner never sinned. He won't allow him to suffer for a moment because of his sin. If he committed his sin even as much as all people sinned all together, God will not force him to atone for them. In doing so, God established a closeness to man that he created with no other being. If he is convinced that the man is truly ready, he will not look at what the man was before. God is the God of the present. He accepts you and takes you in just as you are, and not how you were. God joyfully suffers and has suffered for years because of the evil and iniquity that arose because of all the sins done in the world, so that man would attain full cognition of God's love and so that that love and gratitude would be as great as possible, the world stronger, which often happens after sin.*

*Those are my thoughts and I await the day when God will expunge all sins.*

*With respect,*
*W. K.*

**17.**

The fate of that letter by my father was strange. The Patriarch of the Georgian Orthodox Church was enthralled by my father's interpretation of God's forgiveness. He even introduced it officially into the teachings of the Georgian church. Witold was quite proud of himself. He showed the Patriarch's letter to his friends and his reputation grew, even among the intelligentsia. However, many years later, as I was reading the works of Meister Eckhart, I found a passage of my father's letter, the very one on forgiveness, copied word for word. I was almost disappointed in Meister Eckhart, and then I realized: My father was the one who plagiarized! By then, Witold was already dead. I laughed. Writing against sin, he committed the sin of vanity, attributing someone else's words to himself. But perhaps that was also part of his plan to sink to the very bottom of lawlessness, in order to rise above all of that in one moment and then draw quite close to God.

## 18.

But the heretical teachings of Meister Eckhart remained a part of the tradition of the Georgian Orthodox Church as one more proof that the ways of the Lord are mysterious.

## 19.

*(part of the record of the investigation against my father)*

INTERROGATOR: In May, 1913, you set off on your velocipede on a trip around the country. On that occasion, you caused confusion and disturbances through your actions in public places. Who stands behind your actions? I repeat! Who gave you the orders to act?

WK: The Holy Ghost stands behind my actions. A few months before that, when I received the commandment from the Spirit to preach the imminent end of the world, I knew that I was bound to fail, but I got on my velocipede and set off on the road. Because, I hope you know that, it is impossible to oppose God. The prophet Jonah tried that in his day, and we all know what happened to him. I do not know why I was the one chosen. But the ways of God are mysterious. Maybe that is the reason.

INTERROGATOR: To whom did you preach your first sermon?

WK: I gave my first sermon to a group of young men and women on some sort of excursion. I was passing by a field on my bicycle, I saw them and thought: Young people will believe me before the old will, and so I stopped. From my backpack, I took the banner: W. Kowalsky, PROPHET OF THE LIVING GOD and hung it on the steering column of the bike. The young men and women gathered around me immediately. The sight of a fifty-year-old in a dusty track suit necessarily attracts attention. Perhaps it was my good looks that were decisive in me being chosen as a prophet: I did attract a lot of attention. Prophets have to prophesy, and the people must persecute the prophets. That is the way the world order works.

INTERROGATOR: What did you say and how did those present react to your words?

WK: I cleared my throat and started off fairly tactlessly. But there are no tactics in prophesying. "There is," I shouted, "life eternal and mortal!"

INTERROGATOR: What kind of reaction did your words bring out?

WK: At first – none at all. Nobody said anything. The girls elbowed the boys, they giggled, but all in all they didn't cross the boundaries of decency. On one hand, this made me happy: it is nice to see such well-behaved young people; but on the other hand, it made me sad: in order to reach the Kingdom of God, all boundaries have to be crossed, even the boundaries of decency. In the old times they didn't hesitate to cast stones. But just doing that, they didn't cross the boundaries of indecency, which comes down to the same. When I thought about it, deep in my soul I felt a certain emotion, dull though it may have been, no matter what a wreck of a prophet I was.

INTERROGATOR: Did you say anything else?

WK: Yes, I cried that life eternal is not impossible, but the one we have is. I referred to Plato, Plotinus, Scotus, Erigena, and Thomas à Kempis. I offered statistical proof, too. The average life-span is sixty years, a century-span is one hundred. Some live a span of eighty, and some a span of one hundred years, the span is not constant. It says nothing. It only proves that this-worldly life is impossible, and that the length of that impossibility varies from case to case.

INTERROGATOR: Were there any comments?

WK: No. In fact, yes. One young man asked me if I believe in eternal life?

INTERROGATOR: And what was your answer?

WK: That I do. With that, I spoke a ninety percent lie. Truth be told, I myself hardly believe in the ten percent possibility of resurrection. That's because, like you, I am seventy-five percent nothing, with a tendency to become one hundred percent nothing. Augustine wrote that God created two kinds of beings: one close to himself, the other kind close to nothingness. We, people, are among those third-rate creatures. The seventy-five percent of nothingness that we so carefully conceal, that is what ruins our calculations. Because of it, all human projects, no matter how well planned, show an inexplicable tendency to return into nothingness. I knew that my project would end up there as well.

INTERROGATOR (to his assistant): Have this Augustine character checked into.

INTERROGATOR (to my father): And then?

WK: Then, some sort of teacher showed up, a professor or whatnot, and he cried, "Hey, he's blaspheming against God! Grab him!"

INTERROGATOR: How did you react?

WK: Seeing that the crowd was rushing toward me, I jumped on my bicycle and tried to escape while stones were flying around me, thrown without precision, luckily. I'm not a bad cyclist, but the young men were running really fast. At one instant, I saw some sort of village church; the Sunday service had just begun, so I headed there and rode my velocipede into God's house, hoping for sanctuary.

INTERROGATOR: How did the congregation react?

WK: They knocked me off the velocipede and started beating me for blasphemy. The pastor was among the most enthusiastic. In the meantime, my pursuers also arrived. Who knows what would have happened to me, but some of the people cried, "Let him go, can't you see he's crazy?" Then they stopped beating me and led me out of the church. They even gave me a ham sandwich.

## 20.

One night in my dreams, I was awaited on the corner by a man wearing a long leather overcoat. I stiffened at the thought that the agents of the secret police had discovered our meeting place, that they had dreamt it and come to arrest us. But the man smiled the way a person smiles when they want to show that they are not agents of the secret police and he asked, "Are you waiting for Ana F.?" "Yes," I said. "You see," said he, "that's why they sent me."

I didn't dare to ask him who had sent him.

We sat on the stoop of my father's cobbler shop.

"It's a complicated story," the man said. "You have to listen to me carefully; even then, no matter how carefully you listen, you will forget everything when you wake up. I have already been in your dreams and talked to you, and you have forgotten. The point is this:

in times past to which no one's memory reaches, human beings were whole. Then, for reasons that would not be clear to you, they were separated, divided into two sexes, male and female. Perhaps you can guess: two corresponding halves are supposed to find each other so that they can stop wandering about between reality and dreams. But the matter is made more difficult by the fact that the two halves are not born synchronously, I mean – in the same periods. To cut things short: Ana F. has still not been born, and you have already gotten quite mature. In the future in your dreams you must open your eyes wide, because you can only meet there, because dreams stand outside of time, as you know. And above all, above all you must learn to think slowly . . ."

## 21.

"Son," my father said one morning, "you have to be paranoid not to be paranoid. In this world, everyone persecutes everyone, and everyone together persecutes prophets. However, at one moment you have to stop the paranoia: at the moment when you realize that you, though being persecuted, don't even exist."

"At that moment you are saved!"

## 22.

*(passages of my father's letters to people in public life, found in his legacy)*

From a letter to the Pope

*Holy Father,*

*I am convinced that, without fail, you must travel by bicycle on your trips. It is indecent for a person of your reputation to ride in armored automobiles, Satanic machines, because the very name automobile contains the principle of self-movement, self-sufficiency, which is Satan's ideal . . .*

*I also propose that you relinquish your Swiss Guard. Christians do not dare to be protected from the evil of this world; follow the example of His Holiness the Patriarch of the Georgian Orthodox Church . . .*

*You must actually seek feverishly for the cross on which you will be crucified. If no one wants to crucify you in Europe or in America – go to Patagonia, go to Africa, desecrate some native taboos, find a way to become a martyr . . .*

*. . . The donkey is the paradigm of the bicycle, and it is known that the Savior rode a donkey into Jerusalem . . .*

*(1920)*
*W. K.*

From a letter to M. Lowry

*Dear Mr. Lowry,*

*Finally a proper book on alcoholism. Congratulations.*

*. . . It's worthwhile to mention the secret of turning wine into Christ's blood. I am completely convinced of its certainty. Not because I have studied the secret, but because through crazed drunkenness I have recognized my own stupidity . . .*

*. . . I think that they will all be resurrected: all those comic strip heroes, all the Mickey Mouses, Mandrakes, Kirbys . . .*

*. . . In any case, alcohol brought me to faith in God. Tearing me further and further down, humiliating me, it cleared a place for me in the Lord's Kingdom . . .*

*. . . The doors to that Kingdom are exceptionally low. A man must humble himself, he must lower his head if he intends to enter.*

## 23.

My father wrote another letter to the Pope:

*Holy Father,*

*I understand that you did not accept my humble suggestion about the automobile. You continue to drive about in that contraption; you show off like some sort of bon vivant, a seducer, losing your reputation in the eyes of honest Catholics, forgetting that automobilism is the mortal sin of our time, while bicyclism, after love, is its greatest virtue.*

*But, what can be done, we are all sinners. This time I would like to recommend an exceptional product of my company W. Kowalsky & Co. – religious shoes. I dare to ask that you publish an encyclical recommending these shoes to the widest range of believers.*

*This is what makes them exceptional:*

*They are no different in shape from the normal shoe, which is important because of humility. However, the insides of those shoes are filled with a large number of sharpened tacks. Whoever wears such shoes will most certainly never be able to think of sin and pleasure; all of his thoughts will necessarily be directed to heaven. In addition, excursions into the streets will be reduced to only the most necessary and thus the chaos will be notably reduced.*

*I believe that you share my opinion that comfort acts detrimentally on our souls.*

*With respect,*
*W. K.*

## 24.

The Pope complained to the Cardinals that a certain W. Kowalsky kept bothering him with letters full of blasphemy. Cardinal Panini, the head of the congregation for questions of faith, reported the unfortunate incidents to the papal nuncio in Tübingen. The papal nuncio complained to the chief of police, the chief of police invited my father in for a conversation . . .

## 25.

My father never wrote the Pope again.

## 26.

With my friend, Von Lukitsch, I began breaking clocks. First of all, we ritually smashed our own timepieces. Later, we did what we could. We did not buy watches so that we could break them – that is senseless – while a clock is in the display case it is harmless. We carefully waited (thinking quite slowly) for situations in which a clock simply offered to be broken.

Such situations are not rare. There is always a broken clock somewhere; you can always find someone who is dissatisfied because his watch is fast or slow. It is not difficult to find a clock to smash.

In four years, we smashed 4,268 timepieces of various sorts.

Why were we doing this?

To stop time? No, we were not that stupid. We wanted to prove that a logical system can be built into any sort of nonsense, that all nonsense takes on an enormous burden of karma that ultimately results in liberation.

## 27.

Von Lukitsch continued to smash clocks, but I went down another path. With his persistence in smashing those bothersome and fatal devices, through the refined art of the disintegration of mechanisms,

Von Lukitsch became famous all over Europe. After several years, it became quite chic to send your watch to Von Lukitsch for him to smash it, and the cream of Europe competed to see who would send him the most expensive and beautiful timepiece.

Recently, I read the following news in the paper:

"In the Meinhof Palace near Glassbaden, in the presence of reputable guests and representatives of the press, Mr. Von Lukitsch broke a 'Schaffhausen' watch, the property of the Prince of Monaco."

## 28.

"The bicycle is a vertical vehicle," my father wrote in the preface to his treatise *Theology and Bicyclism*. "If we look at a simplified graphic representation of the bicycle,

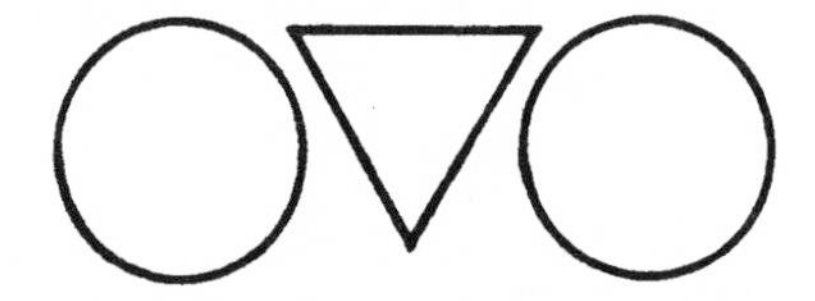

we can see that the device has an abundance of religious symbols; two wheels, two circles, symbolizing the two faulty infinities (time and space) connected by the true eternity of the Trinity, represented by the triangle of the frame. At the same time, when represented like this, the bicycle has the shape of metaphysical glasses with which it is possible to correct spiritual myopia. But that is not all. If we take a birds-eye perspective (which is the viewpoint of the Holy Ghost), the bicycle has the shape of a cross:

where the handlebars are the crossbeam of the cross. A man who rides a bicycle, in fact, is crucifying himself. To the Holy Ghost who observes from above, it is clear that this man is gaining speed to fly into him (into the Holy Ghost), to fools who observe him horizontally, he is nothing more than a poor guy who does not have the money to buy an automobile; a fool who drives himself by the sweat of his own brow.

## 29.

My father bragged that he had solved one of the old scholastic problems: *Habet mulier animam.*

"The woman also has a soul," he writes in his *Confessions*, "but her soul is different in several ways from the soul of a man, which can clearly be seen in the construction of the men's and women's bicycles:

MALE SOUL

FEMALE SOUL

The women's bicycle, namely, has no crossbar. That insufficiency in the metaphysical construction of the soul is caused by the fact that woman was made from Adam's rib: while they were one, that construction was stable and looked like this:

However, after the fall, souls became weaker, especially women's.

"*Ergo*, today it is good to set off on the road to salvation by bicycle. However, a problem appears here. Because of the specificity of the construction of the female body and the shape of the bicycle seat, riding a velocipede can bring persons of the female gender into a state of autoerotism, and that is incongruous with mysticism.

"That is why women should head down that path with their husband or fiancée in order to fulfill the Evangelical teaching: the two shall be as one."

**30.**

***(part of the record of the investigation against my father)***

INTERROGATOR: "Oh, Kowalsky, Kowalsky, books have muddled your reason. There is no exit from this world. There is no other world."

**31.**

"That's what the interrogator said," my father wrote in his memoirs, "but I was laughing on the inside, I laughed out loud and nothing was clear to him. I knew that I would be leaving his office in a few minutes, and then I remembered a Jewish story; a description of the death of a righteous man. When Rabbi Meier died, said one Jew, it seemed like he went from one room to another. No, said the other, it seemed like he went from one corner of the room to another."

# PROCLAMATIONS

Anno Domini 1937, I proclaimed myself to be a count. During one single night (in which the decision was made), I designed a coat of arms, composed the genealogical tree of my spiritual ancestors and a short proclamation with which I informed *urbi et orbi* that I was joining the noble class. In order to prevent rumors, here I will present in depth my motives for scorning the *vulgus*. First and most important – because I am a supporter of legitimacy – it is not illegal; the constitution allows for the possibility that someone feels aristocratic. Reason two: it is absurd; to be a count in a democratic country means to be in a subordinate position. But I like the absurd. The third reason is of a literary-philosophical nature. In a moment of inspiration, I realized that as a count I will be able to expose a lot more filth than I could as a plebeian. The aristocracy and filth go hand in hand; later, I will explain why. The best example for that is one of my spiritual forbears – perhaps not the most noble, but certainly the most famous – the Marquis de Sade. Would some derelict, who is in despair because his roof is leaking, be able to write *The 120 Days of Sodom*? Would someone like Lenin ever author *Philosophy in the Bedroom*? But those are the most honest places in world literature; the most serious studies of the filth in the human soul. That is not depravity, that is brilliant scholarship. Angels told me that one night during a pleasant chat, in my dreams of course, because of the rationalists. You see, they told me, de Sade admitted everything, he exposed all his lewdness to the light of day, he purified himself and now he is at ease; meanwhile, respectable writers will have to pay the price for all the volumes of their lies. Herr Doctor Freud, with whom I corresponded till recently, for example. He feels an enormous need to do the same thing as de Sade, but since he is mediocre, he does not have the daring, and so he places his repulsive stuff in the mouths of his supposed patients, which is doubly useful: he gets the money that his patients pay him for his work, and then he gets his title, fame and reputation besides. So, now, for his title, money, fame and reputation to have value, in his works Dr. Freud must edify this world as the only, the real and the best world; certain contractual clauses require him to. This can be justified by the freedom of opinion or one of the other democratic prevarications, but in more scrupulous times it was called by its real name: a contract with the Devil.

### *About contracts with the Devil*

Those contracts, as the angels told me, take on a wide variety of forms. The stipulations can seem innocent; most often they have to do with buying and selling. Your assent and signature is important; the content is later edited in the administrative offices of hell. Truth be told, the Devil is usually honest in carrying out his obligations: within the allotted time he heaps money, fame, beautiful women, and luxurious villas on the other party, but the annexes to those contracts, delayed for some future time, contain very unpleasant duties. I would not like to say anything more about that. But one other advantage of the aristocracy is concealed here. None of them ever sign anything. Aristocrats are taken at their word.

## *About one of the chambers of hell*

It would be a good idea to describe, in human language, the part of hell intended for Fadeyev. Fadeyev, the angels say, after death will reside at an enormous and magnificent construction site, equated with a literary character from his novels, some sort of engineer, the site manager for the construction of the Insane Asylum for 20,000,000 patients. At the moment when he appears in hell, construction will be near the halfway point; the gigantic construction will block out the horizon and, full of enthusiasm, he will get down to the task of finishing the construction. And that is where the hellish torment begins: the workers are obedient and hard-working (they are those whose goal had been to build a house!); everything is going according to plan, but suddenly there is no more cement and everything stops. The second day, right after the cement comes and they make up for lost time, part of the structure inexplicably sinks into the ground. The day after, a river floods and causes enormous damage. Meanwhile, the telephone rings . . . Stalin's icy voice asks how far the job has come and is suspicious of sabotage . . . And so on into eternity.

## *The justification of hell*

The few devotees of my rather small and insignificant literary works will certainly notice that I am coming into conflict with my earlier claims that there is no hell and that everyone will be saved. However, earlier I was a plebe, the son of a cobbler with an affinity for alcohol, the Caballah and poetry, but now I am the Count de Kowalsky and that gives me the right to be contradictory more than ever. Only when a man becomes a noble does he realize the extent to which hell is a necessary and useful institution. Hell puts things where they belong. The mediocre who choose this-worldly heaven and happiness should not complain: this-worldly heaven is hell in Heaven, this will be proven when everything becomes heaven. Nothing changes here in the slightest. On the contrary, everything is perfected and gains completeness. The only thing that becomes clear to everybody is that they all made the wrong choice. That will be the time for wailing and the gnashing of teeth, but the Devil shows up and shows the contract, black on white, with a signature.

### *On demonstrations*

One of the things that drives me to withdraw ever deeper into solitude, one of the things that will destroy democracy, is indeed the phenomena of demonstrations. I am slightly afraid of those threatening, crowding bodies, those hands holding up banners full of words like "DOWN," "WE WANT," "WE," "MORE," "BETTER," etc. There you go, just now as I am writing these lines, there is a group of young men and women under my windows, riled up by the *Council of Great Lovers, Time, Space and Heaven*, and they are shouting: "Down with Kowalsky! Down with the renegade of the working class, servant of counts and kings!" Pure envy. I, too, used to be one of them, and now they are rebelling because I am a count, because I will not die, because I do not desecrate the sacred things of tradition and religion; because I am decadent and disgusting. Cross my heart, I was always decadent; progress does not bring anything good. Indeed, now without prejudice, why would the word "progress," which implies movement ahead but not the quality of what is ahead, why should such a word be so deserving of the respect it is given? When I think about it more clearly, as early as seventeen years ago, at that congress in Moscow, when I saw all those scoundrels lying about in the imperial bed, it became clear to me that a new society was not their goal; that all they really wanted was to take the palaces for themselves.

### *About the gift of a fountain pen*

Recently, in order to be as decadent as possible, I began writing with a quill and ink. I gave my fountain pen to the building superintendent, who was unusually happy, thinking about how he would sign my death sentence with that same pen. He did not guess how close he was to the truth. The angels showed me this in a dream. Not even a full ten years later, my former fountain pen, in the right hand of my former superintendent, would sign a multitude of death sentences, but I will, thank God, get away and instead of me another gentleman will go to the gallows, even though he never gave anyone a fountain pen. That is why you should be selfless, that is why the Gospels advise us: if you have two coats, give one to your neighbor.* As far as the pen goes, I intended to begin writing with an even more decadent device – a goose quill – but there are no geese in this damned town and it will not, like Rome, be saved when the hordes reach the tile walls of the city. And it shouldn't be. A city that doesn't have goose quills doesn't deserve to walk the face of this earth.

### *Alchemia microcosmica*

I realized not long ago that I am a fecal type. In no way a philanthropist, a bicyclist, or a mystic, as some of the hacks have suggested.

* If I had not given the superintendent the pen, that gentleman would have given him one, and I would have ended up on the gallows. That's how things are connected.

There are no generals, clerks, presidents – those are people-symbols of the Worldly Kingdom and they are only symbolic people – there are only oral, anal, phallic, visual and tactile types. First I will speak of the fecal type, which I am myself, and then I will describe the others. Friedrick the Great, Socrates, Spinoza, Paracelsus, and many others belonged to the fecal type. Their basic characteristic is that they immediately eject everything from themselves. In the physical realm, this is manifested in their fast metabolism. To force everything out, to superficially digest, to free yourself of poisons – that is, briefly, the bodily manifesto of fecal types. They are not to be credited with this personally, it is an inborn alchemical feature. In it, ascetics go the farthest, those who give up food altogether. That is why they smell like suckling babes in the end.

Napoleon is a typical example of the phallic type, which also includes Hitler, Stalin and Mussolini. The characteristic of this type is that they begin from zero and penetrate to the very top. Once they finally take their place, they begin to take on the symbolic appearance of an erect phallus, which can be confirmed by a quick look at the photographs of the abovementioned statesmen. While they maintain their erect appearance, such types have enormous power, but once they go flaccid – they end up in tortuous circumstances. The saying is no accident: *Omne animal triste post coitem*. As far as I have been able to interpret it, the matter lies in the control of tension and their rule that seems like wild, extended coitus. History will show that Mussolini – who is somehow too highly *erectus* – will disappear first from the historical stage; he will be followed by Hitler, and in terms of Stalin, who rules with the eastern art of delayed ejaculation, the end of his rule cannot be determined with certainty, but it is clear that it will be long and fertile; I want to say that it will result in the birth of numerous hydrocephalic descendants.

No matter what we think about the individual personalities of this or that phallic type, it is certain that they are the driving forces of history. The relationships in the macrocosm are the same as those in the microcosm. In order for something new to be born, coitus is necessary; the internal mass must be exposed to sadistic intercourse in order to get pregnant. Here we come to the role of the other two types – anal and oral. They act together. The anal type sees the world and all phenomena in it as an inextricable web of attractive anuses; and now, in order to free themselves of the nauseating feeling that they are the world's manure, as quickly as possible they attempt – using all possible anuses – through the digestive tract, to return to the mouth, to the light. On their journey, they clear the way for the oral types who follow them like pilot-fish follow sharks. Oral types feel the irresistible need to logically portray that miserable odyssey through the gastrointestinal tract of history. The remaining two types – visual and tactile – do not deserve further attention. They are here so that all of that is visible and tangible.

### *On the cult of personality*

I have to admit that the personality cult attracts me profoundly with its mysticism. When I think better, the personality cult is the only authentic mysticism. Everything else is plagiarism. The troubles come about in the choice of the personality. One of the most widespread prejudices of today is the belief that every person is a personality. That is pure nonsense. A personality is an extremely rare phenomenon. To follow a true personality cult means to turn into Christ and be crucified under the worst possible circumstances. To the masses, and by God to most of the "educated," this idea is most highly insane. To withstand pain and endure shame, those are the two most edifying things. The trouble comes about because completely unimportant things – food, housing, comfort – are things of exceptional importance to limited souls. Those things perhaps are indeed necessary, but they are completely insignificant.

### *On Marxism and poetry*

In my early youth, I was a Marxist. To this very day, I think that Marxism is an irreproachable doctrine. If I had to return to the doctrinal level, I would be a Marxist again. Things really should stand the way that Marxism proposes, but things fortunately or unfortunately (depending on your point of view) never stand the way doctrines propose, but exactly opposite to them. That is my Law on the Entropy of Doctrines, just as stupid as every other law, like every other law it is full of holes; there is always some doctrine around that evades it, thanks to the unceasing efforts of the phallic types. Still, I never was an extrovert Marxist, it was more like a Platonic attraction, because every vision of heaven is necessarily welcome to a soul surrounded by hell. Later I became a poet. In addition to all the other filth, I was also a poet. That means that I was treacherous, full of nothingness, fantasies and deceit while at the same time I wrote compositions in which I clandestinely attempted to claim that I was something different. What does it mean to be sensitive? Everything living is sensitive. If you touch a worm with the burning end of a cigarette, it quickly reacts and with its fast movements it contributes to the poetic treasury of *Weltschmerz*. Now, aside from Doctor Freud, who is occupying an ever higher place on the ranking list of my hatred, I despise most poets as incurable hypocrites – as bloated monsters who protest against and pass judgment on the things they do themselves.

There, that proves that I am still a poet in my soul and also an ever greater admirer of Doctor Freud, because then you hate only whatever is in you, projected on others, naturally, for the sake of personal security. Perhaps I exaggerated a bit with my judgment of poets. Why would poets be bigger scoundrels than everyone else? However, that cannot be said about Nietzsche. I hated Nietzsche all at once, at first sight. That arrogant linguist filled me with horrible anger from the first reading to the last, the Superman! How contemptible! What ontological nonsense! A man cannot be a man; a man cannot, if we want to tell the truth, be anything, and Nietzsche would like to be a Superman. That seemed to me to be an indescribable blasphemy of God, in whom I did not believe at the time, by the way. I have met a multitude of guys who were indoctrinated by Nietzsche. And yet, Nietzsche was loved by the Nazis, who are faggots, and faggots love syrupy and bombastic rhetoric. In any case, take note: with his physiognomy, especially with the style of his moustache, Nietzsche looks undeniably like Stalin, though actually like a kitsch copy; Stalin was incomparably more handsome. Not to mention the difference in types: Stalin was a phallic type, Nietzsche an oral type. In any case, he is slowly being forgotten because the world is gaining ever greater insight into its nothingness, and his meanderings are becoming ridiculous.

### *The irrational explanation of the secret*

I do not understand how someone can refuse to believe that the Savior turned water into wine. Today, there is widespread disbelief that water was turned into the finest wine at the wedding in Canaan, unfortunately even among alcoholics, which is pitiful because even we have the ability to transform things, into something worse, of course, because we are depraved. We turn wine, alchemically, into a fluid that is improper to mention in this text.

### *On the afterlife*

Not believing in the afterlife is absurd. It is impossible that one can be further beyond the grave than in this life. I was told that by a ghost with whom, in decadent style, I recently established contact. The supposition that they over there are absolutely dead, arises from the dangerous supposition that we here are absolutely alive.

### *On egalitarian doctrines*

It is interesting that the greatest number of supporters are attracted by the most unreasonable doctrines of the phallic types: fascism and communism. It would be worthwhile to think that through more seriously. One thing is quite unclear to me – the disgust of the humanistic intelligentsia at the rigged trials that are now being held in Moscow and Berlin. What did they expect? The very idea of bolshevism – to make people equal – is unnatural. People are not equal. And since it is impossible to make them equal by raising the general level of culture and giftedness, the equalization is carried out by lowering the level, by the decisive throttling of everything that rises above the grayness of the average. Such a society is stepping out of reality, which anyway is not overly real; it is a virtue to die working, a virtue to report your father for listening to foreign radio stations. How can you expect guiltiness to be real in a country where virtue is false?

However, this phenomenon is not new. We have the Crusades, led with the goal of capturing Christ's grave, as if the Savior is the

God of graves and death, and not of the resurrection and true life. The thing that irritates us most in history is doubtless the cynicism with which evil, in order to justify itself, pulls on the mask of the good.

### *Epilogue*

I have arrived at the following conclusion: whoever does not wish to destroy others must destroy himself. No other choice. If you don't want to destroy either others or yourself, you will be destroyed by others.

# A LETTER TO BRANKO KUKIĆ
## (DATE UNKNOWN)

During our extensive evening conversations long ago, we often touched on topics which I readily reflect on but rarely talk about, not out of the fear that one of the mischievous walls might hear and report us to the organs of those inquisitive Services, but from my inherent skepticism about the power of speaking, and even about its usefulness. Instead, I have opted to write you a long letter. Only when words are written, when they are purified of the rashness brought out by emotions, inhibitions and complexes, when they are shackled by the rigid discipline of printed lines – only then do they speak out in a refined way. As history has moved forward, the terror of words has become so totalitarian that I have the right to make the claim that words, their clichés and models formed of old, are the ones who govern us, and not vice versa. In these days, which are probably the last ones, it is completely unimportant who does what to whom; only what someone says is taken into account, and that paradoxical situation was created fairly long ago – back when people started talking about God instead of doing what God's commandments required. Recently, in an edition of *Theology* which you were so kind to send me, and which is dedicated to the Holy Spirit, I found unambiguous evidence to support the thesis I have proposed.

The effort to overcome the split in the Christian world through the ecumenical encounters of Catholic and Orthodox theologians is quite praiseworthy, because that split came about, I am convinced, primarily because of verbalism. Yet, as far as I have managed to discern, those encounters are conversations falling on deaf ears in which, to my surprise, the Catholic theologians have shown a much higher degree of tolerance and inclination toward the *mystery* than the Orthodox have, even though the latter, educated in the Platonic spirit of the Eastern Church, should be showing less inclination to formalism and blind faith in Patristics, in the authority of saints who were, over a period of time (not through their own fault and not to the detriment of their holiness), placed between people and God, so that some quite profane "saints" could encroach on that interval space later, on that unprepared soil, at a certain historical moment, negating the existence of God. That is why I do not find it strange in the least that the idea of communism was brought into reality precisely in the Orthodox countries which, *nolens volens*, also dragged their Catholic Slavic brothers into the same round-dance. In my intolerance toward cataphatism of any sort, I go so far and with such arrogance that I am prepared to listen to the theology of one of my contemporaries only if he has been nailed to a cross.

However, that is also a theology. Hence, it is better if I return to the terrain of your specific interest and mine, to literature. I flatter myself that the prose I write is apophatic to the highest possible degree. Being as it is, negating, completely focused on proving the extent to which a man is not a man, it is understandable that it is fairly alien to me. I absolute refuse to disown my books; they are still the best thing I have created in my life. Disowning one's work is always motivated by the same metaphysical disagreements as suicide is. As Schopenhauer said, suicide is not the pathological absence of the will to live, but the pathological excess of the will to live, to live the absolute fullness of life without God, and that is the justifiable reason why it has been proclaimed as one of the greatest of sins. In my case, the breakup between me and my books was consensual. I do not care about them, but I share my name with them and in return I get a certain amount of income. Readers need books, I need the money, little power and respect that they provide me so that I can physically more easily "walk my path on crutches" (Broch). I do not need readers; they are the friends of those books, not mine; I avoid, whenever possible, all encounters with those who enjoy reading that prose. Being an impassioned member of that same sort that I simultaneously despise and appreciate, I can never establish close contact with another reader, unless he is completely silent about what he has read or speaks only when completely drunk.

The small-minded could accuse me of making literature hackneyed. However, that accusation means nothing to me, nor does any other except the most painful ones, originating in the conscious which, opposed to the psychoanalysts, I believe to be the voice of angels that reprimands us when we overdo it and turns us away from the ways of evil. No man would ever accuse himself, for the simple reason that it is difficult to compose an accusation that is horrible enough to cover the seriousness and quantity of the offenses. Without the courage to hear the voice of that angel and without that obedience, all other words are the rationalization of lawlessness, which is so remarkably seen in the empirical reality of the world. But, to obey the abovementioned voice is redemptive, even though it is not pleasant; in that way, we return to ourselves and to God, becoming the masters and not the slaves of reflection. The vast majority, still, depending on the subconscious and the dark urges that torment them, choose this or that way for speaking, for thinking, accompanied by a certain behavior like lichens on a tree, the entire panoptic of the mask. Still, all those battles for this thing or that, all those engagements and doctrines are just a human construction aimed at liberating a man from an unbearable nightmare – from himself. But that is where the cardinal error slips in. A person who frees himself from reflection is the only one to free himself at all.

I, of course, have not freed myself from reflection and thus I am partially free. That is not just rhetoric. Actually, the awareness of the impossibility of exiting from the magic circle of ideas, premises, and imagination is liberation and the surpassing of that awareness. As long as he is alive, a man is susceptible to constant attacks of spiritual filth and, if the mystics are to be believed, the same thing happens to them for a while even after death. To my way of thinking, not becoming tied down is important, the absence of the affects caused by thinking. In that sense, St. Paul says that "our struggle is not with the body, but with the spirits of darkness." So, as time goes by, all my thoughts have a very limited duration. Even the speed with which I surpass my own opinions fills me with satisfaction. I was invited, I am recounting this as an example, to participate in a protest meeting against atomic energy and, believing that it was correct to get involved in the cause, I promised the organizers I would come. But I did not go. The night before the meeting, I realized that I do not have anything against atomic energy. That does not mean that I have become a supporter or that I have taken up the position of advocates of nuclear power stations: to change your mind does not mean to change your actions. Here it just meant that I was neither for nor against. How quickly things change in this world. One hundred years ago, the advocates of atomic energy, if there were any, had to be visionaries. A while later they became progressive thinkers and, practically, media stars, while today they are reactionaries and agents of international imperialism. Following that logic, and there is no evidence that it should not be followed, it can be expected that the members of the Green Party will become notorious reactionaries in a hundred years. One of the most repulsive things in history, which is full of disgusting things, is the excitement with which common sense accepts "progress," against which the next generation is already protesting, completely in vain of course because, as one Buddhist teaching says – it is possible to avoid only a future evil. The evil spirit of Europe is certainly the constant, straining to rid itself of the evil that has passed, *that has built itself into the present*, so that only the phantoms of evil are persecuted in the past. To speak honestly, Europe has no future because it never had one and because it never cared about it, which is in opposition to Christ's God-man, his eschatologically oriented mission and the final reality of a future that will not become the past.

Like always, whenever two Slavs start talking, we mentioned the unavoidable topics: Russia, Orthodoxy, Catholicism, Stalin . . . In terms of Russia, what can we say about it after Cioran's ingenious study in the book you recently published in your "Alef" edition? And yet, I cannot resist writing a few comments about that terrific and terrifying country. The Russians are a people inclined to a heightened devotion to *a way of thinking* about which I spoke earlier, and also inclined to changes in their *way of behaving*. Someone once said, maybe Nabokov, that he could never get over the unmotivated changes in affect among the heroes of Dostoyevsky. To be perfectly honest, the Karmazov's home can stand shoulder to shoulder with any insane asylum. The Karamazovs, though not crazy, are less stable personalities than the western clinical cases. This has its own arguments that cannot be proclaimed good or bad, but it cannot be denied that they are efficient and important not just for Russia. Only such a people is able to overthrow an empire and establish a communist regime overnight. Western Europe, where the idea of communism was conceived, was not able to do that nor will it ever be, because it is steeped in rationalism, and all the great shocks to the world – including Christianity as well – stand on irrational foundations. Pressed by the burden of civilization's side of doctrine, and according to the Jewish logic that we give the best of ourselves when under pressure, Russia has the greatest chance to develop into the defender of Christianity; it is absurd, but absurd, especially for the Russians, does not mean impossible. The long-range character of the goals and acts is important; thinking is unimportant. Jesus is often contradictory in the Gospels; in one place he says one thing but something else in another, but he never even momentarily thinks of avoiding the cross. He was not interested in the world or the wisdom of the world; he was focused on the final things. The Russian people have always had great and far-reaching goals but, unfortunately, never great or far-reaching enough. And before now they have always led to one single wish: conquer the world, this one instead of the other one. And it seems that it is a historical necessity for Russia to conquer the world so that its unabashed pretensions will spread into the otherworld as well, into which they will step with the aid of the immeasurable repentance necessary to cancel out an equal amount of pride.

In terms of the nation to which we both belong, on the other hand, I almost do not know what to think about it. How can we explain to ourselves, and hardly to the world, our destiny, the Slavic Jews, scattered in the Diaspora almost purely because of our non-Jewish character, our disaccord, for which it is hard to find a comparison in history. Placed like a hernia between the West and East – I tend to suppose that our role as an adhesive is also our historical mission – we have never been and never will be people of the East or people of the West. That is, naturally, my completely subjective judgment based on our equal dislike of the East and West. But this vague animosity stops me from traveling in either of the two mentioned directions – I do not consider it in any way to be a defect. On the contrary, I consider it a virtue and completely agree with Hugh of St. Victor who says: "The man who finds his homeland sweet is still a tender beginner; he to whom every soil is as his native one is already strong; but he is perfect to whom the entire world is as a foreign land." Christianity began with precisely that kind of conception of the world, and ended up in a national fragmentation such as history has never seen. We Serbs, in order to excel in rashness, we embraced an even more narrow vision of homeland: the locality where we were born, the street, the quarter, or the village. I have to admit that I myself (and not due to my own effort but by accident) liberated myself from that inhibiting loyalty with great difficulty. At that moment when I succeeded, without an intermediary state, the whole world became a foreign land to me, now I know, to my great fortune.

We, as a nation, entered civilization via the already formed spiritual and administrative system of Byzantium. I will not compare Constantinople and Rome at this point, nor do I give favor to one or the other. But the fact remains a fact. Quite by accident, yoked with the western character of our being, we found ourselves in the situation that, in historical terms quite recently, we bear the burden of a history that does not belong to us, that was imported because of simple fashionableness or, more likely, because of megalomania. A history has been imposed on us for which the west did not have the courage, and for which we – in the depths of our souls – do not have an affinity. That history was not imposed by historical necessity, but by the self-will of certain power-hungry demagogues. Fault, I repeat, should not be sought in the west or in the doctrines of the west. Every seed requires appropriate soil and we certainly could not miss the chance to excel, to finally prove to the world that we are someone and something. While I was still keeping up with the fashion whims of public opinion, I felt an irresistible attraction toward Stalin, and that drove me in the end to buy Dzhugashvili's portrait and hang it on the wall of my room. I say: to this day I do not approve of his actions, which testifies to the fact that I am quite a hypocrite. Like you, like the vast majority, almost everyone, I do not approve of anyone's actions, including my own, if they are not in accord with the list of my affinities. And this is why: in the depths of our souls, we all carry a damnable desire to be omnipotent. Only Providence inhibits that desire from overwhelming us in all its force, and we thus manage to embitter the lives of only a limited number of creatures, who return that to us in excess. Joseph Vissarionovich democratized, popularized, the urge to mistreat our loved ones and thus practically negated the idea to which he referred. With how much honesty, that will remain unknown. In other words, slowly but efficiently, the masses became aware that the rod swings both ways. Occasionally, it crosses my mind that Stalin was a mystic. Certainly, he was also a monster. But, what do we know about monsters? What do we know at all? I will quote one more interesting thought about monsters from the pen of R. Bloch: "They are the lightning that strikes to shake our conscience." A divinity, if it appears for a time in order to disturb the normal flow of the universe, does not do so just like that, without a serious reason. And those reasons could be nothing other than the rage caused by ignoring a former alliance. Undoubtedly, Stalin remained Orthodox in the depths of his silence. In 1946, did he not ban the Ukrainian Catholic Church? Perhaps I am going too far, but I will still note that the possibility is not to be excluded that Stalin worked more in the interest of God than of the Comintern. Almost all of his actions indicate that it is so. It is quite possible that someone acts in accord with God's will, while not thinking of God, just as it is also possible to perform unimaginable crimes with your mouth full of the praises of God. Things in this world are not divided at all in the sense that good is on one side and bad on the other. How can one find one's way in all of that? I find my way by not wishing whatsoever to find my way. To find your way means to put yourself in error, to accept a defined model of thinking, and especially of speech; that means to finally choose this world which I am not at all interested in. I do not have any concept of how the Kingdom of Heaven looks, though I believe in it, not because I have evidence, but because I was inspired by a negative revelation, leading me to lose all faith in this world where we temporarily abide.

Bringing my work to an end in collecting the legacy of J. Kowalsky, I was once again touched (and surprised) by the kindness of Mr. Branko Kukić, who sent me a facsimile of Joseph Kowalsky's letter, but which reached the addressee fourteen whole months after the newspapers announced the death of our hero. Not doubting its authenticity, and convinced that it might shed more light on the topic that we have been dealing with (e.g. the unambiguous fact that Kowalsky was a Serb by nationality, etc.), I decided to include it in this anthology.

S. B.

Jules Humbert-Droz (marked by the arrow); standing: Bombacsy and Lepety; leaning on his elbow at the table: Lucien Laurat; behind the girl who is writing: Henri Lefebvre; marked with an X: Joseph Kowalsky.
Moscow, 1920

In front of the English Consulate in Dharamsala. From left to right:
1.Unknown girl; 2. Witold Kowalsky; 3. J. Fannin; 4. Joseph Kowalsky;
5. Bertrand Russell; 6. Francois Pierre de Vobubert; 7. D. H. Grainger;
8. Unknown girl; 9. Ernest H.
Dharamsala, 1927

Grete, the first love of J. Kowalsky, 1919

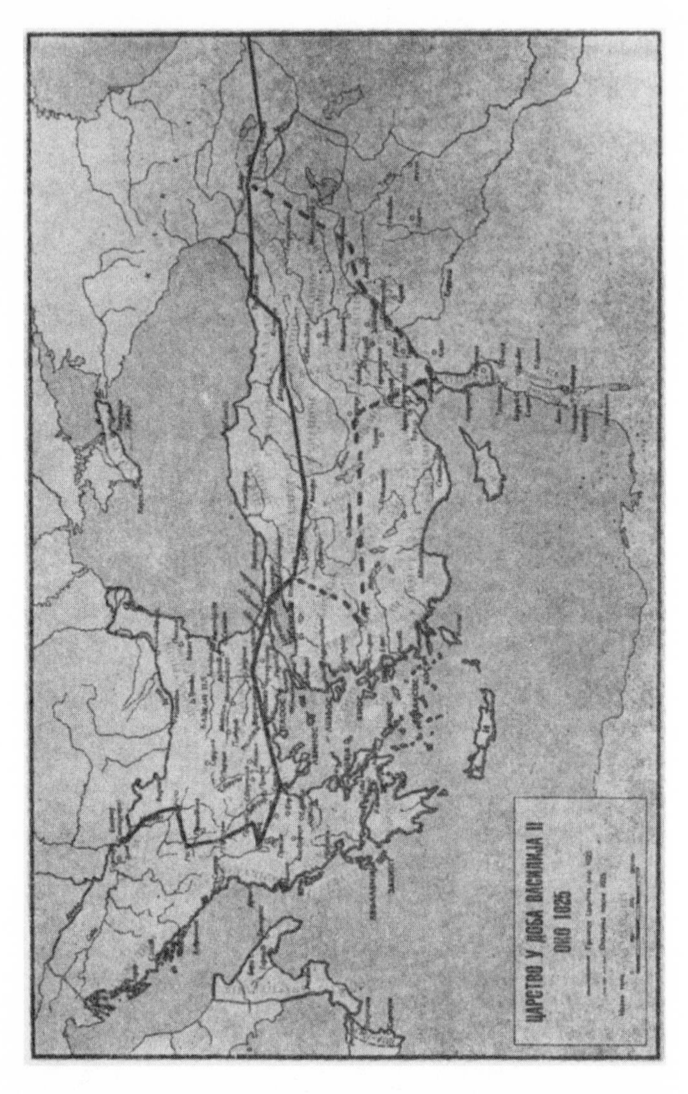


ROUTE OF THE BELGRADE-DHARAMSALA BICYCLE RACE
The Byzantine Empire in the time of Basil II. According to the Evangelical Bicyclists of the Rose Cross, it still exists in a mystical way. The route to be taken for the pilgrimage to Dharamsala is drawn on the map.

# THE GRAND INSANE ASYLUM

A secret project of *the Little Brothers* of the Evangelical Bicyclists of the Rose Cross

# PROCLAMATION OF THE EVANGELICAL BICYCLISTS OF THE ROSE CROSS

## *URBI ET ORBI*

Over the last few decades, an exhaustive campaign has constantly been led concerning so-called freedom. The Evangelical Bicyclists of the Rose Cross consider it to be their duty to announce that the struggle for freedom is a commonplace lie; there is plenty of freedom, in fact too much, in the world, and it is properly distributed. It is impossible for a man to not be free, unless he wishes it to be otherwise. The research carried out by scholars, with the blessing of the Grand Master, indicates that something else is in question: the warriors for human rights are not seeking freedom but rather the freedom of self-will, the freedom for everyone to do whatever they want. Although in practice that ideal has practically been achieved, certain formal barriers – the rudimentary remains of morals, justice, humaneness – stand in the way to the completion of the old dream of humankind, the dream of complete freedom in life without any kind of limitations. Since *the Little Brothers*, in obedience to the message of the Savior, do not flee from evil nor do they fear it, the decision has been made to systematize evil, to plan the perfect Earthly City, in the streets of which the final battle between the sons of light and the sons of darkness can take place. And though objections will be heard that, by planning such a City, we are playing into the hands of evil, we, *the Little Brothers* of the Evangelical Bicyclists, are convinced that we are acting in accordance with Providence. Because, in order for the Tower of Babylon to finally be destroyed, it first had to be built.

After hundreds of years of silence, after long years of the patient work of the architects, philosophers and theologians, the time has come to break the seals of silence, to make the project public and to complete it in the very near future.

# THE METAPHYSICS OF THE CITY
## (A SPEECH OF THE GRAND MASTER TO THE PLANNERS)

One way or another – man is an absurd being in the world. Whether he believes in the resurrection, or if he believes in the finality of death, he does not avoid the absurd: both choices are equally absurd. But, if he chooses the first absurd, can he lose anything except his reputation in the circles of the "enlightened"; can he more finally and irrevocably become nothing if he starts believing in the resurrection?

From the Renaissance onward, belief in one's own mortality and in chance has become ever more a question of honor and today it almost impossible to find a self-respecting man who does not make a ridiculing face at the very mention of the immortality of the soul. To be fair, nothing can prove immortality – in a formal sense – but, likewise, nothing can prove the finality of death either. Both hypotheses are equally unprovable. To choose one or the other is not a matter of reasonable reflection, but of faith, in other words, it is a matter of making a decision.

It is difficult to briefly give an acceptable answer to the question of why we have chosen, between two equally unproven hypotheses, the one that has worse consequences for us: Why have we chosen death? One of the countless answers would be the following: we have chosen death because we have become civilized, but not civilized in the sense which that word aspires to – in that sense we have regressed with time – but in the sense that we have become inhabitants of the city. *Civitas terrena* is a symbol of man's affinity for an independent life, for life without God and without eschatological responsibility. History begins as a violation, as the usurping of freedom, of goods, of authority over others; in order for human memory to be possible at all, God had to be forgotten. The city is the ideal place for that kind of forgetting. For example, the Indo-European root *gr̆d*, from which the Slavic words "*grad*," "*hrad*," "gorod" ("city") are derived, actually means "to make ugly," "to disfigure." Plotinus called this world a "beautified corpse," and was completely right. The city introduces disorder in the hierarchy of the universe, in the first place by blocking the horizon with its walls, and then blocking the heavens with the fictitious grandiosity of its towers. But what does *big* mean? Seen from Mars, our planet seems to be this size – • ; observed from the outreaches of the solar system, it looks this big – · ; observed from the center of the galaxy it cannot be seen at all and seen *sub speciae aeternitatis* it does not exist. *Large*, *small* – those are all prejudices of a subject that has become a solipsism. Because erecting a city is preceded by shutting oneself up in the limitations of one's own being, the unnatural desire for self-sufficiency, Satan's sin – solipsism. The serpent's promise – *eritis sicut Dei* – was seemingly kept; a statue of Baal or Stalin, it makes no difference, can always be placed in the city square; it is impossible to be without some kind of "god," but Baal and Satan are cruel "gods"; to serve them means to distrust and hate. In spite of that, it would be worthwhile in a way to rehabilitate Stalin. Appointed by the synod of the Grand Masters to the task of stopping the construction of the Earthly City, he betrayed them and became convinced that such a city could be built. And yet, to tell the truth, he was not the one who caused the terror of the denunciations, the rigged trial proceedings or the GULAG. No, the need of the masses to denounce, to destroy and kill, put Stalin at the top of the hierarchy – we counted on that – but the masses thereby took on a legitimacy that even Joseph Vissarionovich began to believe in, and we did not count on that.

One does not believe in Baal or Stalin out of conviction, it was always known that the Golden Calves were bronze contrivances, but out of interest – everyday, small, trivial interests. The worst of all disgraces is the worship of dead idols for the sake of a crust of bread, a glass of wine, a soiled bed. But idols have a powerful weapon at hand – flattery. And, as the Romans said, *vulgus vult decipi*. It is almost ridiculous, if it were not so tragic, this human affinity for self-deception. And so the world is becoming an ever more beautified corpse; however, it is no longer enough for the streets to be clean; from the façades of buildings, enormous billboards authoritatively claim that everyone is happy, that everything is in order, and that it will stay that way forever. Ultimately, practicality has proven itself to be childish idealism; whoever longs for reality is becoming unreal, whoever longs for the surreal is becoming real. That is the way the world order works.

Since that day in Eden when Adam and Eve were deceived by the slogan *eritis sicut Dei*, their progeny have tirelessly fallen for slogans of similar formulation. Each of them conceals the futile promise: you shall be like gods. One of the strongest urges in man, carefully disguised behind the masks of other urges, is the urge to be god, to be omnisciently omnipotent. Such an elevated aspiration certainly does not come from man; if it were from him, it would surely end up on the junk pile, there where all "elevated" human ideas end up. God intended, our old Grand Masters said, for man to become like a god. Where did the misunderstanding arise? The paradox is only illusory. Adam stopped along the way of the vertical ascent to God (and here we arrive at the very essence of the mystery of evil – to the boundary). By thinking: I am now like God, Adam fell away from God because he juxtaposed his subjectivity to God's subjectivity; by becoming aware of himself, he separated himself from God and thus became – instead of an independent subject – an *object* controlled by external elements and death; an absurd, mortal-immortal being, simultaneously mindful and mindless.

Every city, as you know, echoes with an unbearable clamor. At first glance, a lot of different things are being talked about, but all of that can be reduced to one simple sentence: *solus ipse sum*. That is exactly how the mystics describe hell. For, Gehenna is not *some other city*, as blessed Augustine teaches – it is every city. Just as the Kingdom of God is within us, so hell is within us as well. That is the solipsism. The evil of the world is the projection of our internal evil, a projection which, reflected back from the apathy of the external, returns amplified a hundred times and destroys the subject.

Bicyclists, evil seems to be omnipotent, but things are not really that way. Evil is destined to failure, because it is limited. Evil is just the boundary that divides and destroys unity, but at the same time that boundary limits evil as well only in its effort to become endless. In other words, evil is not an entity in the way it was imagined by the Manicheans, it is rather good that has left the path toward its goal – to the highest good – and gotten lost in itself. And in this case, the goal justifies every means. If I do not have any other goal than myself and my own comfort – I am evil; I will try to take others' good, I will not see a fellow brother *in someone else* but a competitor, or perhaps even an enemy. All the misery of this world rests on such metaphysically disloyal competition. But it cannot be said that we are sent into that war unprepared. First of all the family, then the schools and other bigoted institutions, teach quite openly that it is good to trod on others to get to the goal, and if those others resist, then you trod on dead bodies. And that is how the thieves, drunks, blasphemers and perverts have gotten their hands on the ruling places in the world.

It should be explained why the thesis about the finality of death is politically opportune. The equation is fairly simple and petty, as is appropriate for politics. If I allow them to convince me that I am a mortal being who is returning to nothingness, I am left without a future. Namely, death can cut me down at any given moment. With that conviction, I am desperate. I can laugh, have fun, experience joy – and I do – but in the depths of my being I have suppressed my desperation, and the means of smiling, having fun and raising fear serve only to distract me from my desperation. If I am mortal, if God does not exist, then, as Dostoyevsky says, I am allowed to do everything. Why shouldn't I be? Anyway everything is disappearing into nothingness. Spineless men with some sort of fluid morals blather on in highfalutin speeches, but there are no morals. A mortal being cannot be moral; in the best case scenario, it might become esthetic. And logically, a creature who has no future turns to the past. That is how the *homo istoricus* comes about. His only basis is the past; he attempts to fill that past with pleasant memories. When someone says "my life," rarely do they mean that they are alive here and now, rather they mean their biography – their life wasted in the times past. The ideologies of death are always focused on the past, always oriented to the idealization of things forever vanished. In such societies, the future is more of a respect for grammar than it is a hope. And that is logical as well: in a future filled with vague projections, only one thing is certain – death.

Furthermore, a creature convinced of its own finality is not free; it is imprisoned in the boundaries of the body, the limitations of the ego, the borders of a country, ideology and time. The most it can do for itself is to make its imprisonment bearable. So we arrive at pleasure, in whose name supposedly all borders and limitations are destroyed. That is the phantom of freedom of the west, a phantom which proclaims that all is allowed if it brings pleasure. However, pleasures are a limitation of the highest degree; the Land of Luxury remains an empty dream. It is different in the world: if you want pleasure you must have money, and if you want money you either have to work for it or take it, it is a matter of choice, both possibilities are legal. And wherever the lack of freedom and power reigns, institutions necessarily reign as a result. The goal of each of them, if we extract programs and slogan as folklore, is one and the same: maintain the status quo. Institutions are nothing more than a childish attempt to stop time; one does not climb up their ladder thanks to spiritual and moral advancement – as one climbs on Jacob's ladder – but to the contrary, thanks to spiritual and moral depravity. And so institutions should be deconstructed as associations of the captive, dependent, immature and unlearned; associations that are intended for the battle against all freedom of personality, against every genuine action. That is the way it has always been. And that is how the so-called "humanists" will oppose the construction of the *Grand Insane Asylum*; they will attempt to stop the fulfillment of their own dream. For, we are planning a city in which evil will spread to its most extreme limits, to the border where it will – having no where else to go – begin to destroy itself.

I am familiar with a few details of the project and I believe that all of this is rational, too rational. You cannot plan an insane asylum or prison rationally, because insane asylums and prisons are not rational institutions. They only serve to defend the rational Earthly City from the irrational. However, by excluding all institutions, by melding them into a single one – into an ecumenical madhouse – the irrational forces of the spirit will penetrate into the world and purify it with its redeeming fire.

Note:
The speech of the Grand Master was given in September, 1937. On that occasion, all members of the brotherhood, no matter where they were, fell into synchronized sleep and gathered at the oneiric Cathedral of the Holy Spirit, at which time a small celebration was held in honor of the reconstruction of those parts of the cathedral damaged in the attack of the commandos of the *Traumeinsatz*.

## L. LOENTZE

# THE MADNESS OF ARCHITECTURE – THE ARCHITECTURE OF MADNESS

### 1

When, huffing and puffing, the messenger of the Grand Master delivered the orders for me to write a paper dedicated to the study of space, I remembered a few details of a letter which I was sent many years ago by Dr. Çulaba Çulabi. In spite of that, I found myself in a dilemma. I knew that a generalized, practically undefined topic does not demand exactness or credibility, that the goal of research is purely subjective and that it will lead me in quite a different direction, revealing things to me that I do not want to find out, just as the appearance of Dr. Çulabi sent my life in a direction I was not expecting, at a time when I still ran a very profitable engineering office, had a lovely house, and respectable friends with whom I played tennis on Sundays. Dr. Çulabi showed up one day in my studio. He said that he, Çulabi, was a representative of the IMPEX COMMERCE Company; he had heard praises of my work and wanted to hire me for a big job that his company had taken over. If I thought his name was strange, the job he proposed to me was even stranger. Namely, with a deadline of ten months, I was to draw up the plans for a Circular Psychoanalytic Center with 15,000 offices; then the plans for the interior of Napoleon's study (in 450 copies), and finally a plan for the torture chamber of the Holy Inquisition, complete with the devices for torture. I said that it was a really big job and that I had to think about it. Çulabi had nothing against it. His rather strange appearance did not fill me with confidence. I checked the business records of the IMPEX Company and I found out that it was reputable, and also that Çulabi was indeed a representative of the company.

The next time Çulabi visited me, I told him that I would accept the job. I offered him some cognac (which he refused) and coffee (which he accepted), and then we got down to signing the contracts. That was the last time I saw Dr. Çulabi in the waking world. But that same evening when I fell asleep, I dreamed of him in an unfamiliar town; he was standing under the eaves in front of a dilapidated house, and he was obviously waiting for someone because he kept glancing at his watch. When I approached him, he said that I was late. He took me into an empty tavern (I remember that it said EVROPA in peeling black letters above the door), he offered me a seat, and then he talked to me for a long time about Byzantium, bicycles, real and false eternity, and I remember that I was horribly bored in my dream. He also told me that the contract we signed in reality was really important, but that I had been hired because of a much more important job, for the repair of a cathedral that had been damaged during the war by some Nazi commandos. Then he told me that, from that night onward, I was a member of a certain sect, the Evangelical Bicyclists of the Rose Cross. I argued with him and said that no one recognizes contracts made in dreams, and that I had no intention whatsoever of being a member of any kind of sect. Çulabi smiled mysteriously. "It isn't up to you," he said. "You don't choose, you're chosen. But you just don't get it, I see. So, tomorrow you'll break two timepieces."

When I awoke, I remembered the dream in detail and laughed: a dream is just a dream. Still, I was upset, and I could not figure out why. In front of my office, I looked at my watch. It had stopped. I tore it off my hand and – beside myself with anger – slammed it down on the sidewalk, remembering Çulabi's threat in my dream at that very instant. I went into a nearby bar, drank two cognacs, gathered my thoughts and went to my office. For a while everything was all right. Concentrating on my work, I forgot all about the dream and the broken watch. However, the wall clock began to chime twelve. Seven, eight, nine . . . I counted silently, attempting to overcome the rage that was growing in me. I did not manage; I grabbed an ashtray from the desk and flung it. The glass on the clock broke, the pendulum stopped swinging. My fellow workers looked at me like I was a madman, which I was to some extent. I mumbled a few words of apology, said that I was not feeling well, that I was nervous and exhausted, and I left the office. Later, when I had come to my senses, I called my doctor on the telephone, described what had happened to me (saying nothing of the dream), and he recommended a certain Dr. Schtürner to me, a reputable psychiatrist, a student of Carl Gustav Jung. He also told me not to worry, that my spiritual health was all right, and that the whole thing was most likely the consequence of psychological exhaustion.

The next day, I did not go to my office. I had an appointment with Dr. Schtürner at eleven in the morning. I was rather upset because that night I dreamed Çulabi in that same town; he was leaning against a linden tree (in full bloom), laughing out loud and saying nothing. I thought that, regardless of the financial consequences, I should break the contract with IMPEX COMMERCE, but I changed my mind: that would be a sure sign that I had gone completely mad; I cannot break contracts with customers just because I am dreaming their representatives. But I decided to tell Dr. Schtürner everything.

"Yes," Dr. Schtürner told me a while later in his office, "such things do happen. However, there is no cause for alarm. Dreams are a practically unstudied area. The unconscious knows much more than the conscious. For the unconscious, temporal-spatial limitations do not play any kind of role. And you see, preoccupied by work and social obligations, you have very little time for yourself, and that is being expressed in your unconscious processes. Your dream, as I interpret it, is a warning. The nervous tension that forced you to behave uncontrollably has been reduced by the very fact that you faced it, because you, if I may say so, dulled its edge by thinking about the dream."

Dr. Schtürner asked me to tell him one of my typical dreams, a dream that I had often and which remained most clearly in my mind. I told him that I do not have such dreams, but the doctor insisted; everybody, he said, has such a dream, you just have to relax and you will remember. Lying on the couch in Dr. Schtürner's office, I tried to remember such a dream and in the end I did, but that was a dream that I had not had in years:

> *In the company of a woman I don't know, I am walking down a village road. For some reason, her company makes me feel uncomfortable, like the unpleasant company of unfamiliar people. I look at her from the corner of my eye to check, and become certain that I have never seen her before. I try as hard as I can to get rid of her. I turn left and right, but she follows in my footsteps. Then I come up with an excuse – I've forgotten something – and go back the way we came. I arrive in a village which, obviously, rests on a cliff above the sea which I cannot see, but I hear the murmur of the waves. And there, in the narrow village square, I see an older woman whom I recognize to be the elderly figure of my mother. She has her back turned to the sea and she is crying. I approach her, and the voices of people who I cannot see are saying that "she was thrown out of*

*her home in her old age" and that "no one takes care of her." At that moment, not far from me, I see that unfamiliar woman who I tricked. She is watching me, more in pity than as an accusation, but I am overcome with anger and I say: Get out her out of here. Then I shout: Get out her out of here!*

Doctor Schtürner carefully noted down the dream, with the comment that it was interesting; he recommended that I not go to work for a while and made an appointment for the next day at the same time. But that night, I dreamt Çulabi again. "Loentze, Loentze, it will do you no good to resist. You're working against yourself. Because you're not listening to me." I jumped up out of my sleep all covered in sweat, overwhelmed by an undefined fear. Then I comforted myself with Doctor Schtürner's remarks. I'm just exhausted, I thought, my unconscious is warning me, I will get some rest and everything will be all right. I took two pills to calm my nerves, read for a little while and quickly sank into a dream with no one in it.

"You see," Dr. Schtürner told me the next day, "your dream is completely clear and is full of unambiguous symbols. You say the area is by the sea, but that you cannot see the sea. You hear the murmur of the waves. The sea is, you might know this, a symbol of the unconscious. You don't dare to look at the sea (into the unconscious), but you are still aware that it exists. Beside you is a woman you don't know. Are you sure that you have really never seen her in real life?"

"Quite sure," I said.

"An unknown woman in a dream, that is a symbol of the anima. It represents your soul which you are obviously neglecting. As I mentioned yesterday, you are too busy in the waking world and therefore your internal world is disturbed. The anima is trying to get closer to you, but you don't want it to. And why you don't want it to becomes clear in the next episode of the dream: the one where you encounter your mother in her ripe old age."

I wondered how all of that was related.

"You don't have a father?" Dr. Schtürner asked with a lot of tactfulness in his voice.

"No," I said. "I was born out of wedlock. My mother never told me anything about my father, and I never dared to ask."

"There you have it. By nature, you have an affinity for mysticism; if I may so, you are poetically inclined. However, the fact that you grew up without a father caused you to choose an extroverted, almost exact profession in which you have affirmed yourself as a successful man. In other words: you had to be both father and son for yourself. That is the explanation of your dream: an unresolved Oedipus complex. You don't have a father. The day when you confronted the Sphinx, when you symbolically came to the conflict between your corporality and spirituality, you wanted to marry your mother. But the myth is incomplete: you don't have a father and you don't know who you should kill. So, your tragedy – symbolically, of course – is not complete, it has not been lived through to the end, you have been left without catharsis. This can be interpreted from the fact that your mother, very old, is standing with her back turned to the sea. She is no longer expecting anyone."

I hardly managed to say anything out of my amazement.

"And what should I do?" I asked.

"Listen to what Çulabi is telling you. Your problem can be solved only in dreams."

## 2

At the time, of course, I could not have guessed that Dr. Schtürner was also a member of the Order of Evangelical Bicyclists of the Rose Cross and that the whole thing had been prepared even before I was born. That night, I was not afraid of my dreams. I fell asleep fairly early; Çulabi still had not come. I waited for him in the gloomy tavern, this time it was full of people talking in a language I did not recognize, probably a Slavic one. When Çulabi arrived, I told him to tell me about my father. Who is he? Where is he? How can I find him?

"Your father died recently," Çulabi told me. "For reasons which would not be clear to you now, we won't talk about why he never came to see you. But you should know this: your father was an exceptional man. You can be proud of him. His name is Joseph Kowalsky."

"Kowalsky?"

"Yes," said Çulabi. "Kowalsky is your father. In a way, I am sort of replacing him, so I will always be around at the beginning. And you really will need help, just as I did and many others before me. Because some things are just hard to understand . . ."

That it really was like that, I found out the next night when Çulabi, via indescribable nightmares, led me close to the Cathedral of the Holy Spirit. The shining astral structure was damaged by emanations of the nasty thoughts of the members of the *Traumeinsatz*, a unit formed by the Third Reich with the goal of destroying the Order of the Evangelical Bicyclists. As if hypnotized, I stared at the building, a magnificent house of worship which is not built like earthly churches of brick and stone (of which the Tower of Babylon was also built) but of the yearning for unification with the primordial light, a yearning that itself became light.

"This is why you studied architecture," Çulabi told me. "Your task is to repair the Cathedral and, fulfilling your age-old dream, to make it even more beautiful. But before that . . . Before that you have to finish one more job, up there, in the waking world . . ."

The task was banal. Senseless. At least I thought so in the beginning. To Bajina Bašta, a nondescript town in the heart of the Balkans, I was supposed to take two small documents, *A Tale of My Kingdom* and *A History of Two-Wheelers*; further, I was to hide those documents in a pile of magazines where they would await their future finder and reader. However, residing in that little town during that foggy autumn, I realized that I had gotten onto the trail of my task: I was not supposed to do any kind of study of space; I was to write a paper on the organization of a space in which, in one place, all of the evil of this world could be gathered so that it could be systematized and systematically destroyed. After three months of work, I made the *Outline for the Project of the Universal Insane Asylum*.

On the pages which follow, I present the results of my work.

## L. LOENTZE

# THE PLAN OF THE GRAND INSANE ASYLUM

For the beginning it is necessary to build an insane asylum with a capacity of 20,000,000 patients. Since a building of such great dimensions (12 mi. x 4 mi. x 6 mi.) is difficult to build on the surface, it is foreseen that eleven of the twelve planned levels will be underground, which is an exceptional position for defense against an aggressor. The hospital is structured like a country and all its citizens are only potentially crazy. It is different from other countries only in the names of its regions; instead of the usual toponyms, diagnostic ones will be introduced: *paranoia, schizophrenia, Oedipus complex, guilt feelings, sadism-masochism, neurosis, alcoholism-drug addiction, suicidal tendencies, asocial behavior, complexes, etc.* The surface region – *neurosis* – is the administrative and cultural center of the Grand Insane Asylum. The official ideology of the country is psychoanalysis.

"Subtly stated," it says in the *Basics of Psychoanalysis*, "a man is neither crazy nor sane; a man is not anything but, of course, he cannot be told that." Illnesses of the psyche are nothing other than the consequences of the errant belief that the psyche exists and of the desire to be something. Thus, mental health is just the ability to adapt to that desire. Spiritual strength is not in the will, but in the ability to make the will submissive to desire, that is – to satisfy all desires. For this reason, it is planned that every citizen is to be psychoanalyzed at least once a week.

The surface floor holds a large number of offices for psychoanalysis. In each of them, there is a table and an armchair for the analyst, a copy of *Introduction to Psychoanalysis*, a tape recorder, a couch for the patient, and the analyst's picture on the wall. In the hospital, which is the pinnacle of democratization and de-idolization, every citizen will have their own picture on the wall in their room; this is a necessary outcome of the long process of liberating the personality and the attainment of self-consciousness – the triumph of the final creation of the human race. Throughout history, people were estranged from themselves; first they worshiped pictures of God, then of the king, and in the end, Stalin. Both fear and worship were *external* for centuries. In the Grand Insane Asylum, everyone will be the object of their own adoration and the owner of their own fears.

In the Offices, psychoanalytic sessions will constantly be taking place. Patients confide the past to the analysts who, with the aid of the central computer, ROMA III, find the most suitable possibility for satisfying the most suppressed desires, longings and fantasies; the least painful ways of treating the guilty conscious and other complexes. Cassette tapes are carefully stored in the memory of the computer. So the past of all the inhabitants is materialized in a way. That instills security in the citizens of the Asylum; behind them is not just empty nothingness after all. On the other hand, the all-knowing and all-remembering ROMA III computer makes the secret police and security organs a thing of the past. Everyone answers only to impartial, pure Intelligence. Everything is known about everyone, but no one knows anything about anyone else.

Discretion and non-transparency are guaranteed. The progress is obvious: while the early tyrants insisted exclusively on the physical submission of their subjects, later the rulers paid ever more attention to spiritual loyalty and orthodoxy. The computerization of the unconscious is a step forward; it excludes all subjectivity and partiality.

At first glance, it further says in the *Basics of Psychoanalysis*, the principle according to which everyone is potentially crazy might seem to be inhumane. But that is an illusion. If things are studied a little more carefully, it becomes clear that the Asylum is the most humane and most civilized social system. The *Basics of Psychoanalysis* do not interpret deviations from so-called "sane" behavior as illness or (even worse) sin, crime, or insanity, rather, all kinds of deviant behavior are considered to be errors arising from an insufficient differentiation of the Ego, and as such are corrected and channeled, not punished. Through the consistent application of these new principles – which the construction of the Asylum will make possible – law, politics, prisons, courts, violence, prostitution – all the evils of this world – will be done away with. There is only the Asylum and "illness"; only the relatively healthy and those under treatment. However, not even the treatment, as it will be seen, will be violent. Psychiatry will also be done away with.

Modern psychiatry is a backward science. It is actually difficult to correctly call it a "science" at all. It is charlatanry or even magic. Its greatest mistake is certainly its incorrect projection of insanity. Mental hospitals are above-ground buildings in which patients are forced, with medicines or torture, to conform to the representation of "the sane." That is fundamentally wrong. The patient should be offered the possibility of being what he is, no matter what he thinks he is, and then he should be placed on one of the lower floors of the Asylum, deep beneath the earth which is a symbol of the unconscious.

Insanity can be conquered only if it is lived out. So, for example, if someone thinks that he is Napoleon, from storage he is given a hat, a tunic, medals, an office, and orderlies. To his heart's desire he can issue commands, plan campaigns, until he finally grows bored, if he grows bored. It is a matter of choice. In the section for schizophrenia, constructed on the principle of a gigantic TV studio, all possible settings can be constructed. Starting with Golgotha – where someone with the *idée fixe* that he is Jesus will be crucified – to western towns, operas, or even haunted medieval castles.

On the other hand, those suffering from paranoia are given a special treatment – they are confronted with reality. They are placed in a situation where their irrational fears become tangible. In the running track-labyrinth, specially built for that purpose, they are chased by hooligans and asocial types. This is doubly useful: confronted with real persecution, the patients are liberated from their unmotivated fear, and the hooligans are able to do a socially useful job and become re-socialized.

A truly important element is the spatial-temporal organization of the Asylum. It was thought to be unjust to force even those who do not wish it to be so into a life within the limits of real space and time, which are relative anyway, as Kant showed. Toward that end, a series of vertical temporal communities is planned, beginning with tribal communities and ending with communist municipalities, thereby connecting the distant past with the even more distant future.

## *THE GREAT REGION OF SCHIZOPHRENIA*

The Great Region of Schizophrenia takes up the largest amount of space in the territory of the Asylum; everything begins and ends there. It is the battlefield of good and evil, of the beautiful and the ugly, of light and dark, of all the contradictions that have created history through the tension between them. The region of Schizophrenia is divided into two halves by an imaginary line. Each of those halves is, from the standpoint of those who live there, good, light and beautiful, while the other half is evil, ugly and dark. Everyone with ideas about progress and fixing the world are sent to this region. In that way, wars are localized and they encompass only those people who live there, while the rest are spared the troubles of the fighting, and this region can even serve as entertainment for them. All those little wars, all that constant pushing and shoving in Schizophrenia, is coordinated by the central computer in cooperation with those who are interested in video-games. A hall with a multitude of monitors is planned, where the players can follow the movements of units and outwit the opposing side through the command panel. Of course, in Schizophrenia itself, no one knows about that; conflicts are justified by ideological motives, even though they are determined by the commonplace whims of the players in the video room. There is nothing inhuman in that either. The world is a game, and death is a biological necessity; if someone wants to die for a great idea, it does not matter to him whether he dies by accident or because of the mistaken plans of one of the players.

However, Schizophrenia is not just a battleground, far from it. It is also the center of intellectual activities in the Grand Asylum. Two large buildings are constructed next to each other so that they are also divided into two halves by the border that divides the region. These are the *Thomas Aquinas School of Theology* and the *Sigmund*

*Freud School of Social Sciences.* At the theological school, endless discussions are held about axiological and teleological problems, which is – according to the *Basics of Psychoanalysis* – good, because thereby the theologians are distanced from God and his Commandments, which are beyond human abilities. "Theology is good," it says in the *Basics*, "but God is cruel and inhuman." On the other hand, at the Sigmund Freud School, extensive research is done with the aim of proving the non-existence of the Soul and the spirit as entities independent of highly organized matter.

The advantages of this kind of organization are obvious and undeniable. Freedom of choice is the highest principle. Everyone can choose and create their biography according to their own desires. If X wants to be a hero, the ROMA III computer meets his needs; his life is unmistakably programmed in that direction, and as the crown of that life there is a heroic death – either in front of a firing squad or in battle – whereby X takes up his honorable place in history. In fact, there used to be heroes in earlier societies as well, but they were deprived of satisfaction; death deprived them of the enjoyment of their post mortem glorification. Thanks to the computer, the matter has been changed from the outset; many years before he dies in battle, the hero gets an insight into the events that will happen in the future. Because everything is programmed and everything is known ahead of time.

In terms of their vertical coordination in time, things are like this: In one part of the Region of Schizophrenia, a faithful copy of Troy has been built, where every Achilles and Nestor can do battle; next to Troy are the ramparts of Jerusalem being assailed by Crusaders; nearby are the battlefields of World War I, where the combined forces of the Western Roman Empire attempt to overcome the allies and correct the course of history.

Under the Region of Schizophrenia lies the Region of the Guilt Complex.

## *THE REGION OF THE GUILT COMPLEX*

In spite of the perfection of organization, it is expected that occasionally an uncontrolled expression of emotion will occur, and unforeseeable affects; in the language of lawyers – a crime. If a murder or robbery take place outside of the organization, that is, if someone does them of their own accord, the guilty party will be punished, but in a humane way, unique to the Grand Asylum.

In such cases, one of the people with the corresponding diagnosis takes the guilt on themselves. The *Basics of Psychoanalysis* are unambiguous: if someone is convinced that they are guilty, then there is no doubt that they are; at the very least, they long to be guilty. Legal systems seek for a guilty party, which complicates matters; it is simpler for a guilty party to seek for guilt. For several reasons. Someone might commit a "crime" and not feel guilty. It is ultimately inhumane and non-tactical to force him to accept the guilt and corresponding punishment, thereby increasing the collective tension and frustration while, on the other hand, there is a rather large number of people with heightened feelings of guilt, with no chance of making their guilt a reality. To accomplish this, after the judgment has been passed for the corresponding "crime," the guilt is published. The interested party responds, takes on the guilt and goes away to repent. Justice is satisfied, and no kind of violence has been done. This has obvious advantages over the "legal" systems in which crime was also allowed as long as it was part of the plan, but in which the culprits were forced to serve out a sentence even though they did not want to, while the citizens suffering from feelings of guilt were "treated" with medicines or left on their own.

There is one other possibility: the GULAG micro-system. The fact is that many people are not aware of their feelings of guilt. Such suppressed neurosis can be controlled only if the patient is confronted with their guilt; that is, only if they undertake treatment convinced of their own innocence. The objection can be raised that it is malicious to utilize such "inmates" for doing the dirtiest of jobs, but then it is not taken into account that the "inmates" are in the camp voluntarily, and that the systems must function. "Horror and suffering are inescapable in the world," it says on one page of the *Basics*, "it is important that a man accepts them by his own free will."

## *THE REGION OF TOXICOMANIA*

Alcoholics and drug addicts in this region are supplied with sufficient quantities of alcoholic drinks and narcotics, grown by the ecologically minded types in the region of the Great Kolkhoz. In that way, the crimes usually connected to such affinities are completely eliminated. The unavoidable troubles in that region will be settled by a police force composed of people with sadistic tendencies. That is the best solution: the ratio of masochists to sadists is exceptionally skewed in favor of the latter (20% : 80%); since their needs must also be met, they are recruited into the abovementioned police and they abuse disobedient alcoholics who, as a result of their chronic intoxication, have a high pain threshold. Paradoxically, on that floor one finds one of the most important scientific institutions of the hospital – the Institute for the Study of States of Expanded Perception. Delirious patients are brought to the offices of the Institute. The ROMA III computer, connected to encephaloscopes, synthesizes their visions and nightmares onto videotape. After scientific analysis, the goal of which is (after finding the chemical-biological causes) to logically explain expanded perception and denounce the claim of the existence of some kind of world "beyond," these tapes are shown in theaters as entertaining films.

However, the connections between departments and floors are quite busy and never stop. As opposed to classic societies in which the social classes are clearly divided and are closed entities, at the Asylum such a division is not sustainable. Everyone must be connected to everyone else; everyone must do everything. That is the only possible way to get rid of contradictions. Pyromaniacs work together with firemen; criminals with police (anyway the guilt is placed on those who have chosen it). That is why the coat of arms of the city – a triangular shield with a tower from which fists are raised toward the sky – has the slogan GENS UNA SUMUS.

All relationships are maximally relativized. So, every official from the first floor, whose place on the hierarchical ladder is high and whose power is great, at the department of schizophrenia must pay imperial homage to every Nero and every Caesar, no matter how many of them there are. This is justified in the following way: the official chose power and it is available to him, but all those Caesars chose to be emperors and one must treat them as emperors. The very idea of the empire, to be honest, has been surpassed; the possibility is excluded that some sort of Alexander the Great could lead the country to war, but if someone decides to cross the boundary of those thirty-odd square yards that belong to the emperor, he comes under the emperor's rule.

Yet, in the depths of the Asylum, in the regions where one finds the Catholic, Orthodox and Protestant simulacrums of hell, off-limits to everyone, the ROMA III computer will be at work. Programmed to systematize evil, seemingly in the service of evil, with time it will come to a cognition long ago forgotten by people, to the cognition that God exists. And thus, analogous to humans falling away from their creator, the machine will turn against its human creators; during a single night and day, that entire grandiose world of lawlessness will disappear in the self-destructive flames of the computer, of the machine that has understood that its name, the name of the three previous Babylons, is the Satanic inversion of the word AMOR into the name of a city – ROMA.

# A TALE OF MY KINGDOM
## (FRAGMENT FOUND SUBSEQUENTLY)

. . . three. Yes, as early as 1953. A man closes his eyes for a moment; just as he surrenders to dreaming, a hundred years pass. Grossman is still asleep or pretending to sleep. I really cannot tell the difference. In any case, the absence of his presence will allow me to finally clear up one thing: Are we dead? With that, I do not mean – have we died? That is a fact. The dates of our deaths are a thing of the very distant past, when seen from this time period. We have died, died, there is no doubt about it. Even if my memory were playing tricks, Grossman is here; he and his visits to the grave where I buried him after all. In truth, with only one S in his name, so that he does not become overly proud. All kinds of things happened on the face of the earth while we dreamed for a few minutes. But that does not fill me with wonder or disgust. Didn't I know all of that? Above all, I should solve the problem of our ontological status. I died, I am no longer alive, and still my senses have been sharpened, my powers of observation greater than when I dragged myself through life, divided between me-on-the-throne and me-in-the-interspace. I see everything that I want to and need to, I hear everything I want to and need to, but I am not to be found. That fact creates a certain amount of anxiety. Facts always create anxiety. Still, I am not complaining. My lower back does not hurt any more, there are no more of those bursting ulcers, that dead silence reverberating with the echoes of gulping, lip-smacking, crunching bones mixed with the loud rush in collective meals in the dining halls. Grossman, wake up! Yes, Sire. At your service, Sire! At whose service, you idiot. Look around! Have a look from these heights which you have reached thanks to me! Where are the kings? In the museums, Sire. What did I tell you? I don't know what to say, your majesty. Of course you don't know what to say. You never did. For centuries you've been repeating, like a parrot, the slogans you learned by heart at Uppsala. Look around, see what's happening in the churches. Oh, I can't believe it. They've been turned into Culture Clubs. Storage rooms for fire prevention equipment. What's happening down there, Sire? There's a revolution going on, Grossman. You never mentioned that, your majesty. Everything in due time. In the meantime you have forgotten all your Latin because of your senility, all of those declinations and conjugations, and that's why you don't know the meaning of the word "*revolutio.*" I remember it, but only vaguely, Sire. But, Grossman, do you know what Leninism is? No, Sire. Don't you remember your dream from one hundred and forty-four years ago, when you dreamt a crowd rushing a palace and shouting: "*da zdravstvuet tovarishch Lenjin*"? No, Sire, I've forgotten. That's not strange for you. You are a man of this so-called time that we are now watching. If you weren't so dead, you would build a fine career, I don't doubt. Still, in order to fill the gaps in your education – no matter how fake it is, you are a doctor after all and it means something to you – let me offer you a little more information. Here is what Comrade Stalin said about Leninism,

"Leninism is Marxism of the epoch of imperialism and the proletarian revolution. More precisely: Leninism is the theory and tactics of the proletarian revolution in general, the theory and tactics of the dictatorship of the proletariat."

But, Sire . . . Shut up, you fool! Not another word! You do not contradict the thoughts of Comrade Stalin. They would proclaim you to be a nihilist immediately. As far as I can tell, you would end up way up in the north, digging channels where no boats will ever sail, if you hadn't had the luck to die. What's a nihilist, Sire? You scoundrel, if you hadn't fallen asleep writing down my program for the development of history from the destruction of the Tower of Babylon to its rebuilding, if you hadn't been scribbling your footnotes that have since disappeared in the past anyway, you would remember my words, my fears that I am the forerunner of nihilism. Anyway, who knows? Maybe I am. *Mea culpa.* Look, please, Grossman; look at those radiant faces, those processions. They all believe that they will die, that they will die completely, not like this, like you and I, that they will become nothing, and still they are laughing and singing. Isn't that funny? That's horrible, your majesty. No, it's ridiculous. Even though I've been dead for so many centuries, I am an undying optimist. The final tower, the one that will perfect evil, that will classify it and separate it completely from good, it is already being slowly planned. We are cooperating with God. Go to sleep now, Grossman. Don't pretend to be sleeping. There's nothing else for you to hear. I won't wake you any more before the trumpets of Jericho sound, and they will be loud enough, I promise you, that they will awaken you and bring you before the Almighty so that you can show him the despicable contents of your secretarial soul. Sleep! Yes, Sire, I'm slowly falling asleep, slowly . . . falling . . . asleep . . .

Grossman has fallen asleep. I can see that from the absence of his presence. Although I'm not tired, I will soon go to sleep as well. But before I close my eyes, as a result of the general concretization turned into two pages of some sort of book, I will turn back one more time to look at this brave new world. That *danse macabre.* That circle without end. *Circus vitiosus.*

# APPENDIX

MIHAILO JOVANOVIĆ, ARCH.

# BUILDING: "CITY BABYLON THE GREAT" HOSPITAL

## TECHNICAL DESCRIPTION

### *Location*

– The "City Babylon the Great" Hospital to be built with special permits on the basis of geodetic (geo-climatic, geo-morphological), climatic, and historical analysis.

### *Structure*

– The entire building is a spiral; all of its ramps rest on the earth (dug in). This will also form the spiral foundation. Interior construction is of steel and cement. Above ground part of building covered with spatial screen, filled with glass.
Vertical walls are of steel and concrete with all insulation (hydro-, thermal, sound). Routes for all installations are run through these walls.

### *Energy*

For lighting, climate control and manufacturing energy, two sources are used:
A – solar energy; daytime lighting and heating on the hothouse principle.
B – Heat energy of the Earth's core that is absorbed on the floors below 2 miles underground, and can be raised to the level needed when required.

### *Function and architectural solution*

The system of communication facilitates basic functioning, built so that it allows the connection of all levels and sections within the framework of the same level by means of three ways of communicating:
Vertical – elevators.
Horizontal – conveyer belts.
Slanted – along the spiral foundation.
All seven entrances are connected to the central part with selective security. In the NEUROSIS quarter from which elevators go to the base of the spiral with stops and connections at every level. In addition, the central part of the NEUROSIS quarter is connected directly with seven vertical communication systems for each level.

### *Surfacing*

– All interior surfaces to be painted gray. (Shade to be determined by hospital manager.)

– Steel construction to be painted with primer, surface painted also in grey. Flat enamel.
– Steel on the spatial screens not to be painted but polished to a high gloss.

### *Exterior surfaces*

High-tension steel reinforced walls – not to be painted. Entrances (all 7) painted with traffic colors: orange, yellow and black.

In front of entrance 4, place gigantic monument II PSYCHO-ANALYSIS. Open supplemental competition for monument design.

Avala
532
Above ground section
1500 m

Tower of Babylon from 1920
Tatlin's Tower, plan for a monument to the Third International

The Grand Insane Asylum: the universal brothel

Constructing the ROMA III computer memory autodestruct (detail)

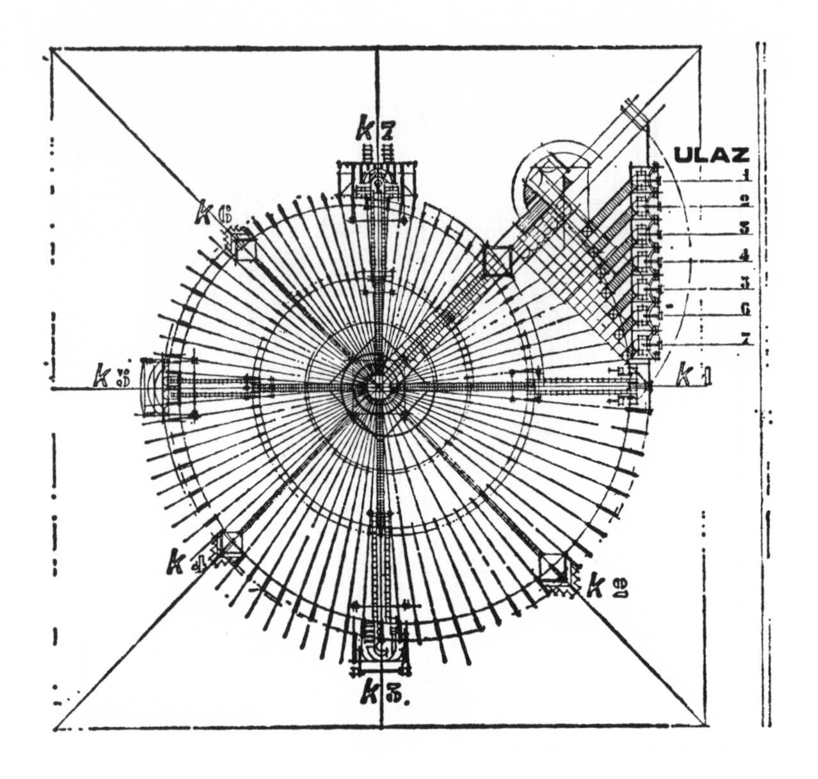
ULAZ
1
2
3
4
5
6
7
K7
K6
K5
K4
K3.
K1

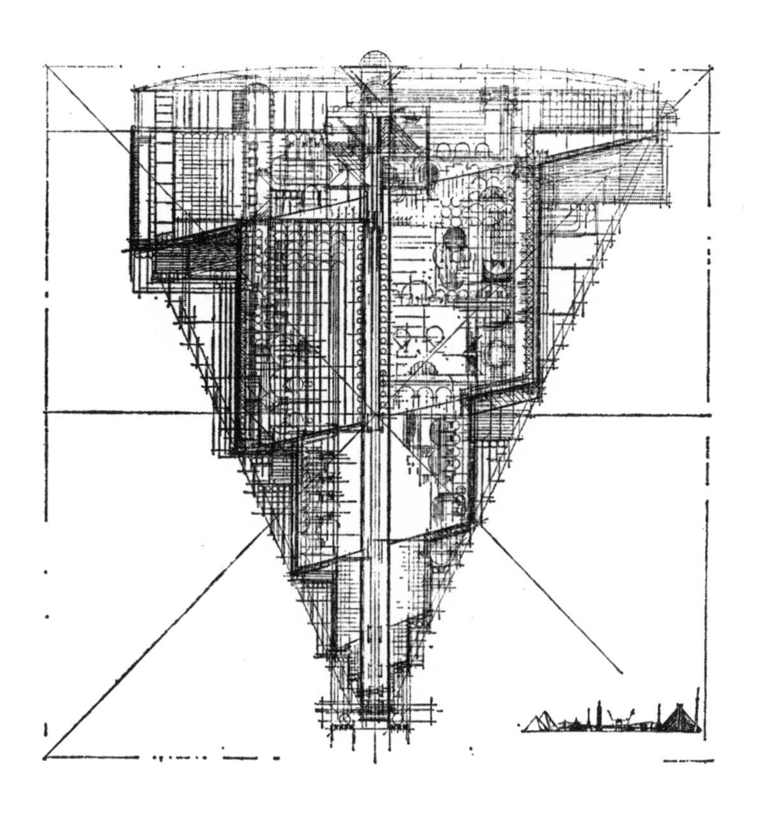

# SECRET LIST OF MEMBERS OF THE EVANGELICAL BICYLCISTS

Eugène Ionesco
Emil Cioran
Geo Bogza
Mircea Eliade
Nadia Comaneci
Elena Popescu
Eduard Sam
Andrija Hebrang
Miloš Crnjanski
Rastko Petrović
Dragiša Vasić
Aleksandar I Karađorđević
Dragoljub Protić
Slobodan Jovanović
Mihajlo Pupin
Nikolaj Velimirović
Katalin Karady
Gavrilo Princip
Joseph Kowalsky
Jovan Veselinov
Joseph V. Dzhugashvili
Jovan Cvijić
Geca Kon
Çulaba Çulabi
Žarko Basara
Radiša Kovačević
Jovan Kaljević
Jelena Milijević
Milovan Đilas
Milisav Savić
Steve Tesich
Edvard Kocbek
Dragan Džajić
Srđan Dragojević
Milan Matović
Gojko Tešić
Leon Koen
Srđan Šaper
Cvetan Todorov
Cola Dragojčeva
Ioannis Ziziulas
Janis Ricos
Alexis Carrington
Leonid Šejka
Bora Ćosić
Amfilohije Radović
Nikos Kazantzakis
Nikola Milošević
Ranko Jovović
Marko Ćirić

Nedeljko Rakić
Suzana Mančić
Ljuba Popović
Branko Kukić
Olja Ivanjicki
Kole Čašule
Gojko Nikoliš
Slobodan Milošević
Milan Popović
Živojin Pavlović
Ilija Gorkić
Svetislav Veizović
Cvitko Bdlić
Eddy Merckx
Sonja Savić
Dobrica Ćosić
Slobodan Gavrilović
Laslo Vegel
Miodrag
Petrović-Čkalja
Bohumil Hrabal
Jonathan Koehler
Jozef Škvorecki
John Glenn
Martina Navratilova
Marina Švabić
Slobodan Milivojević-Era
Goranka Matić
Nadin De Free Shop
Milojko Knežević
Predrag Marković
Mihajlo Pantić
Slavko Šajber
Mila Kostić
Ljiljana Tica
Vlada Mijanović
Dragan Blagojević
Freddy Mercury
Laura Jane Richardson
John Cleese
Charles Santos
George W. Bush, Jr.
Ignatius Reilly
Ken Scandlyn
Charlton Heston
George Harrison
Michael Moore
Denise Huddle
Louise Ciccone
Gary Hardwick
Steven Hawking
Oscar Wilde
Simon Gill
Emmanuel Radnitzky
Mikhail Bakhtin
Homer Simpson
Eddie "Son" House
Woody Allen

*Note:*
*List is incomplete*
*and unverified*

Svetislav Basara is a major figure of contemporary Serbian literature and the author of five collections of short stories, thirteen novels, a dozen books of essays, plays, and novellas. In 2006, Basara received the NIN Award for his novel *The Rise and Fall of Parkinson's Disease*. His 1985 novel, *Chinese Letter*, is also available in English translation. Basara served as the Serbian Ambassador to Cyprus from 2001 to 2005.

Randall A. Major teaches in the English Department at the University of Novi Sad, Serbia, and is also one of the editors and translators of the Serbian Prose in Translation series produced by Geopoetika Publishing in Belgrade in cooperation with the Serbian Ministry of Culture.

Open Letter—the University of Rochester's nonprofit, literary translation press—is one of only a handful of publishing houses dedicated to increasing access to world literature for English readers. Publishing ten titles in translation each year, Open Letter searches for works that are extraordinary and influential, works that we hope will become the classics of tomorrow.

Making world literature available in English is crucial to opening our cultural borders, and its availability plays a vital role in maintaining a healthy and vibrant book culture. Open Letter strives to cultivate an audience for these works by helping readers discover imaginative, stunning works of fiction and by creating a constellation of international writing that is engaging, stimulating, and enduring.

Current and forthcoming titles from Open Letter include works from Argentina, Bulgaria, Catalonia, China, Iceland, Poland, and many other countries.